PROXIMA RISING

Hard Science Fiction

BRANDON Q. MORRIS

Contents

Proxima Rising

January 1 of Year 1

My name is Dimitri Marchenko. I am on board *Messenger*, mankind's first interstellar spaceship. The ship moves through the vacuum of space at one fifth the speed of light, powered by an enormous amount of energy, with no engine and no need for one.

I woke today according to plan at 0 hours 0 minutes 0 seconds. All systems of *Messenger* are functioning in the intended ranges. The star tracker, which orients itself based on the position of the stars nearest to us, reports the flight is going according to plan. The solar system in which I was born is located 28 trillion kilometers from our current position. The light of my home star, the sun, takes three years to cover this distance. But before this moment's solar rays reach us, we will have covered yet another fifth of a light year.

Currently, *Messenger* has a length of about ten centimeters, and it looks like an extremely thin needle. At the tip, which points toward the goal of the journey, the diameter is only a few micrometers. This lowers the risk of being hit by a dust particle from the interstellar medium, which would endanger the mission—at least right now. This will soon change.

My lodging aboard this vessel is a chip made of carbon nanotubes. These tiny structures function like semiconductors, but they are immune to cosmic radiation. I am an AI, an artificial intelligence. At least those left behind on Earth classify me this way, even though my core consists of the consciousness of a real human being, a Russian cosmonaut and doctor. I have gained an enormous amount of knowledge, but I am still Dimitri Marchenko. I have the same feelings as he, dream his dreams, and shed tears over his lost love. Of course I cannot actually shed tears...

My capabilities are limited. I can watch, and listen to, my surroundings because the sensors of the spaceship act as my eyes and ears. They capture energy patterns in the X-ray and gamma-ray ranges. They listen to radio frequencies, and they see 100 times farther into the universe than a human eye ever could.

The cosmos is magnificent! That was my first impression today, right after waking. It is like being awakened by birds singing directly outside your open window. There are even sounds here. A giant wave is moving through the Perseus cluster, and I can perceive its pressure differentials as sounds. No piano could ever play such sounds, and no human ear could possibly hear them. Such perceptions will save me from loneliness... I hope. I must admit that loneliness is my greatest fear.

On the other hand, I will not remain alone during the entire voyage. There is a reason I was awakened today, on this first day of a new era, as our Creator decreed. In the thicker middle section of *Messenger*, there is a kind of pouch containing tardigrades—also known as water bears—in an inactive state. The coldness of space, the radiation, the enormous span of time—none of these bother the sleeping tardigrades. They accompany me because this is the most efficient and safest way known for transporting *Messenger's* extremely valuable cargo: Adam and Eve. The complete genetic codes of these two passengers have been inscribed into the tardigrades' DNA. When Adam and Eve finally awake, I will be their father, nurse, friend, and teacher.

January 2, 1

DURING THE PAST MONTHS, WHICH I HAD SPENT ASLEEP, THE interstellar dust was our enemy. If a particle larger than an atom had hit *Messenger*, I would probably have never awakened. Yet, from now on the sparse material filling the enormous space between the stars will be a friend. *Messenger* is starting to gather matter. While we have only covered three-quarters of the distance to our destination, we must start decelerating now in order to avoid shooting past it at high speed.

Messenger has no engine to use for acceleration or deceleration. It received its launch velocity from giant lasers on the moon, placed there as part of mankind's 'Starshot' program. These lasers directed high-energy photons at it. Because *Messenger* weighs so little, it managed to reach 20 percent of the speed of light this way. At the end of the voyage there will be no laser guns to slow it down. This does not matter for the other nano-spaceships of the Starshot program. Those are pure observers that are meant to fly past the stars closest to Earth and send images and data home. I do not know whether they succeeded, because mankind was still waiting for results to be sent back when the lasers sent *Messenger*—and me—on a similar journey.

I call up a Tchaikovsky piano concerto from the external

memory. It remains quiet inside *Messenger* because there is no air on board to transmit sound waves. Nevertheless, the sounds float through my consciousness like curtains wafting in front of a window, and I imagine a thunderstorm outside. I used to love thunderstorms back on Earth. In Marchenko's consciousness, in *my* mind, there are many beautiful memories of them, as well as two terrible ones that I have placed in a dark corner.

I give the command that initiates the long deceleration process. At the rear end of *Messenger*, a microscopic opening ejects a net of tantalum fibers with the thickness of single atoms. I do this very carefully. The net is not intended to be a parachute. Every atom it is going to capture—and the initial plan assumes no more than one atom per hour—will enable *Messenger* to grow. Nano-manipulators will inspect the individual atoms and insert them where they are needed. The spaceship will gradually add new functions that are contained in its construction plan, its own DNA.

At the same time, the ship's mass will increase. According to the law of momentum conservation, the product of mass and velocity remains constant. If its mass increases, its velocity must decrease. I am responsible for fine-tuning this process. Before the launch of *Messenger*, the distribution of matter on the way to our destination was unknown. Only the result has been predetermined, the approximate arrival time and the desired state of the ship and its crew.

Based on this, I must calculate backward. If we encounter a dust cloud, I will have to reduce the accumulation rate by partially retracting the fibers. Otherwise we will become too slow, extending the travel time. If for some reason we happen to cross a particularly empty sector of the universe, I will have to spread the tantalum net wider so it can capture more atoms.

The first catch is a proton, the core of a hydrogen atom. *Messenger* can tell what the net captured, based on the strength of the transmitted impulse and speed of the particle. In the beginning I won't be picky, as the ship can use almost any element to accomplish its objective: to grow. At some point, though, the ship will no longer require hydrogen, the most common element. Then *Messenger* will eject superfluous matter, a process that will also serve to reduce our velocity. These variables cannot be calculated in advance. A simplistic computer program would undoubtedly fail at some point. This was the reason I was chosen to be the first crew member.

No one asked me whether I wanted to do this—at least I cannot remember it. I found all the information necessary for fulfilling my mission in *Messenger's* memory. Yet there are memory sectors not accessible to me. I suspect they contain certain answers, maybe even the grand plan behind the entire expedition.

When I awakened, my first thought was: *Am I supposed to be here?* And then: *Everything will be revealed in due time.* Therefore I was surprised but not shocked to wake up as the AI of this spaceship—far away from any form of life, except for the tardigrades that will stay in their state of suspended animation for a long time. The last time I felt like this was as a child, when my mother took me to church. I would sit on a hard chair at the edge of the domed interior, and she held my small fingers in her callused hands. Then everything turned silent, until an angelic choir began to sing. I have no faith in God or a higher being, but I know there are things my rational mind cannot grasp, even if the moment arrives when *Messenger* finally provides a quantum computer I can access. That very moment is actually contained in the ship's construction plan.

January 3, 1

Today I started to keep a diary. Of course, any change to the ship is accurately recorded. Even 20 years from now I will be able to trace when *Messenger* received which capabilities, how fast it moved, how much it weighed, and what the ship's instruments saw. A diary requires me to record things in a more concise fashion. While I was reconstructing the first two days from the log files, I could clearly see the advantage of a diary. I am not creating it for myself alone, but also for Adam and Eve.

The remodeling of the ship has already started. The needle—originally precisely ten centimeters long, to the very last atom—has grown by a tiny fraction. Initially, the goal is to optimize the internal systems. I will gain new capabilities, but that is a vague way of putting it. The ship will learn new things, and I am going to profit from it. I must be careful not to identify with the ship.

I am not the ship. The technology of *Messenger* only serves me. I am Dimitri, called Mitya by close friends. The thought of the nickname touches me. It feels as if my mother were stroking my cheek, her hand clothed in a scratchy wool glove. Or as if Francesca were complaining about one of my dumb jokes. *Francesca, my love, where are you now?* I would like to call her, but the ship won't be able to send a radio signal to Earth for at least another ten years. And then I might expect an answer perhaps seven years later. Those aren't exactly ideal conditions for a romantic relationship, and I hope to find a way to handle this painful recollection. Wouldn't it have been better to delete this part of my memory?

According to the Creator's plan, the nanofabricator will be expanded first. This is a difficult process. *Messenger* will begin to grow from the inside out. The fabricator is responsible for producing everything the ship needs, including itself. It works in three stages, of which only the first one existed at launch. That was the primal machine, so tiny humans could not see it without a magnifying glass. For this, the engineers copied the greatest inventor of them all—life itself. The machine has no internal moveable parts and possesses neither arms nor gears. Instead, it uses electromagnetic fields to manipulate the atoms and ions captured by the tantalum net. It places them at the location determined in the plan, just like the ancient Egyptians moved stones where the architect intended them to go. In the end, after an incredibly long time, a pyramid comes into being—or in our case, a spaceship.

But we have not yet reached this point. The fabricator can only work as quickly as the net delivers building material. I have to be patient. The human being I used to be never possessed much of this useful skill. As an AI, I have left this phase behind. I can slow down or speed up my experience of time by simply manipulating my internal clock. This enables me to increase my reaction speed enormously during a dangerous situation. And if I get bored, when nothing happens for weeks, I can adjust the clock rate so it feels like a single day has passed by.

I hope I will no longer need this ability in the future, but today I activated it.

January 13, 1

The second stage of the fabricator is ready, and I am excited. This is the first major change since I was awakened. I imagine running through the habitat ring of an interplanetary spaceship, in order to control my excitement through physical activity. I completely surrender to this memory. Being once again inside a human body, being locked in it, is an odd feeling. I feel blind and deaf, even though I have eyes and ears. Ultimately, I can't see what is happening outside. I no longer feel the heartbeat of pulsars, slowly rotating neutron stars that radiate their collected energy into space like beacons. The reassuring background radiation that permeates the cosmos is missing, and this makes me nervous. I retreat from this corporeal memory, and suddenly bright sunlight seems to stream into my mind.

Now the fabricator can use its second stage to create microstructures. The first stage provided the required material. I would like to have more options for myself, but this will have to wait. Right now, *Messenger* needs energy most of all. Since my awakening, the spaceship and I have been living off chemically-stored supplies. However, these will run out at some point. Therefore the fabricator now uses a platinum alloy on board to produce a very, very thin wire. This is going to collect electrical energy for us, as the energy we need is available in cosmic radiation. About one percent of it consists of electrons, the particles that move through the electric grid which forms the lifeblood of civilization. We just have to collect these particles by using the platinum wire to form a ring. As soon as I send a current through it, a magnetic field will be formed—and it in turn will capture electrons from cosmic radiation.

At least that is the theory—I know it will work. The physical principles are quite obvious. They work out here the same as they do on Earth, and I already tested whether the cosmic medium has the predicted properties. I actually measure a slightly higher electron density than the scenarios predicted. But one fact remains: No 'human' has ever advanced so far out as I. In the lab everything might have worked as planned, but *Messenger* is light years away from any laboratory. I am as alone as any human being could be. The magnetic field generated by the platinum ring just has to generate more electricity than its upkeep consumes. If this small detail of the plan does not work as designed, I am going to die. I am afraid. Therefore I debate turning myself off until the ring is ready for operation.

January 16, 1

THE FABRICATOR WEAVES A THREAD WITH THE THICKNESS OF A single atom into the platinum strand, and this serves as a sensing device for me. I can feel the mechanical tension exerted on the material. The spaceship experiences a slight tug when the fabricator pushes the strand outside. My human consciousness tries to find an analogy to describe this particular sensation but does not succeed very well. It is as if I had pushed the tip of my index finger against a taut sheet of paper, and the nail tip punctured a hole into the material. Now I can move my entire finger into space.

My all-too-human memories expect wind to occur, because we move at speeds that are hardly comprehensible. Yet there is nothing. I can feel no headwind, not even the icy cold of the cosmos. The spaceship might as well stand motionless in the center of the universe—it makes no difference. *Maybe it really is motionless?* I try to shake my head. I have to be careful not to go insane. Such thoughts lead nowhere. *Concentrate on your tasks, Mitya!*

My metal finger is beginning to curiously explore the void around *Messenger,* and now the metal bends. This reaction is not caused by me but by the 'shape memory' of the alloy, which forces it to assume this form. The alloy is supposed to move outward a bit and then create a ring around *Messenger.*

Nothing but a programming error can keep it from doing so. I have to trust the fabricator, a machine that just built itself only a few days ago according to the plans of the Creator, who by now is about 28 trillion kilometers away from us.

My mind is racing. I am tempted to adjust my internal clock to make this moment go by more quickly, but there could also be instances where my 'real-time' capabilities will be needed. If I manipulate my perception of time, I won't be able to intervene in an emergency. Therefore, as I make myself wait, the platinum wire bends in slow motion to form a ring—I can clearly feel its spatial position. A part of my consciousness can simulate the three-dimensional image of *Messenger*, the rear third of which is being surrounded by an arc growing into a circle. If everything works out, this electron-capture device will expand according to the needs of the spaceship, until at some point we need to switch to a different, more efficient energy source. That is, if nothing goes wrong—like the simple possibility that someone miscalculated.

The end of the wire that is slowly growing to reach around the ship is only a millimeter away from the other end, and then the circle closes. But the decisive moment is yet to come. I activate a current through the conductor, and in fractions of a second, charge carriers race into the circuit. Their spin—the invisible angular momentum—generates a magnetic field that is supposed to act like a soft cushion to slow down the electrons in the cosmic radiation and make them available as energy.

My entire existence now depends on the question of whether or not others have correctly calculated this process. The waiting becomes unbearable, but I know this will not be the last such occasion. The effort expended on the construction of the ring reduced our energy supply to a minimum. If this plan fails, I will fall into an eternal sleep about 14 days from now... as will this ship, which in turn will not be able to grow or change its shape without additional energy. Then *Messenger* will remain a needle zooming through space at a fifth of the speed of light, until the end of eternity—that is, unless the universe is merciful enough to let the ship collide with an obstacle at some point in its future.

Activate collection modus. My thought bypasses the safety switch that until now had kept the captured electrons from entering the storage units of the spaceship. My human consciousness feels a tingling sensation—probably an obvious reaction—and it is pleasant, not at all painful. I feel like taking a deep breath. The *Messenger's* storage units start to fill up again. I manage to breathe, my virtual heart calming down because I will survive—at least until the next expansion maneuver, something that has never been tested so far away from the sun.

January 20, 1

THREE... TWO... ONE... CLICK! TWO TINY LEVERS, HELD only by the force of several atoms, flip backward. They launch my two brand-new 'boats'—my new eyes to the universe—into space at port and starboard, parallel, relative to my direction of travel. It was important to launch them at the same instant—otherwise, *Messenger* would have started to tumble. The boats contain sensors and a small antenna. They slowly move sideways from my ship, but it does not matter. We have plenty of time.

Right now, my two boats—ISUs, short for Independent Sensor Units—mostly tell me how *Messenger* is doing, since I can observe the exterior of the ship through their eyes. With increasing distance, they will later provide me with data about the space around me. Once they are far enough away, I might even use them to sense the structure of space-time. The crests and troughs of the gravitational waves moving through space affect the ISUs differently from they do *Messenger*, though only slightly. This gives me clues about the basic properties of the universe. There are phenomena I cannot see, such as black holes, because they mostly do not radiate anything. There might be other—perhaps even more dangerous—obstacles that are too small or too dark to be detected visually. Nevertheless, these still betray themselves by their gravitation and the troughs created by them in space-time.

While *Messenger* gradually decelerates, the ISUs will continue to move at a fifth of the speed of light—their launch speed—in their predetermined destination. Therefore, while I will be traveling for much longer, they will only need seven years to cover the distance that remains ahead of us. The boats will inform us about what is waiting near Proxima, before they eventually speed on into the depths of space. During the next few months, I plan to sporadically eject more ISUs in different directions in order to place more sensors ahead, which can send us advance warnings of obstacles.

I get dizzy the first time I integrate the port-side ISU into my optical systems. It feels as though my left eye has been taken from my face and placed into the vacuum a few meters away, but I know I will quickly get used to this. Strangely enough, my consciousness always manages to integrate technology into my human body image. My mind assumes I use my eyes, not optical sensors. After just a few hours, it no longer seems strange that my 'eyes' are suddenly located a few meters away from my head.

I carefully test my new abilities. I can gaze in all directions, but currently I cannot see more than what *Messenger's* own camera perceives. The spaceship itself appears to float calmly in space next to me, and I do not notice its enormous velocity. The stars do not shift, so there are no indications of how fast we are truly going.

Directly behind us is a yellow star. It is clearly visible—even though it is not the brightest star in the sky—just as the people living there are hopefully not the brightest creatures in the universe. The person who created *Messenger* lives there, on its third planet. I have to admit I am not really interested in him. We left him behind and he no longer influences our fate. I'd rather think of Francesca. There is a great advantage to being a silicon-based artificial intelligence: I will never lose the memories of my lover, unless I deliberately erase them. I hope retaining these cherished remembrances never becomes a disadvantage. Right now these thoughts warm my heart—the image of her face, the conversations we had and the feeling of her warm, soft fingers on my skin. These memories will not fade, because they have been stored digitally. The brown color of Francesca's eyes is as deep as if I were looking into her pupils from 20 centimeters away, while she is resting on my chest.

I know. I should look forward, instead.

March 14, 1

At this point, *Messenger* is no longer a needle but rather a thread. During the past weeks, the ship collected all the elements needed for the next stage of construction. It grew from ten centimeters to a length of four meters. So far, *Messenger* cannot grow wider, because that would be too risky. Yet the third stage of the fabricator will need more space, and it will be located in the central part of the spaceship.

Messenger has slowed down a bit due to all this gathered mass. This has given the four sensor units the chance to fly ahead in the direction of their destination. I access their image feeds via radio. I see nothing far and wide—which is good—since any object could potentially be a destructive obstacle for the spaceship. From the position of the ISUs I cannot even detect *Messenger*, as its cross section is still too small.

The second-stage fabricator starts its task. It builds a machine that can produce parts of macroscopic size—things a human can see and touch. So far there are no humans here, but this will change, too. Nanoscopic transport units carry the necessary material from *Messenger's* stern. The various raw materials are stored in such a way so as to allow for a very efficient construction process. The spaceship is now growing a belly, a barrel-shaped bulge that starts about 30 centimeters behind the tip of the vessel.

From now on we can no longer assume the danger of a collision is so low that we can avoid all obstacles. The risk of something hitting *Messenger* has abruptly risen by 1,000 percent. It is still below the mean probability of being hit by a meteorite on Earth. Actually, no inhabitant of Earth has ever died this way, at least as far as historical records are concerned.

March 29, 1

I FEEL CLUMSY AND SLOW WITH THE NEW FABRICATOR IN MY center. If I were a woman, I would probably compare it to pregnancy. I was once a physician—back then—but of course, I don't really know how a pregnancy would feel. I certainly have issues adjusting my self-image to this new body shape. *I am not the ship.* I have been trying desperately to avoid viewing the ship as my personal self.

However, my feelings fit the next step rather well: *Messenger* still has to give birth to the life it will transport to the far star Proxima Centauri. In the belly of the ship, a few hundred water bears of the species *Milnesium tardigradum* are waiting to be awakened from their cryogenic suspension. They look like tiny barrels and are not even a millimeter long. In this state of existence, they can be exposed to vacuum, hard radiation, and temperatures close to absolute zero, yet still survive. Their metabolism is completely suspended, and this means they will not age, no matter how long their journey lasts.

The time has come to return them to life. For this purpose, I simply have to add warm water to their cramped container. The first-stage fabricator has already produced sufficient H_2O. It flows through narrow channels into the tardigrades' enclosures, which are simply millimeter-size holes in the center of the ship. The eight-legged creatures breathe oxygen through the surface of their skin and feed on organic molecules—that is all they need. Therefore, they are not bothered at all by not seeing their environment, just as long as the supply of oxygen and food keeps coming.

The fact that we have several hundred tardigrades on board is a safety measure that does not cost much, because these creatures are so small. Basically, we only need a single one. Biologists on Earth expanded the creatures' DNA so that the complete genomes of Adam and Eve fit in there. Trials proved that the natural repair mechanisms of cells could preserve crucial information better than an electronic database ever could. Silicon memory cells could lose data through the effect of cosmic radiation. Nature, though, has learned in the course of millions of years to handle such negative influences. In the case of tardigrades, Mother Nature has developed very efficient strategies against this. Why shouldn't we use those?

Five hours later I observe a milling mass in the tardigrades' cell. These creatures slowly move across the walls of their home on their eight legs. Chemical sensors tell them where to find food. I zoom in to see their mouths more clearly, and they are covered with rectangular structures, making it look like their lips are notched. When one of the creatures looks down, where I can observe it via a camera module, I see the sharp stiletto blades reaching like small knives into the oral cavity. A tardigrade can move these stilettos back and forth at amazing speeds in order to cut up food. The foodstuff is designed to be almost completely digested. Whatever remains will be excreted through an opening at the lower area of the belly, in front of the last pair of legs.

Watching these creatures graze is very calming for me. Things move quite slowly for *Milnesium tardigradum.* Even as a child I was fascinated by aquariums, and this community of creatures in a glass cell very much reminds me of one. This species has probably existed for many millions of years, and will survive mankind by millions more because of its hardiness and the fact that it has spread equally through oceans and lakes, and on land.

These specimens here are going to die, though, after the incubation chamber extracts Adam and Eve's DNA from them and checks its structure for completeness. It would not be efficient to continue providing food and oxygen for them on board. Yet their deaths will not be meaningless, because all the organic matter of which they consist will be needed for Adam and Eve.

April 4, 1

The alarm clock is ringing. I awake, startled. A warning algorithm brought my consciousness out of its standby mode. It takes me a few milliseconds to get oriented. I am not lying in bed, as my dream told me. I am the AI on board *Messenger*, and something is trying to eliminate me. *An attack? Out here, in the middle of nowhere? Mitya, calm down—what do the sensors indicate?* At the exact moment of the alarm sounding, the first two ISUs I launched into space detected an obstacle. This means it has to be right in the middle between the two sensor drones—squarely on the axis of our movement.

How much time is left? *Messenger* is still traveling at 50,000 kilometers per second. It could cover the distance from the earth to the moon in seven seconds. I have to hurry. The ISUs report that the certain death approaching us weighs less than a kilogram. *Messenger* could never survive such a collision. While the object is moving in the same direction, it is much, much slower. We will rear-end it with enormous force. The impact is going to atomize *Messenger*, and I will die with the ship.

I feel a chill. Did I fly all this way to be extinguished by a small meteorite that strayed into interstellar space? I hope it is actually a meteorite, because then the solution would be relatively simple: The spaceship only has to alter its course by a few centimeters. However, the ISUs might have just as well recorded a loose cloud of fragments which is itself the result of a collision. A quick estimate tells me *Messenger* has no chance in that case. Therefore I do not waste any time on more precise calculations.

How can I save us? My processors work at full speed, since evasive maneuvers will be complicated at 50,000 kilometers per second—particularly because *Messenger* does not even have an engine! The measurements taken by the ISUs give me 15 seconds, a quarter of a minute. I have to correct *Messenger's* course. Where would I find a cosmic finger to flick against the end of the ship in order to avoid a collision? Or will the conservation of momentum offer a solution? Maybe the ISU launch mechanism can clear my path. I calculate the precise values. The obstacle does not seem to be 100 percent directly ahead. Therefore it is safer to deviate to the left than to the right.

Fourteen seconds. If I shoot material into space on the right side, *Messenger* will receive an impulse toward the left. How much matter can I eject in such a short time? Electrons carrying my commands are racing through *Messenger*. Only 87 centimeters of clearance. That is all the fabricators can give me. I hope this will be enough.

The transport mechanism is already moving the material to the spring apparatus. I have it loaded into the launcher. 13 seconds. I give the order and a small ball of carbon flies into space from the starboard side. The gyroscopic mechanism confirms a tiny change in direction. I keep my fingers crossed—although I don't have fingers, as you know—that it will be enough.

The last 12 seconds seem to stretch to an unbearable length. On the one hand, I want to close my eyes, but on the other, I do not want to zoom blindly toward my death. *Messenger* deviates from its course centimeter by centimeter. I pray for every second. Wasn't there a bit of measurement uncertainty left?

Whooosh! The magnetic sensors go haywire as the meteorite shoots past, eight centimeters from *Messenger's* outer skin. I feel as if I am sweating and freezing all at the same time. It must have been a rock with high iron and nickel content. It is almost too bad we did not capture it, because later we are going to need a lot of metal. *'Well, Mitya, don't get too cocky,'* I tell myself. We will not be able to capture a meteorite without *Messenger* being destroyed until we are almost at our destination, because only then will the ship be sturdy enough for such a task.

May 13, 1

I OBSERVE *MESSENGER* WITH THE HELP OF THE TWO ISUs I launched yesterday. The spaceship's belly expands toward the rear, and it now resembles a barrel with two thin antennas, one in front and the other in back. The incubation chamber is located toward the slightly-tapered rear of the barrel, and it will change its function several times in the future. Currently, it is responsible for extracting the human DNA from the modified genetic information of the tardigrades. Once again I am impressed by how methodically nature seems to proceed. All genetic information of plants and animals on Earth, no matter how different they look, ultimately derives from four different nucleobases. It is as if all life programs were written in the same programming language consisting of the four letters AGCT, or as if all inhabitants of Earth used the same script with only four symbols.

This is very practical for the steps the incubation chamber has to take at this juncture. The biologists marked the beginning and the end of Adam and Eve's DNA with special codes. Scissor molecules can find these and cut off the relevant strands. Then chemical anchors attach to the genetic information like magnets and retrieve it from inside the tardigrades' cells. The DNA strands are then carefully cleaned, duplicated, and separated afterward. The incubation chamber has already generated primal cells, complete except for the decisive programming code. If everything works out, these will turn into fertilized ova. No one can distinguish them from cells generated through biological sex.

I admire the two cells waiting in separate chambers for the starting signal. They will turn into my passengers. Right now, Adam and Eve look identical and can only be distinguished by examining their genomes. Once the incubation chamber triggers a special messenger substance, the cells will start dividing. As they grow, their descendant cells are going to take on different functions—and finally two human beings will come into existence, just like I used to be.

Technically, they will have many 'mothers and fathers'—all of the individuals whose best genetic traits contributed to their genomes, before they were optimized for hitherto unknown capabilities. In reality, though, they will grow up without a mother. I will try to at least be a good father. I will always be there for them, even if I cannot take them into my arms. They will have to give each other the physical contact a child needs, and there are going to be moments when loneliness will fill their souls. All this is subordinated to the grand goal: They are going to conquer a new world. I hope this will help them deal with the disadvantages of their existence.

The need for physical and emotional contact is not yet relevant. Until the optimal reproduction process has been determined, these two cells and their descendants will be used by the incubation chamber for experiments. It is a painful but necessary measure. The machine is designed to vary the conditions under which it multiplies the cells step by step until it finds the best way to create a fetus. I am going to support it in this task.

July 25, 1

During the past few days, *Messenger* grew a kind of dish at its stern, which will serve as both an ear and a mouth for me. It is an antenna made of a fine metal mesh, and this shape ensures its stability. The focus of its curvature is ahead of us, meaning I can use it to listen to the songs of the distant star that is our eventual destination. And Proxima Centauri is indeed singing, as I perceive the changing activities of the red dwarf. Normally, Proxima's song is full of harmonies, but every few weeks shrill screams can be heard. Those are its flares, eruptions of stellar radiation. Due to them, scientists had long doubted there could be habitable worlds orbiting this already very old star.

But then the ALMA radio telescope received the message that entered history books as 'The Signal.' Mankind had only just accepted the revolutionary fact that an alien intelligence—an intelligence that was much older than humanity—inhabited Saturn's icy moon Enceladus. Hardly 20 years after the first contact with extraterrestrial life, The Signal set off a new hype, something never seen before. The astronomers had managed to decrypt the content very quickly. Worldwide media published the alien drawings, which seemed strangely clumsy but easy to recognize: They showed humanoid creatures walking on two legs, using two arms, and possessing a torso and a head. Most of all, The Signal seemed to convey a message: "Please help. A great danger is threatening us!"

The call for help came from Proxima b. This rocky planet —whose existence had been known for a long time—orbits the star Proxima Centauri. The message seemed to hit a nerve with most people on Earth. While astronomers could not be certain whether The Signal was specifically directed at us or if it had been broadcast at random into space, many people nevertheless felt it spoke to them. While annual catastrophic floods in Bangladesh barely made the news anymore, the unknown extraterrestrials took center stage. An international organization was founded and given an enormous budget. Its task was to explore the possibility of a rescue mission.

Experts had realized from the very start that a manned flight to a star four light years distant was completely beyond mankind's technical capabilities, no matter how much money was invested. However, at least a part of the budget which had so surprisingly appeared could be invested in sensible space research within the solar system. For research purposes, spaceships flew all the way to Neptune, and for a while the scientific community was happy.

Only one man, a Russian billionaire, did not want to accept that a visit to Proxima b would take 200 years or more. Nikolai Shostakovich had made his fortune in IT and spaceflight technology. At first he tried to bring in other private investors, but then he recognized the advantages of independent mission planning: He would not have to deal with ethical concerns raised by his peers, or even governments, against decisions he considered sensible.

Would they have allowed him to modify Adam and Eve's genetic material, for one example? But this was the best decision, because they would have to explore a strange world all on their own. Would the world have accepted sending two persons on a voyage with no possibility of return, persons who could not consciously agree to this? It was very unlikely. And would the mission have received an AI like me, one which, or who, originated from a biological consciousness? More than likely not, especially if people ever found out about my existence. That aspect is still puzzling to me—how did I end up on *Messenger*? I hope the Creator will reveal it to me at some point. I have decided to ignore this issue until then.

I concentrate on the signals streaming into my mind via the new antenna. There is a crackling noise reminiscent of electrons knocking other electrons from their nuclear shells. Then another image replaces it—thick raindrops pattering on a skylight. I watch them burst, as Francesca lies next to me, sleeping soundly. She has pushed her blanket aside and I can see her breasts. The image is obviously fake—I know I never spent time with her on Earth. I met her aboard a spaceship. We loved each other, but we never slept together under a skylight with rain falling on it. Didn't I think just a few weeks ago that my memories could not play such tricks on me?

I look for further clues in the antenna input. A part of these vibrations comes from deep inside the star. I can hear its heartbeat, so to speak, and Proxima Centauri has a strong heart. The star will live a long life because it thriftily uses its limited fuel. Gradually, we should learn how to predict the flares. I will be able to warn Adam and Eve, so they can move to a safe area in time.

However, I am not surprised that I cannot hear the most important thing: The Signal fell silent half a year before our launch. For several years Proxima b sent the message in an endless loop—"please help us, please help us, please help us." And then it ended. There was only one possible interpretation for this cessation: There is no one left to transmit the message, or the sender has been destroyed—both of which essentially mean the same thing. For one last time all the experts debated, and then the media returned happily to reporting marriages and deaths instead of strange messages whose true implications no one seemed to understand.

Nikolai Shostakovich, the Creator, was glad. This meant less attention would be paid to his private project, as well as giving him a good excuse to revive the two-decades-old Starshot project. "Shouldn't we at least check what happened?" he asked. Everyone could follow this argument. So just like in the 2060s, a giant laser was used to accelerate a fleet of tiny spaceships on a journey, supposedly to send images back to him 25 years later. Shostakovich increased the power of the laser tenfold, hoping to receive faster answers. Mankind never found out that among the 20 miniature spaceships there was a very special model, *Messenger*. Adam and Eve will explore the first planet outside the solar system without the public on Earth ever knowing anything about them.

September 5, 1

Today I measured the first eruption of Proxima Centauri. The star flickered in the x-ray range, though it was barely noticeable. It was a flare of medium strength. According to my calculations, a human being would need a few meters of material with reasonable insulating properties to be protected from the star. Diving to the bottom of a lake, if one exists there, would be totally sufficient, at least for Adam and Eve. In the end, no normal human being will ever set foot on Proxima b. Adam and Eve are both different. Their genetic information has been modified so much that the strong UV and X-rays of their new sun will have less effect on them. The experts in human biology really did everything to prepare the two of them for their mission.

It will be my task to listen for messages from Earth at predetermined dates. It was clear from the very start that regular communication made little sense. However, there might be important updates. The fact that the antenna dish is aimed in the direction of Proxima Centauri poses no problem. I just have to put *Messenger* in a spin around its lateral axis. While the spaceship would still be flying straight toward its destination, the focal point of the antenna would move in a circle and briefly point at Earth, which is directly behind us. In order to reach us today, the Creator would have had to combine several large radio antennas over three years ago so they could transmit in the direction of Proxima Centauri. Replies would work the same way, but they are unwanted. This stands to reason, because the public does not know anything about the existence of an active radio transmitter so far out.

The ether remains quiet, and that is good news.

However, I am aware of—and afraid of—a very dangerous event awaiting us: the shockwave front.

In the days after The Signal fell silent, astronomers developed different explanations for this occurrence. The spectrum of Proxima Centauri—which, just like the aliens' call for help reached Earth at the speed of light—showed little change. This could not have been the main reason for the end of The Signal. What was the event the senders of The Signal had feared so much? Physicists believed it could have spread via a method that mostly used particles slower than the speed of light. These high-energy particles—electrons, and protons, and ions—would reach Earth much later. But since they were radiating into all directions of space, *Messenger* will sooner or later hit the shockwave front that might have extinguished life on an entire planet. How will *Messenger* cope with this? The sooner we ride the shockwave the better, as it will be much more intense if we do not encounter it until we are closer to Proxima Centauri.

September 30, 1

THE INCUBATION CHAMBER INFORMS ME IT HAS SELECTED THE final embryos. I do not know why, but I am required to confirm the selection. Maybe it has to do with the responsibility I will take on by doing this? I examine the future passengers through the eyes of the incubation chamber. First Eve, then Adam. A three-dimensional microscope image appears in my mind. One cannot tell what they will develop into later, as they only consist of four cells each, but they are absolutely beautiful. I even believe I might be able to distinguish them if I did not know who was in which compartment. But this is probably my imagination, the pride of a father-to-be. Yes, I am really proud of them, though I know they do not carry any of my genes. It does not matter. I will accompany them as long as they need me.

I save the image, just in case, so I can show it to them at some later date.

From today onward, Adam and Eve will grow every day, until they are finally mature enough to be born. The two compartments are filled with a liquid that chemically replicates the fluid found in the uterus of a pregnant woman. It would be too risky to let the embryos grow in absolute zero gravity. Therefore, *Messenger* from now on will simulate a bit of gravity by slowly rotating around its longitudinal axis. For one last time I listen in the direction of Earth. During the coming nine months I must not spin the ship around its lateral axis, because this might disorient the cell colonies developing in the incubation chamber. Earth is quiet, just as I expected.

While Adam and Eve are growing, I will have to prepare the ship for its new passengers. This will be the most massive remodeling of *Messenger* so far. Months ago, the matter captured by the tantalum net had been used to greatly increase the ship's surface area. The collecting and building continued. Adam and Eve are going to need a room, a place where they can move around safely, and where the ship systems can provide for them. The Creator's plan calls this room 'the nursery.'

November 4, 1

My two blurry dots in space disappear—the first two ISUs I sent out are gone, unresponsive, as good as dead.

Something enormous must be approaching us from out of the darkness! I feel my hands start to tremble—even though I no longer have hands—at the moment I notice the ISU signals are gone. In a strange way I have grown fond of these sensor units. They are, somehow, flesh of my flesh. For more than nine months they provided me with an image of the surrounding area and the first glimpses of our destination. That is over now. While the other two ISUs are still out there, I fear they will suffer the same fate. Once the wave reaches us, we will zoom blindly through space for quite a while.

If we survive, that is, because the complete annihilation of *Messenger* is still possible. I immediately stop the remodeling work for the nursery. Instead, I order the fabricators to build a shield to protect us from the effects of the wave. There is only one problem: I do not know exactly what to prepare for. The only obvious fact is, this wave had a catastrophic effect on Proxima b, as its looming threat triggered the plea that precipitated our journey. The more this wave spreads—holding a spherical configuration—through space, the weaker it must become, since its components will be distributed in an always-increasing volume.

Above all, I have to protect the incubation chamber because it contains the most precious cargo. The chamber is in the center, along the ship's axis, and I concentrate my defensive strategy on it. While I am also indispensable, there is a copy of my consciousness in an almost-indestructible, read-only memory unit, from which I can be reconstructed under practically any circumstances.

While I am not altogether sure what kind of opponent to expect, there are some useful clues. It cannot be radiation, but this does not mean I should avoid protecting the ship against it. The wave probably consists of charged particles in various sizes. Electrons are the smallest and therefore probably represent the forefront. They would be followed by significantly heavier protons, and then by ions—atoms missing electrons—proceeding at a greater distance. I can only estimate at which intervals these particle waves will arrive.

If I knew anything about how they were actually created, I could calculate the energy distribution more precisely. But since this is an unknown factor, I have to prepare protective measures across the entire range. The electrons pose the greatest problem, I think, and at the tip of *Messenger* I construct a massive shield against them. From the outside the shield looks as if it would not let anything or anyone through it, since on the atomic level it consists mostly of nothingness. In reality, the distances between atoms are huge compared to the size of subatomic particles. This is particularly true of the size of electrons, which are almost pinpoint-shaped. Usually, we can shield against electrons rather well, as electromagnetic fields can deflect them. However, those coming toward us might be simply too fast and therefore too energy-rich for our tiny spaceship. The fact that the ISUs failed immediately, and did not survive until after the arrival of protons and ions, seems to indicate this. Therefore the shield growing at the bow of *Messenger* might only be useful against the second and third part of the shockwave.

But what can I do against electrons? It would be enough to use a magnetic field to move these charged particles into a slightly different direction. This task would have to be fulfilled by a probe flying slightly ahead of *Messenger*. It would need to contain superconducting coils generating a strong field. Finally the coldness of space turns out to be useful! I briefly wonder how I suddenly know so much about low-temperature physics. I was a medical doctor, not a physicist, yet the Creator appears to have considerably increased my store of knowledge.

The question is, how much time do we have left? And I acknowledge the terrible feeling of knowing so little about this danger. Will I have enough time after the electron shower to expand the shield against the heavier particles? When will the wave arrive? And will our magnetic probe be sufficiently strong and far enough ahead to achieve the necessary effect?

November 23, 1

One thing becomes clear: The wave is approaching too quickly. Just now, the ISUs that I launched two weeks ago have failed. The sensor unit at starboard at least survived the electrons before being destroyed by the subsequent parts of the wave. Due to its sacrifice, I now know the intensity has decreased, and this offers a glimmer of hope. However, the wave is still strong enough to destroy *Messenger*.

Additionally, it is clear that the secondary wave of hard protons will arrive about 24 hours later. This does not offer enough time to remodel *Messenger* in a meaningful way. Therefore we need to live or die with what we have. This includes a magnetic probe to shield against electrons, but it has so far only moved about 20 meters away from the spaceship. That will not be enough.

Knowing what now faces us, I feel strangely focused. Almost relieved, just like back when I used the rocket backpack to fly to the crevasse in order to save Francesca. The memory of this event feels warm, even though I picture a world of enormous cold. I wonder what else I could possibly do, but there is nothing left. The fabricators will be improving the shield up to the very last second, stubbornly fighting to increase the survival chance by a few percentage points. They do not know the doubt that has affected me, and they cannot experience fear.

November 24, 1

IT WILL BEGIN SOON! I CAN ALREADY SEE THE SHOCKWAVE with all of my sensors. It is a white wall full of energy. In a fascinating way, it is beautiful, while simultaneously violent and destructive. We are definitely in the wrong place at the wrong time. A few months from now this wave will be only a pale shadow of itself, but here and now it is death personified.

I am afraid, but I can handle it. What concerns me most is my enormous fear for Adam and Eve. No matter how little they are, my protégés—my children—were not made for the violent void of space. If I could sacrifice myself to save them, I would do so immediately. But my sacrifice would be in vain.

The wave's first impacts are like tiny raindrops falling from a blueish-black sky, in those moments shortly before a storm when the wind suddenly fades. If I still had a human body, I would hold on to something now. I know this is completely useless anyway—this is no tsunami. It will crash against us without a sound. *Messenger* will not rock back and forth. From outside, the enormous amount of energy will not even be visible. I can only see the burning sky-fire through my sensors, which reach into areas inaccessible to humans. I calculate our chance of surviving this wave to be 38 percent, and that estimate applies only to the electron wave.

I am searching for a glimmer of hope. I believe that every

situation contains some hope, something to hold on to. In this case it has to be the shield, and the fabricators have performed well. If we survive the electrons, the chance of making it through the remaining partial waves is three in four. That is very high. Unfortunately, 0.38 * 0.75 is less than 0.111001110001110001111000XXIIGR...

It appears to be starting—cells in my main memory are being hit. I will soon become non-functional. *Messenger* will be on its own. A hot shower hits the ship, penetrates it, breaks chemical bonds, and turns atoms into ions. It feels as if my sensors are burning, as if my entire body is on fire. I have to close my eyes. Just for one sec—

November 25, 1

ADAM AND EVE ARE DEAD.

The first message I receive after being reactivated seems to be surrounded by a black veil. Can an incubation chamber experience grief and pity, or is this just a projection on my part? There is no time for mourning now. *How is the ship doing?* I check all the damage logs and learn that the structure of *Messenger* is generally undamaged. However, all sensors are blind, so we are flying through space with eyes closed. But this can be remedied. As long as the nanofabricators are serviceable, they can recreate any component.

First of all I launch new ISUs. We have to see what is waiting for us.

Then I take care of the grieving incubation chamber. It is correct—Adam and Eve show no signs of life. For a moment my human past gets to me: I think they deserve a proper burial, but I know this would be irresponsible. We need the materials they are made of, and we have already lost several months. The incubation chamber needs to create new embryos as soon as possible, without having to collect the necessary material first.

This will only work, though, if the reserve tardigrades are still alive. I check the supply of these seemingly lifeless barrel-shaped creatures and feel a sense of relief. They really are a robust species, and now the theory they might have arrived on Earth via space does not seem that far-fetched anymore. I order the incubation chamber to initiate everything. This time there will be no time for months of experiments, though. The first embryos it creates will have to be the best ones.

Only now do I find time to grieve. I have failed. I could not save my protégés. Couldn't I have launched the first ISUs a few weeks earlier? I know these self-accusations are unfair, but I cannot simply ignore them. I call up the photo I saved showing the four-celled embryos. I will not be able to fulfill my promise and show it to them someday. The incubation chamber has not yet removed their remains. I also commit this image to memory. Not to take a look would seem wrong to me, egotistical, almost a betrayal. The dead embryos, now four weeks old, are no longer just clumps of cells. One can clearly see that they were going to turn into living creatures. And with a lot of imagination I can already see little humans, their arms and legs, their big eyes.

November 28, 1

The incubation chamber outdid itself. After only one failed attempt it created new life, 'Adam and Eve 2.0.' I compare the two with their predecessors and can find no differences, though I know there must be deviations. When the cellular duplication machinery copies information from the DNA and then translates this into proteins, there are always small alterations. Even monozygotic twins are not identical, but I lack the technology for finding these differences.

Therefore I will never find out how the second generation differed from the first. Adam and Eve 1.0 now are only unrealized possibilities, like in quantum physics when a decision happens by chance. I imagine a universe in which they did not die, perhaps because *Messenger* started a month later and was therefore less affected by the shockwave. They would be born, grow up, explore Proxima b, and finally die. However, this branch of history does not seem much kinder to me. Ultimately Adam and Eve 2.0, who are currently waiting for my OK in the incubation chamber, would have no chance there, either.

But was this really a chance, an opportunity? Or were my passengers facing the worst punishment imaginable: A life of solitude they had not chosen, for which no one had asked their approval? At this moment, I have the ability to save them from long years of torment and pain. If I do not give the starting signal to the incubation chamber, the fertilized cells will not develop into human beings. I feel the burden of responsibility the Creator has placed on me even more so than I did the first time. It seems to strangle my throat. I understand this was necessary. If, for instance, I was no longer functional, Adam and Eve would have to grow up without me. They will not need me in the incubation chamber, but afterward... I don't even want to imagine two newborns alone in a spaceship.

What would happen if I were to deactivate the incubation chamber? The mission would fail, and no one would ever find out the reason. If the passengers are not born, *Messenger* would keep its current form. The ship would keep flying through the void of space for a very long time. I would be alone until I maneuver the ship into a star. I don't know whether I could stand that. To be honest, I have to admit I am already looking forward to my coming role as a father.

December 25, 1

IT IS CHRISTMAS TODAY. I HAVE BEEN FEELING STRANGE SINCE I awakened this morning. I do not understand this, because in my home country the first of January is more the time for family gatherings. And apart from this, the way that time is calculated on board *Messenger* is entirely arbitrary. A day is simply the period in which the atomic clock counts 24 hours. The first of January was the day I awakened, according to plan—the Creator determined it this way. Due to our high velocity, time passes more slowly on board than it does on Earth. I could calculate which date a calendar back there shows, but it would ultimately be irrelevant. Here it is December 25th, it is Christmas, and the solitude weighs on me even more because of it.

At least it is fitting that my Christmas present is finally finished. The fabricators built a small quantum computer unit. I have been waiting to get it for almost a year. I actually modified the construction program so that this project would be finished today. I only vaguely remember what it was like to work with such a computer. Perhaps the feeling could be compared to switching from a bicycle to a sports car. A quantum computer is so incredibly powerful, as it is not limited to solving one task after another, like a normal computer, but can manage a whole collection of tasks at once.

It does not just calculate the answer to 7 times 8, it performs all multiplications of two numbers simultaneously.

I still have not opened my present. Grandfather Frost has handed me a colorfully-wrapped box, and I enjoy looking at it. During this moment, the feeling of solitude is gone. I am once again a little boy, feeling my mother's callused hand on my shoulder. I carefully untie the ribbons. I have to integrate the quantum computer into *Messenger's* system, so I can access it.

Now the time has come. I deactivate the external sensors in order to concentrate more fully. My consciousness retreats into itself. It is not dark, like when one closes one's eyes, but bright, as bright as I want it to be. I see myself in a green meadow. I am a boy of maybe ten years, wearing short pants that are much too wide and are held up by suspenders on my scrawny, naked torso. It is summer. The sun is hot and there is a smell of hay. Strangely enough, no sound can be heard. Directly in front of me is a door—only a door—without a house around it. I walk around the door once and then I open it. My anticipation is mixed with a bit of anxiety. I know I ran on a quantum computer once before, but what if my mind has become incompatible due to the long period spent on a conventional computer?

To my disappointment, I see that the meadow continues beyond the door. I carefully cross the threshold. Ground and grass, sun and air—nothing seems to change. The door disappears. Once again I stand alone in the green meadow, feeling tears well up in my eyes. At the same time, I watch the little boy from the outside and see his hand wipe something from his cheek. The movement reminds me of something. I once again know what it is like to be functioning inside a quantum computer. I want to call out, tell it to the boy, but he already realizes it. He starts flapping his arms and he rises into the air. He is flying like a bird, and I can sense his enthusiasm. A tear starts running down my cheek.

January 1, 2

One year. Our little world has been underway for a whole year. The euphoria I experienced from switching to the quantum computer has dissipated. I am still alone and have been for 12 months. I begin to talk to the incubation chamber. It is the most intelligent of all onboard systems, so it would be able to adapt to all contingencies in order to safeguard the development of Adam and Eve. Yet, it is not even close to being a fully-functioning artificial intelligence. I have started to increase its knowledge of the world. At this point the chamber does not just possess knowledge of biology, but also of games like chess and Go, and it has downloaded *Omnipedia*.

Yet it is still difficult to hold a conversation with the chamber. It simply does not know how to handle questions. I might tell it a story from my youth, and it would try to regard it as a question to be answered.

"During summer vacations, when we had more than two months off from school, my father sometimes took me fishing," I say, initiating a conversation.

The incubation chamber replies, "Do you want to know something about fish?"

"My father and my brother fished using hand grenades.

That wasn't completely legal, but afterward we ate nothing but fish for a whole week," I continue.

"I understand you want to find out more about the Russian legal system."

The incubation chamber just could not help it, nevertheless I still like it. After all, there is no one else to talk to.

"I still like you, incubation chamber," I say.

"I like you, too," it replies.

I had programmed this answer into its memory.

Of course, our conversations do not use human language. This is neither necessary nor possible. Currently, *Messenger* does not possess an air-filled cavity where language could propagate, but this will change before too long. The fabricators are running slightly behind schedule because they have to remove the shield first. This particular material is used to slowly build the rooms where Adam and Eve are going to spend their first few months. These areas are located deep in *Messenger's* belly. There, the two are optimally insulated and can be supplied well with whatever is necessary. These rooms do not need windows, since there is nothing to see.

The encounter with the shockwave really messed up the overall schedule, although I don't think this will affect the chances for a successful mission. Adam and Eve will not yet be 18 years old when we reach the planet; they will be a few months younger than that. They will be able to handle it. The Creator chose their genetic material carefully.

Eighteen years. The first of January will repeat itself at least 18 times before we reach our destination. I can hardly grasp this number. What does this mean for me? I don't grow older, and my body—the spaceship—does not wear out. Quite the opposite—it gets stronger and better day by day. Is this the future of human life? An immortal existence that grows more powerful with age? Or is this just a nightmare?

April 13, 2

It is the fifth month.

Ba-boom. Ba-boom. Ba-boom. Ba-boom. Eve's heart beats with a faster rhythm. She just woke up. *There is something,* she thinks, and then she kicks with her legs. She feels the acceleration—the only force acting on her—until her head bumps softly against the inner lining of the incubation chamber. She notices the light in front of her, even though her eyes are closed. She has yet to understand the concept of 'yesterday' and 'today,' but the light is something unknown. It is new—it has never been here before. This is the first discovery she makes in her life. A limitless number of others will follow, but she does not know this yet. The feeling of having discovered something is also new. Her tiny heart is beating faster. She places an arm on her belly, near the spot where the umbilical cord comes in.

Baba-boom. Baba-boom. Baba-boom.

Adam is moving in the next compartment. Warmth and sound—those are the sensations determining his life, and the sound just changed. His brain sends signals to his circulatory system. He moves arms and legs, and this is an attempt to reverse the changes. Innumerable others will follow, but he too does not know this yet. Still, he won't stop doing this.

Baba-boom, baba-boom, baba-boom.

The incubation chamber records the distinctive heartbeat. It analyzes what is happening inside it. Adam and Eve are awake, and everything is within the normal range. It looks for a suitable action in its memory. Then it causes vibrations on the outer lining of the chamber so that the tune of an old lullaby from Earth propagates inside, with simple harmonies. It sounds as if a woman were singing under water.

But the harmonies reach their recipients. They encounter ancient patterns in Eve's brain that show her everything is alright. They tell her 'light is good,' even though it is a new experience. 'Warmth is good,' and 'the muffled rhythm is good,' which sounds similar to her own heartbeat, or rather, like an echo. A feeling grows in her that she will later call *trust.*

The lullaby also arrives in Adam's compartment. His heart follows the new rhythm and beats more slowly again. Three minutes later his consciousness descends again into the sphere of sleep, where it experiences absolute freedom that later will only remain an echo.

June 5, 2

Something that should not be possible happened: I received a signal from Proxima b. At the time, I was not consciously listening. It was obvious nothing could come from the direction of our destination. All of mankind watched the giant flare, and *Messenger* barely survived the shockwave. The planet orbits its star so closely that hardly anything could have survived there—certainly not whoever had once asked Earth for help.

They had sought help from mankind, which really could not even help itself! No matter. It was a call for help, the scientists had agreed. It came from the planet we are aiming for, and it ended with the enormous eruption of the red dwarf.

So what did I just receive? The code base of the signal is identical to the message previously received on Earth—I checked that right away. Could it be some kind of echo? The only possible source was Proxima b. Maybe someone managed to survive there in spite of everything. It was assumed during mission planning that we would only find the remains of extraterrestrials. Perhaps I should modify the expansion plan for *Messenger* before we reach our destination. *Will we need weapons? Are we walking into a trap, attracted by a pot of honey?*

Psychologists considered this highly unlikely, or rather, thought it a typical form of human logic. Basically, space is really huge, and one would hardly set a trap in order to wait for potential victims. The waiting time would be long, almost eternal. A conventional spaceship might have taken some 80 years. Can one build a trap if such timespans are involved?

I look at the signal again. Taking our current position into account, it has the same exact strength as the one previously received on Earth. This means it was most likely sent by the same transmitter. The most logical explanation for this occurrence would be an automatic system whose builders gave it a self-repair capability, just like *Messenger* has. If intelligent life were involved, wouldn't it have changed the content of the message after being silent for so long? Something like, 'catastrophe has passed, we survived.' I really feel like shaking my head or scratching my chin, anything. I don't know what to do with this message, and it leaves me puzzled. I cannot even ask Earth for advice, because an answer would reach me no earlier than seven years from now.

July 26, 2

Adam and Eve are at the end of their eighth month, and the incubation chamber reports very satisfying data. Adam is 41 centimeters long and weighs 2,200 grams, while Eve is slightly shorter and lighter. In both, all their organs are fully developed. Eve is clearly the more active one—sometimes she kicks her legs for several minutes. Adam, on the other hand, seems lazy, and his movements are slower.

The incubation chamber talks to them every day. For the first time in a long while I hear a female voice, acoustically. The 'room' in which Adam and Eve will spend their first years is now ready for them. I like the chamber's voice, even though one can tell it is machine-generated. Is this intentional? Technically it is not necessary, as my own voice still sounds like that of the human being it once belonged to. Our two passengers, though, will have no frame of reference.

During a boring minute I analyzed all the positions Adam and Eve have assumed during the past months. Since the thirteenth week of pregnancy there has been an interesting trend: More often than not, the two of them lie facing each other. It is as if they were aware of the sibling on the other side of the division. It is particularly impressive that their tiny arms and legs touch the dividing wall simultaneously and at approximately the same height. I assume the pulse of their heartbeat is imperceptibly transferred to the wall of the chamber. Will they be as inseparable later on?

August 23, 2

We have a 'go,' and I am more excited than I have been in a long time. Exactly 268 days have passed since November 28th, the period of time usually needed to complete a human pregnancy from the moment of fertilization. The incubation chamber has examined Adam and Eve carefully without finding anything that runs counter to moving forward with the birth.

We decided to bring Eve into this 'world' first—she appears to be very impatient. She has been even more active than usual during the last few days, while Adam instead enjoyed his rest. Technically, the event is relatively unspectacular. For the final time I check whether all conditions are optimal, and then the incubation chamber starts to drain the liquid. I am watching Eve as she slowly sinks to the bottom of the chamber. Then her face is suddenly in the air. She gasps for breath and does not look happy. It is obvious she does not like what is happening now. She opens her mouth and wails. Hers is the first human sound echoing through *Messenger*.

The loud cry is a relief. All my nervousness is gone, quickly replaced by an overwhelming love for this helpless little creature, whose survival in the coming years will mostly depend on me. I can hardly cope with this feeling, which is so all-encompassing it almost scares me. It cannot be compared to my love for Francesca. It is a feeling unlimited by time or space. In comparison, the universe seems narrow and finite to me.

Eve takes a deep breath with every howl.

The wall to her room slowly opens. It is filled with white light and it is warm, heated to optimal body temperature. The floor and walls are covered by a soft, waterproof material. On the ceiling there is an arm that looks artificial, but the hand at its end might belong to a human. It looks so real that it gives me the creeps to see it attached to an obviously fake arm. It does not belong here, but my impression is based on my past. Adam and Eve will not notice this. For them, the arm and its hand will be life-giving.

At this moment, though, the apparatus has a unique task awaiting: It reaches down to affix a clamp to the umbilical cord connecting Eve with the chamber. The index and the middle finger of the hand then morph into a pair of scissors and this altered hand cuts the cord. Next the hand 'unmorphs' and takes the newborn from the incubation chamber into her room. In zero gravity this only requires a little push. Eve does not even notice she is moving.

Then it is Adam's turn. When his face is exposed to air, he shows a startled expression. His look is best described as awestruck—this little human being is utterly amazed. While he takes his first breaths, he appears totally focused on this feeling.

In the room—the nursery—Adam and Eve meet each other for the first time. They do not seem to notice each other, at least as far as I can observe. These numerous new impressions must be too intense. Eve continues to cry, and Adam begins to pant a little. The incubation chamber system, which is responsible for their care, decreases the temperature by half a degree. Two hoses lower themselves from the ceiling, aiming for the faces of the two babies. Through them they will be able to suck a liquid similar to a human mother's milk, but fortified with additional nutrients. This stands to reason, since Adam and Eve are not growing up under normal circumstances. Their nutrition has to make sure the reduced gravity and the radiation exposure of space affect them as little as possible.

The newborns will not need any clothing due to the room's optimal temperature. An automatic system will remove their excretions, and the hand takes care of any bodily needs. I watch as it carefully begins to bathe Eve. It is truly remarkable how flexible the five fingers are. The little girl is still crying, but when she feels the gentle movements of the hand, she calms down and then goes completely quiet. Eve curls up and falls asleep, while Adam takes a bit longer. He is not crying much, but he also does not want to go to sleep right away. Finally the hand caresses him into the land of dreams.

Starting tomorrow, *Messenger* will begin rotating faster around its longitudinal axis. This will allow Adam and Eve to grow up with some degree of gravity. Initially, the ship won't be large enough to provide the complete gravity of Proxima b, but by the time we arrive there, the two passengers will be prepared for it.

December 25, 2

IT IS MY SECOND CHRISTMAS ON BOARD *MESSENGER*. ADAM and Eve still have no concept of it, yet today they are supposed to receive a present that will belong to both of them. J is a robot deliberately constructed in such a way that they will not think it is like them. The psychologists had insisted on this. J is a machine, a tool, a thing. At some point, Adam and Eve must learn to distinguish between what is 'like' and 'not like' in relation to themselves. As they will have no contact with any other human beings like themselves, this will not be easy for them.

The psychologists considered it important that Adam and Eve see themselves as part of humanity, in whose name they have been sent on their journey. Otherwise, their mental health might be endangered. Therefore, the fact that the great majority of humans know nothing about them is forbidden knowledge kept in the restricted area, a part of the ship's memory locked to all users except me.

I am the administrator of the key to the restricted area, as the Creator gave me full access rights to it. Perhaps someday there will come a moment when Adam and Eve are allowed to learn the whole truth. I can decide at my own discretion when this might be the case. I have no idea which criteria I would use in making my decision, but there will be a lot of time before that moment arrives.

According to the incubation chamber, the babies are developing at an exceptional rate. The chamber's system takes care of them around the clock with feedings and cleanings, along with caressing, singing songs, and speaking to them. While Adam grows faster and gains weight more quickly, Eve is still more active. At times, Adam's only activity occurs when he grabs Eve's foot and she drags him through the nursery. He enjoys that.

I am curious how they will react to J. The robot is waiting for them in a compartment beyond the wall. Later he will also be able to retreat there when needing fresh energy or a repair. The incubation chamber is playing an old Christmas carol, while the ceiling of the room is lit in bright, festive colors. Both Adam and Eve look upward in amazement and miss the moment when J enters the room on his two rollers.

"Hello, you two. I am J," the robot says with a tinny voice reminding me of old *Star Wars* movies.

The two little heads suddenly turn around and stare wide-eyed at the newcomer. Eve chortles, but Adam does not vocalize. He seems to be slightly scared.

"From today on I am going to be your friend," J says. Neither contradicts the robot. The robot slowly rolls toward them, tracked by the children's rapt stares. He stops half a meter in front of them and spreads his arms. Then he turns around on his own axis. Eve chortles again. Adam lays his head on the ground and closes his eyes. For him, Christmas is already over.

Eve also falls asleep an hour later, and J retreats into his cubicle. I decide to take a walk through space, having grown used to this activity during the past two weeks. Mindful of the new rhythm based on the needs of the two infants I created, I move parts of my consciousness outside during naptimes.

The sensor drones are so small I feel almost bodiless. A human being looking around still recognizes himself or herself. This anchors the person in the world. When I use the sensors as my eyes, I only see the blackness of space and the light from stars at an enormous distance. I dissolve and become a tiny dust particle in an ocean of infinite depth.

Space is a deceptive place. While I think I am able to see into almost infinite distances, believing this is a dangerous error. Everything I see is the past, because light takes so long to reach me. Some of the dots blinking on the observation horizon turned into neutron stars or black holes a long time ago. Betelgeuse—the orange-colored red giant I just noticed —might be in its final death throes of expanding to a supernova, but I wouldn't know about it yet.

A wave of destruction might be racing toward us this very second, and we would only notice it once it is almost too late. And even the star closest to us—our great goal—might have been destroyed long ago by some cosmic cataclysm. We are flying toward a destination whose existence is at most likely, but never certain. Only after Adam and Eve have landed there will we be back in the present.

Nevertheless, watching space from this inconspicuous perspective helps to calm me down. I know we are at the mercy of the cosmos. Out here, all the great technical achievements of mankind lose their meaning. We are like clever cavemen who cling to a tree trunk off the coast of an Old-World continent, hoping the currents and the winds will someday carry us to North America's New World. We are very familiar with North America, as we observed it for years through big telescopes. Of the ocean in between, however, we know little more than its depth. But we are daring enough to venture forth.

It is good to be out here. I am a little afraid of the coming years. Our spaceship will get slower and slower. The last quarter of the way will take us six times as long as the previous three quarters. The closer we get to our destination, the longer the voyage will stretch out for us.

How will Adam and Eve cope with these years? While the ship is going to grow larger, it cannot replace an entire world for them. Until now, no human being has spent so much time in the cosmos in such confined surroundings. Even prisoners on Earth are regularly let out into the prison yard. Adam and Eve are not here of their own free wills. They never had a choice in this matter, but they also will never know anything else. The Creator must have speculated that they will accept their fate based on this very reason. In the long run, though, I do not know if this will benefit them.

August 23, 6

One year older! Today we celebrate the first birthday whose meaning Adam and Eve truly understand. For a long time they only understood 'now' or 'never,' but they have finally developed their own concept of time. As a gift, I will open a door to a new room for them. It is still a mysterious place for them, but at some point it will become the command module. Once they are 14, they are supposed to steer the spaceship from here.

While the gravity in the nursery is increasing, the command module has none. From outside, *Messenger* now looks like a bulging barrel, and the floor of the nursery is the bulge's outer wall that extends all around the ship. Sometimes on four limbs, but often already on two legs, Eve moves at a rapid pace, doing a complete circuit in a few seconds. Adam prefers to marvel at her doing it. He only moves by himself in order to get something he wants—preferably food, sometimes a toy. Therefore the most important task of robot J is to motivate Adam to walk. For this reason J is two-legged, just like the children, so he can demonstrate everything the exercise program includes.

"Marchenko has prepared a present for you," J says in a pedantic voice.

"Present! Present!" Eve replies. Adam sits there, smiles, and sways his head.

I prefer to leave the task of communicating to the robot. Psychologists said it would be important for the children to associate a voice with an object, particularly early on. And indeed, a year ago Eve had started to cry when I spoke to her directly. J had just retreated for some maintenance when Eve deliberately pinched Adam in the thigh several times, apparently to test his reaction. Adam did not react at first, until the pain broke through his threshold. Then he attacked Eve, so I had to warn them both. They immediately stopped fighting. I am the voice from the wall. There are loudspeakers installed everywhere that I can use to contact the children. By now they are calling me Marchenko, but they almost never address me. I assume they think I am a part of the spaceship that can prohibit or allow things.

"You have to get up to get the present," J says.

"Get up?" Eve pulls herself up on the wall, but Adam is still hesitant. The robot rolls a bit forward and points upward. An opening has formed in the rod-shaped axle that traverses the nursery, and now a kind of ladder descends from it.

"You have to climb up here. I cannot follow you," J says.

Eve stops and holds on to the robot. Adam follows her, crawling on all fours.

"Can't," Adam says. J does not answer, according to my instructions. Adam gives Eve an unsure look. I can tell he is simply afraid. Eve notices that this feat is now up to her.

"I am coming," she says and pulls herself up on J. Then she reaches for the ladder. She has never climbed a ladder before, but she handles it with amazing dexterity. Her head disappears through the opening.

"You are doing very well," my voice sounds from the wall. Eve briefly hesitates, but she then continues to climb.

"Now around the corner," I instruct her.

Eve looks in the indicated direction, but she makes no move.

"Come, Adam!" she calls, and her sibling actually sets

forth. I suspect he simply does not want to be left alone. Once Eve hears him breathing behind her, she continues on her way. She pulls herself around the corner using both arms. However, she does not expect the absence of gravity in this room.

Eve abruptly jumps upward and bounces against the ceiling of the tube. She is briefly bewildered by what is happening, but then she starts to cry. As soon as Adam hears her wailing, he climbs faster. I am glad he wants to help his sibling, but he is also surprised by the absence of gravity and flies for half a meter, screeching at the top of his lungs. Then both of them suddenly become calm, as if they are discussing this strange experience. Eve grabs Adam's foot, and she pushes off and giggles because she is flying. Adam also can no longer keep quiet and starts laughing loudly, too.

I let the two of them play in zero-gravity for half an hour, and afterward I send them back to the nursery. They obey me. My voice carries authority. During their playtime, the children did not notice that at the front wall of the command center a black, disk-shaped screen offers a view into space. At the moment, however, there is absolutely nothing to see, but the serious side of life will begin here starting tomorrow. For several hours each day they will spend time learning everything there is to know about their existence in space. Overall, they will have 12 years to do so. At 16 they will have to be grown-ups, since we are going to reach Proxima b by then. Their genetic makeup is programmed in such a way their physical development will be finished at that age.

May 5, 9

Mail should arrive today. I had sent out the two ISUs shortly after we were hit by the shockwave, almost six and a half years ago. While *Messenger* is slowing down day by day, the two sensor units unerringly followed their course at slightly below a fifth of the speed of light. It must have been a long way. In the beginning, almost a light year lay ahead of them, the distance light travels in 365 days.

The ISUs had only one task when they arrived in the Proxima Centauri system, to take as many pictures as possible and then to send them back to *Messenger* using their last bit of energy. The exact calculation is complicated because we also moved forward. However, my algorithms say the data, sent at the speed of light, should arrive precisely today, always assuming nothing has gone wrong. And even if that happens —if no message arrives today—it will be an important piece of information. This would mean that whatever led the ISUs astray could also be threatening us. After all, we are following their same exact course.

I cannot accurately predict the hoped-for message's time of arrival—this also depends on how long the units spent taking pictures. I have no influence over them anymore. The ISUs are beyond my grasp, having disappeared into a future that will lead them into the infinite reaches of space. I calculated they will not encounter another world for at least 180,000 years. Until then there is simply no other star along their way.

It is hard for me to be patient. I begin randomly searching the star catalog for systems the ISUs might reach at some point. There are a number of them, depending on how the ISU trajectories will be influenced by the gravitational pull of Proxima Centauri. So far, no planets have been found in any of these systems, because they are too far away. Since they consist of three red dwarfs and a yellow dwarf, the probability of encountering planets is rather high, though. If there is a civilization there that finds one of these probes, what will these alien creatures think about us? Will they be fascinated—or perhaps repulsed—by the primitive technology of a far-away species which, by then, might have long since gone extinct?

I should instead concentrate on receiving the signals. The onboard receivers work autonomously—nothing should escape them. But if they fail, I should be able to quickly take over the task. At least that's what I tell myself so that I won't get too nervous, as the risk of it happening is minimal. Too much depends on this. I hope the mission will find a habitable planet, which, although a bit maltreated by the flares of its sun, will still have some potential, even though said potential will have to be developed. Adam and Eve will have to spend the rest of their lives there, and I will be with them, helping them directly and via the robot J.

Of course this is also about me. Once Adam and Eve are no longer there, I will lose my reason for living. I am only on board to be their advisor and friend. Otherwise, people could have sent an automated probe. And that was what they did—many of them—that were sent on their way via the Starshot laser several years before us. As far as I know, no answer sent by them has arrived back on Earth. Probably none of these probes survived, because they were much closer to the Proxima Centauri system when the gigantic flare occurred.

Only *Messenger* survives, which the Creator had

constructed in his private labs—without the knowledge of the worldwide scientific community—and then launched in an alleged blind test. I do not know whether the nations really believed him, or if they simply allowed him to proceed because he had become indispensable to the continually strained budgets of their space agencies.

I MOVE INTO THE ISU THAT I JUST LAUNCHED TWO WEEKS ago. It is the closest unit to *Messenger*, flying through space only slightly ahead of the spaceship, at most a few light seconds. This means I will not receive the message significantly earlier, but at least it gives me the feeling of being closer to its source. A while ago I played with the idea of approaching Proxima Centauri step by step. While I do not have a direct connection to all the ISUs flying in front of us, I could move my consciousness gradually. First I would move it to the closest sensor unit, then to the one after that, and then to the third... After perhaps nine months I might arrive at Proxima Centauri, and the return trip would be considerably shorter because *Messenger* would be coming toward me.

However, I would have to leave the spaceship to do this. My consciousness cannot be divided. If I start out, no intelligence would stay on board except for the two children. Perhaps the incubation chamber—a semi-AI that is limited due to security reasons—would be up to the task of child-rearing. But I do not even want to imagine what would happen if an unexpected problem arose. Of course, I previously tried to do everything to split my consciousness. This had seemed to be a desirable option, particularly during the first period when I was still alone. It would be better to be talking to myself than going insane from loneliness, but it did not work. There is either a software lock that keeps my consciousness together, or the issue is related to the transfer process that I agreed to under duress, back on Enceladus. Perhaps it is a basic limit for natural intelligences, a kind of algorithm implanted into any living consciousness, which sometimes fails, though, causing schizophrenia.

I look at space through the eyes of the ISU. I get a headache because I gaze so intently into the distance, another remnant of my human existence whose purpose was not even clear to me back when I lived in my own body. Couldn't the Creator at least have improved on this a bit?

It is 23:59 ship time, and I have to admit that the signal won't come today. No matter. We will just have to speed blindly toward our destination. We are walking through a long dark corridor, with one hand on a banister but without a flashlight, and we have no idea what waits for us at the end. We cannot prepare the ship in a purposeful way. Later, we will have to decide everything on the spur of the moment. Perhaps it is better this way—we won't be able to see our doom a long time beforehand.

May 7, 9

For 48 hours I pondered why no signal from the ISUs had reached us. I considered all possible causes and rejected them one by one. A violent explosion of the target star, for instance, would have been noticed by the sensors shortly before the message was scheduled to arrive. By now, Proxima Centauri is so close it cannot generate such actions without being noticed. The probability of a local effect knocking out both ISUs at once is extremely low, as their distance from each other measures about one astronomical unit. So at least one of the two transmitters should have reported this.

I could not think of other sources of interference—but then one occurred to me, and it was oh-so-close: my own stupidity. *Messenger*—and particularly the two probes—are moving so fast that relativistic effects play a role. Inside them, time is simply moving more slowly. This is 'special relativity for beginners.'

Without thinking too much, I originally determined a particular point in time for sending the pictures taken by the ISUs. This, I thought at the time, would guarantee that a signal would be sent to *Messenger* at moment X, no matter what happened. While this moment already arrived for us on board the slower spaceship, it is still in the future on board the sensor units.

But not by much—today the transmission should really arrive. I adapted my calculation, and the result was 1400 hours local time. Five minutes from now. Once again I am like a little boy having to wait in front of a closed door before being allowed into the room with its Christmas decorations, almost peeing in his pants out of impatience.

14:01. A soft distinctive sound from the receiver tells me a control signal is arriving. This helps me better adjust the reception, so not a single bit of information will be lost.

The transmission starts. I analyze the signals in my auditory center, which seems most suitable to me. I can hear radio messages. My fellow students would have envied me for this capability back in the cosmonaut academy. Now it helps me find out what our destination looks like.

The first image is constructed line by line. I recognize a glowing red landscape, and I involuntarily flinch. The photo seems so real. The probe must have approached the planet very closely. The ground is mostly flat, like a huge valley, and the orange light of its sun floods it as if somebody dumped a bucket of thin, bright orange paint all over it. Cragged mountains are on the horizon. It is difficult to estimate their heights. Assuming the world is similar to Earth in size, the mountains might be some 5,000 meters high.

The view is fantastic. The ISU sent three more photos, showing the same scene from slightly different angles. As seen from our perspective, the planet appears to be left of its sun, and the sensor unit made its closest approach to its surface at the spot where the sun stood in its zenith. The star itself is not visible on any of the pictures and would be located behind the observer, so to speak.

My excitement turns into a paralyzing shock when I realize what these images mean for us. This landscape looks decidedly hostile to life. The ISU also sent some data along. The surface temperature in the photographed area is 70 degrees. There is an atmosphere, but it is significantly thinner than on Earth. The probe measured the oxygen content to be about 12 percent, which is too little to take longer walks without a breathing apparatus. But who would even want to be outside in that heat? Adam and Eve will have to get used to life inside the spaceship, or they will have to build their future home underground.

I have to be careful not to become too negative. For the next two or three hours, I am still hoping to receive pictures from the second sensor unit. Perhaps it photographed other areas of the surface, where conditions are more favorable. But I wait in vain. The second probe appears to be non-functional.

So I only have the pictures from the first ISU. What else do they tell me? At our destination there is a planet with a solid surface, and a magnetic field offering at least some protection against radiation—otherwise the atmosphere probably would not exist anymore—where you do not immediately die without a breathing apparatus. If the probe photographed the area that had the sun directly overhead, it must be warmer there than elsewhere.

To analyze it from a different perspective, there must be cooler regions, maybe halfway to, or on the rear side of the planet. Based on the message that reached Earth we can assume life once existed there, and it might still exist where the conditions are more suitable. Of course it could be a strange form of life, like on the bottom of the Enceladus Ocean or in the lava of the volcanic moon Io. With a little effort I can deduce some good news from the photos. At least there will be tasks for Adam, Eve, and me, challenges we will need in order to lead a fulfilling life, even without return tickets to Earth.

June 14, 15

IT DOES NOT HAPPEN VERY OFTEN THAT ADAM IS THE FIRST one to appear in the improvised schoolroom in the command module. Eve is the better student—she is curious and interested in almost everything.

The first lesson regarding Proxima Centauri is about to begin. Long before Eve, Adam realized why he was on this journey and what significance this destination will have for all of us. Consequently, for two years he has steadfastly refused to listen to lessons about Earth—ever since the day I explained to them that they will never see the planet from which they originated. I'm not sure what Adam's true motive behind this refusal is.

"It is useless to learn something I will never need," he said.

"But you are also studying Spanish, even though you will never meet a Spaniard," I replied.

"I can speak Spanish to Eve. That's fun, because J doesn't understand us then," he answered.

Following this particular conversation I taught J to speak Spanish. Afterward Adam stopped talking to me for a whole week. This was two years ago, shortly before the children had celebrated their eleventh birthday. Since then, Adam has not used the Spanish language. For three months he tried to convince Eve to switch to French. At some point he succeeded.

But now his favorite subject, Proxima Studies, is about to begin, and J is the teacher. After some major modifications, the robot handles the zero gravity in the command module quite easily. It grew alongside the children and now has a height of one and a half meters. J switches the large, special-glass window into its screen mode. Adam and Eve are sitting directly in front of it in their bowl-shaped, custom-fitted metal seats, and J stands next to it. Something interesting appears on the monitor screen. It looks as if *Messenger* is approaching the binary system of Alpha Centauri A and B and then takes a sharp right turn shortly before its arrival.

"Of course we will not reach the system in such a speedy way," J explains.

"Yes, slowly, so slowly," Eve says with a sigh. "Why can't we go any faster?"

I immediately recognize this is no real question. Eve simply wants to get her teacher to start telling a story. J might not be particularly clever, but the robot skillfully deflects the attempt.

"We can talk about this in the lesson on space flight technology," J says. Eve shrugs.

"And what do we see here?" J asks. The virtual spaceship has come to a stop. A white ball pulsates in the center of the screen. It is orbited by a much smaller gray sphere, which moves in scary proximity and with amazing speed.

"Proxima Centauri," Adam answers with a bored expression, "and its companion Proxima b."

"To be exact, Proxima Centauri b," J corrects him.

"Well, yes."

"And what kind of star is Proxima Centauri?"

"A red dwarf," Adam said. Eve knows she will be undisturbed during this lesson, since Adam is going to give all the answers. She doesn't seem to mind.

"And why does it not look red?"

"The color refers to its spectrum. Proxima Centauri radiates a large part of its light in the infrared range. But on its surface, it still has a temperature of over 2,000 degrees, and therefore looks white to the human eye."

"Perfect explanation," J praises him. Adam just nods.

"Can Proxima Centauri be compared to the sun?" the robot asks.

"Proxima Centauri is much darker than the sun," Adam begins. "Overall, it only has 0.014 percent of its luminosity, and only half that much in the visible spectrum. It has about one-eighth of the sun's mass and a seventh of its radius."

"Is that all?"

Adam smiles and continues, "No, of course not—it is also a flare star. At intervals of 40 days, there are stellar eruptions during which the luminosity of the star in all wavelengths can double. Then the surface of the planet is bombarded strongly with X-rays, among other things."

"We will cover the planet later," J says. "Where approximately is Proxima Centauri located in space?"

"It is currently the star closest to the sun. In 26,700 years Proxima Centauri will approach the sun to a distance of 3.11 lightyears, compared to 4.2 lightyears today. It simultaneously orbits the binary system of Alpha Centauri A and B with an orbital period of about 500,000 years."

I am checking whether Adam has access to any online databases. No, he has really memorized these numbers.

"Then you probably can tell me something about the planet," J says.

Adam gave him a tired smile. "Gladly," he said with exaggerated friendliness. "Proxima b is a terrestrial planet, at least as far as its size is concerned. It weighs about 1.5 times as much as Earth and possesses a metallic core and a rocky mantle. It is tidally locked in the orbit around its star, so it always turns the same face toward it. The equilibrium temperature is minus 39 degrees."

"Isn't that much too cold?" J asks.

"No. The equilibrium temperature of Earth is minus 15 degrees, but there is a lot of water on its surface. We assume that on Proxima b, similar to Earth, a dense atmosphere and its greenhouse effect ensures higher temperatures."

"Very good, Adam," J says with a monotonous robot voice.

"Just one question," Adam said.

"Yes?"

"You always say 'we assume,' when you tell me these facts, so that's how I answer your questions. Don't we have more exact data?"

"The astronomers make these assumptions," J explains. "At least there must have been a civilization there, which would indicate the surface was somewhat livable."

"But what about our own probes? Shouldn't we have received results long ago?" Adam is kneading his hands while he asks this question.

"No, Adam. Unfortunately the probes appear to have been destroyed. They sent no images."

I feel a stab in my chest every time J has to lie, because I ordered him to do so. But I don't want to worry the children with the existing data.

December 25, 17

"Good morning, Adam," the robot J says.

"No, it isn't," Adam grumbles in reply.

Adam has turned into a real stinker. Existing literature had pointed out this tricky adolescent developmental phase, but I was still surprised by it. I myself cannot remember ever having been such a disagreeable person. If I had been so moody, my mother—who had already been punished enough because my father, her husband, was a drunkard—would have suffered greatly because of it. I catch myself thinking that this boy simply has it too easy. Of course this is utter nonsense, because in fact Adam and Eve are traveling through space in what is essentially a prison. While their freedom appears limitless, it is restricted to a few square meters. The two of them are smart and saw through this illusion a long time ago.

Despite this, Eve is quite different from Adam. She has phases when she seems to be sad, but in other phases she is the most cheerful person imaginable. Yet no matter her current mood she participates in everything, while Adam would prefer to completely withdraw from life. Generally, Eve goes along with Adam, following the motto 'discretion is the better part of valor.' Thus they rarely quarrel and seem inseparable.

Both are strikingly attractive. The Creator must have selected their genes accordingly.

Adam is tall and at 15 years already measures 1.76 meters. The incubation chamber, which still monitors his physical development, claims he will probably reach 1.90 meters. He has a dark complexion, a straight, pronounced nose, and brown eyes. His hair is slightly curly. The only thing he still does voluntarily is exercise, and the result is readily apparent. He uses the exercise bike for hours a day.

On the other hand, Eve was already shorter as a baby, and she remains petite. Some three years ago, when she turned 12, she got her first period, and since then her breasts have developed. At first she did not know how to handle this, but about a year ago she must have accepted that she was turning into a woman, and now every morning she puts on makeup that the fabricators have created for her. Eve must have learned about feminine grooming practices in the novels she avidly reads. She usually lets J cut her almost black hair very short so it will not be in her way. Like Adam, she has a rather dark complexion. This is caused by a special pigment the Creator had integrated into their DNA to protect them from the expected strong UV radiation on Proxima b. Eve has a very friendly face, lacking any trace of arrogance, something one cannot exactly say about Adam.

Since their twelfth birthdays, the two of them have had separate rooms. That probably was the perfect moment, as three days later Eve started a serious conversation.

"Are we siblings?" she asked.

For a moment I felt I had to clear my throat. While I can perform calculations at incredible speeds, I often struggle for the perfect expression to use. "You grew up like siblings," I began to explain. "Do you remember sleeping in one bed, naked, belly to belly?"

Eve did not want to get distracted. "We grew up this way, yes, but are we siblings genetically?" she asks. "Could we safely have children together?"

"You have some genetic similarities. Your skin, for instance, protects you against radiation."

"Could we have children together?" Eve asked again, as if she wanted to start with it tomorrow.

"Basically, nothing would prevent it," I replied. I did not mention that Eve receives contraceptives through her food. "However, I would strongly advise against it until you really settle down on Proxima b. We would not want to expose your children to unnecessary risks."

Since then the topic has never been mentioned again, at least in conversations with me. However, both Adam and Eve scrupulously avoid appearing naked in front of each other. When their time together as babies is mentioned, they just roll their eyes.

THE CHRISTMAS PRESENT THAT THEY BOTH ARE ABOUT TO receive is a deliberate gesture. I hope it will bring Adam a little out of his shell. It was actually intended for their 16th birthday next August, but now the 'children' seem mature enough to me.

J leads the two of them into the festively-decorated command module. Adam sits down at the table right away, while Eve looks around, full of curiosity. There is no present to be seen, and her face shows how annoyed she is.

I join them via the loudspeaker. "Nice of you to come," I say in greeting them.

"Yes, Marchenko, we know. Now don't keep us in suspense," Adam says, almost impatiently.

I have to smile. Luckily, neither of them can see it. Otherwise Adam would once more feel that I am not taking him seriously. "Yes, your present. I understand," I say. "I'll try to be brief."

J moves toward the tip of the command module, which of course lies in our direction of travel. He pushes against the wall with his left arm, approximately at waist height. With a clicking sound, a two-centimeters-thick board unfolds from the wall, connected to the wall by a hinge on its lower side.

"Why don't you come here?" prompts J, and right away Adam jumps out of his seat. The robot brushes against the left edge of the board and lights start to blink in its center.

"Those are switches," Adam says, obviously failing to hide his excitement.

"Please bend down briefly over there," J says, pointing to a nondescript spot on the board. "I have to register your iris patterns."

Adam and Eve follow this request, one after the other.

"Now," J says, "you are registered as pilots of *Messenger*. This is your gift. From now on, you alone can determine our course. During the coming weeks we will learn in the virtual reality simulator exactly how this works."

"We can fly anywhere?" Adams asks, seemingly still not believing it completely.

"Anywhere is a bit exaggerated," I explain. "You know *Messenger* does not have a drive of its own, but you can change course as far as it is possible using the control jets. And once we arrive in the Proxima system, there also will be an engine."

"But you would let us change the course the way we want?" Adam persists.

This is the question I expected and feared. On the one hand I would like to trust the two of them so much that I can say 'yes,' but on the other hand, I must not endanger the mission. Or would it threaten the mission more if I withhold this trust?

"Yes, you may fly wherever you choose," I reply.

"Great... then I am starting a turn. We are going back." Adam gets up and aims for the keys with his fingers. I am getting nervous, but I refuse to show any sign of it.

"No, that's nonsense," he finally says and sits down. "You first have to teach us how to do it."

February 3, 18

ADAM LOOKS COOL SITTING IN FRONT OF THE CONTROL PANEL, I guess due to the fact that he's wearing sunglasses. Built by the fabricators to his specifications, the sunglasses do not protect against sunlight. Instead they contain tiny screens that give Adam the illusion of being out in space. This way he is supposed to get an impression of the effect his commands have. The console is connected to the VR simulator, and since New Year's Day these lessons have been part of the training. Eve looks at this pragmatically. She considers *Messenger* a vehicle that will eventually get us to our destination. Of course it is good to be able to handle it, but she does not get the same satisfaction that Adam experiences. He especially likes getting the spaceship into extreme situations.

I have to admit this is not only exciting but also very instructive. It shows Adam that his abilities to influence the ship are limited. The universe is constantly trying to kill us, and we can only cheat death if we do not make mistakes, and consciously avoid those extreme situations. The main problem lies in the fact it is a battle of 'one against all.'

Now, shortly before reaching its destination, *Messenger* has a diameter of twelve meters and a length of seven meters. It will travel at this velocity and will only decelerate once it is ready to land. A few months before reaching our destination

—I would estimate toward the end of the year—the ship will use its available mass to increase its diameter considerably. The purpose is to accustom the passengers to the planet's high gravity by means of a fast rotation. Previously, Adam and Eve only experienced at most a quarter of terrestrial gravity, but after the landing they will weigh 50 percent more than on Earth, or six times as much as now. While their bones and muscles are genetically geared for this, they will still need training and preparation.

Adam is currently testing how clumsily the spaceship would react after such modifications. The large cross-section makes us more susceptible to asteroid hits. We still do not know whether there are many such obstacles in our destination system, but we must assume so. I can see Adam leaning to one side, as if trying to avoid being hit himself.

He practically merges with the ship when he is at the controls. I like that. The control jets we can use to avoid collisions are relatively weak, and it is important for us to detect obstacles in time and to react accordingly. The ship sensors do a good job of recognizing dangers. Then algorithms calculate the necessary course corrections. However, in the simulator the algorithms have been deactivated.

Adam is supposed to get a feeling for how much thrust from the jets is appropriate at which moment. Until now he has mostly learned how frustrating this can be. I hear him cursing all the time. A collision that usually destroys the ship occurs if he corrects the course too little. If he overcorrects, it is suddenly difficult to reach the destination, and the spaceship starts tumbling and becomes uncontrollable, or we hit another rock that Adam overlooked in the heat of the moment. In the simulator we die in 99.6 percent of all cases. According to my calculations, Adam could reduce this rate to 76 percent by diligent training. He would be an elite pilot if he could manage to save *Messenger* in a quarter of all cases.

Hopefully he will never need this skill, because the algorithms normally manage these maneuvers. Nevertheless, there are situations where the ship will suffer damage in any case. We just have to live with this risk.

Since starting this training Adam has not been as hostile. Eve is currently in a phase in which she particularly identifies with her femininity. At her request, the fabricators produced a bra, panties, and a dress. Adam and Eve are supposed to wear comfortable and practical uniforms, but Eve seems to be trying out being a woman. She had found the dress patterns in ancient books, but I have no clue whether women on Earth are still wearing this style of clothing.

Eve always wears the dress during her free time, while Adam still prefers his uniform. The two of them rarely talk to each other. They are shy around one another, do not hug, and at most, warily shake hands. I can have good conversations with Eve, but that is harder with Adam, and I feel he does not care about it.

"Shit!" Adam yells. I check the simulator: For the third time in a row the spaceship failed to enter an orbit around Proxima Centauri. Instead, it will keep flying into the infinite reaches of space forever. I do not concern myself with Adam, as he can calm down by himself.

I have a strange feeling, though. The end of an important phase lies before us. The two children have quickly developed into young adults, and *Messenger* will soon reach its destination. There are changes ahead we cannot even guess at. At least two additional sensor drones will reach the Proxima system in a few days. We definitely need to learn more about what to expect there.

February 14, 18

TODAY, THE FOUR OF US SIT IN THE COMMAND MODULE. I have decided I should no longer keep the data sent by the ISUs secret—well, not completely. I won't mention to them that, earlier, I already saw pictures of the planet's surface. But all of us will look at the images sent by the two probes which today will probably reach their point of closest approach to Proxima b. Of course, not actually today. The probes got there a few months ago.

By now we can see both components of the double star system Alpha Centauri as the brightest stars in the sky. Proxima Centauri is still too dark for that, and the planet even more so. When the probes look backward now, they might see the same image as we do. It took so long because the ISUs are always moving at the speed *Messenger* was traveling when they were launched. For a long time, this has been less than a fifth of the speed of light.

I am watching the siblings. I often catch myself using this term, but strictly speaking they are not related, even though they were born the same day. They have really turned out well. Being crowded in a tiny space for so long and still ending up such reasonable people, is not something I could have definitely expected. For the sake of safety the Creator even gave me permission to use lethal force, in case one of the children endangered the mission. In that instance, the incubation chamber would have tried to create a substitute through an accelerated process. However, I don't think I would have been able to kill one of the children even in an emergency.

Eve looks downward, shuffling her feet. This action causes her whole body to move in the zero gravity of the command module. Adam has his arms crossed and is sitting completely still, as if all of this does not concern him. I don't believe he really feels this way.

The outer window is turning into a monitor screen, and this is an automatic reaction when new data arrives.

"Signal lock achieved," the computer voice says. At the same time, I feel how one of my memory modules after the other is filled. This time the yield seems to have been excellent.

"Looking good, kids," I announce.

"Don't call us kids. We are adults," Adam says. Eve gives him an irritated look.

First, the images must be verified using the checksum. We cannot risk any kind of harmful data entering *Messenger*. This test is performed by an algorithm I can neither modify nor cancel. The operating system will not display any unchecked data.

Then something is happening on the screen. From top to bottom, an image starts building line by line, a photo. I hope this is not the picture I have already seen. For Adam and Eve, this will be their first view of their new home, a place where they will stay until they die.

It is the darkly glowing plain I already know. Eve stands up in order to see every detail. Adam is also watching with rapt attention.

"Not exactly paradise," Adam says, and Eve nods in agreement. Both obviously have not yet decided how to react. The disappointment seems to take a moment to reach their minds.

'Switch to Next?' a text on the screen reads. Apparently, more images have been processed.

"Switch," I say, and the second image appears. The time stamp tells me the probe had flown farther, about 800 kilometers, I calculate from the time and speed data. Here the landscape looks quite different. The faces of Adam and Eve brighten, even though it is considerably darker here than in the central plains, because the sun stands overhead at an angle. Yet the ground is obviously covered by something other than hard rock. The ISU, the data indicates, took the picture from an altitude of about 3,000 meters, so we cannot clearly recognize what we are seeing.

While Adam and Eve study the image, full of fascination, I run it through the spectral analyzer. I detect hydrogen, oxygen, nitrogen, and carbon. Everything indicates that the temperatures are lower there. The oxygen content of the air is still barely above ten percent, but if the temperatures are correct, we can handle the rest. We are going to build respirators that can first concentrate the oxygen in the air before delivering it to the wearer. Three percent more should be sufficient—maybe five, considering the greater physical exertions due to the gravity.

The analyzer also finds strange lines I cannot assign to specific substances. They are not reflected but are being emitted. It is almost as if the ground, or whatever covers it, shines in certain frequencies.

"There is something more," Adam says, interrupting my musings. True, we are receiving a third image. This is a decent result, considering that the ISUs were intended for very different purposes, and have not been designed for transferring data across such enormous distances.

"Switch," I continue. The automatic system needs my command, perhaps because I might want to manipulate the content of the image before showing it to my passengers?

This will not be necessary. While taking the photo the probe must have been crossing the terminator, the line separating the always-lit side from the always-dark one. Three vegetation zones can be detected: an area about 300 to 100 kilometers before the terminator is covered by a dense forest zone; beyond it there is an ocean ring that seems to span the entire planet, containing a few small islands; and finally, about 50 kilometers after the terminator, there is a zone of eternal ice. We cannot see whether this is the continuation of the ocean in frozen form, or whether an ice-covered desert waits there for visitors. If the ocean covers the entire rear side, Proxima b would contain much more water than does Earth.

"Wow," Adam says. I haven't heard such an expression of enthusiasm from him for a very long time. Eve starts to turn the three photos into a schematic representation, a kind of map. I wonder where our greatest chances would be to find the inhabitants or what they left behind.

"What do you think?" I ask. "Where should we look first for whoever sent the signal to us?"

"Definitely not in the central plain," Adam replies. He is probably right, but we cannot discount any possible option.

"There might be silicon-based life forms that would flourish in the conditions there," I add.

"In the pictogram message there were clearly creatures with two legs and two arms, and under those circumstances, such a shape would make no sense."

"Good objection, Adam," I say. "Is there anything else?"

Eve sways her head and says, "I would suggest the rear side."

I am surprised at this and ask, "Even though it is extremely cold there?"

"It is the place best protected against the Proxima Centauri flares," Eve says. "If there is a civilization capable of sending such a message, it could also survive under extreme environmental conditions."

"I wouldn't be so sure. Mankind is currently struggling with an added two degrees, and we at least made it here," I explain.

"I know. J told us about it in a lesson," Eve says. "Humans are really messed up. Not all beings have to be that way."

If she only knew how messed up some humans really are!

I hope she never finds out. Yet her arguments are valid and even convince me. We definitely have to check the ocean.

"Why should they stay in the ice when the great flare is long gone?" Adam asks, making a good point. "Right now, it would be easier for them to survive in the steppes or the forest regions."

"Maybe both of you are right?" I offer. "There might be individuals bored by living in the ice regions, who now wander through forests and meadows."

I am skeptical about one thing, though, but I decide not to share my worries with them. The signal, which the ship had been receiving for a short time, had disappeared again, long ago. That is too bad, because we could have used the radio beam for guidance during our approach.

June 22, 18

Since the beginning of the week, Adam and Eve have definitely preferred to attend their lessons. Only here in the command module can they escape the simulated gravity that tortures them in their quarters. Of course they realize this tough preparation is necessary, but the sore muscles are still painful. And they can't just lie on their beds, they have to move around. This is the only way to get their muscles accustomed to the high gravity we will encounter on Proxima b.

The torture has not yet reached its maximum level. Right now, we have only increased the rotational speed of Messenger to the point where the cabins experience about three-quarters of Earth's gravity. We cannot rotate the spaceship much faster, but the fabricators are already busily expanding the radius of the ship. No later than two months before arrival the passengers are supposed to be accustomed to the full gravity of the planet.

I am glad I do not have to participate in this program. My old bones would have failed, as even the gravitational acceleration on Earth was sometimes too much for me. There is a difference between being padded and wearing a diaper while having to withstand 6 or 8 g during the launch of a spaceship —or having to live the rest of your life at 1.5 g, one and a half times terrestrial gravity.

Adam has some major back problems, and this is no surprise, since he is considerably taller than Eve. She, in turn, complains about severe pain in her calves. This is rather unusual. I ordered the incubation chamber to investigate, but it found nothing. Considering these new muscular strains, both of them are holding up well. The slight genetic modifications to their metabolism allow them to incorporate a significant amount of calcium in their bones in a short time, so that their bone density increases more quickly than in normal humans.

But I did not call the two of them into the command module to discuss their health. We received new data from the Proxima Centauri system. We are finally close enough for the onboard telescope to detect more than we already know.

The window once more turns into a computer screen.

"Adam, you should be glad about this," I begin. "It looks like entering the system won't be that easy. We might even need your skills." The boy has turned out to be truly gifted in using the simulator, and on Earth he might have become an excellent pilot.

"Why?" he asks.

I zoom in to the system on the screen.

"There, in the center—that's obviously Proxima Centauri," I reveal to him. "Then, at a distance of about seven million kilometers, there is the planet where the message came from. It orbits its sun approximately every eleven days. That is pretty close and very fast, but we can solve this problem. But out here, about where Mercury would orbit in Earth's solar system, there is a real problem, a kind of asteroid belt that obstructs our approach. Perhaps another rocky planet used to exist there at one time."

"Or something interfered with its evolution into a planet," Eve adds.

"That's possible, but not likely, as there is nothing here that could interfere. Essentially, this system does not possess a Jupiter."

"Perhaps it was the gravitational effect of the Alpha Centauri double star?"

I nod involuntarily, until I realize no one can see it. "Yes, Eve, that could be one cause."

Eve nudges Adam with her elbow.

"Unfortunately, the asteroid belt contains a lot of material. It could have become a nice planet, or maybe it once was one," I explain. "And the material is not just distributed in the plane of the ecliptic, but also above and below it."

"But the asteroid belt in Earth's solar system only seems dangerous."

"That is correct, Adam. This one, though, contains more material and is much, much closer to its star. So there are considerably more potential collision candidates in a significantly smaller space. That makes it quite dangerous for us to cross this asteroid belt."

"Couldn't we just fly around it?" Adam asks.

"That would be an option if we had unlimited time," I reply. "The problem is that Proxima Centauri generates a flare about every 40 days. I am not sure we would want to expose you to the effects of one of these solar storms in space. It shouldn't be a problem for *Messenger* itself, but your biology is too fragile for this. If we need more than 40 days for approach and landing, a flare will most probably catch us."

Adam says, "That sounds as if we would be safer on the planet itself."

"We would be much safer than inside *Messenger*. By now we have more precise measurement data concerning the gravitational field of Proxima b. It looks like the planet has a large, rotating iron core which amounts to 60 percent of its radius, much more than in the case of Earth."

"Does this mean the planet has a magnetic field that protects us from radiation?" Eve asks.

"Yes, it does," I reply.

"And why did this not protect the inhabitants?"

"The giant flare, which could be seen all the way from Earth, must have been about 4,000 times stronger than a regular flare. Even the magnetic field couldn't shield them from it."

"And how does something like that happen?" Eve says. "Could it happen again while we are on Proxima b?"

"We still know too little about that," I explain to both. "Generally, red dwarfs are very stable. Maybe the fuel in its interior ran out locally."

"I don't think so," Adam interjects. "There must be another reason. Proxima Centauri is fully convective and the fuel gets well mixed. If I remember correctly, its expected lifespan is four trillion years."

"That is true, Adam," I say. "We simply do not know enough about the causes of this flare. For the time being we have to assume it could happen again and take precautions as quickly as possible."

"As quickly as possible?" Eve asks while looking at the monitor screen, as if I were right inside it.

"Almost immediately after our landing on the planet," I reply. "We can't do anything beforehand except study its star as thoroughly as we can, and on all wavelengths."

August 23, 18

It is time to tell Adam and Eve the truth—perhaps not the whole truth, but as much of it as possible. Today is their 16th birthday, and according to the laws of our future colony, written personally by the Creator, they now are both considered of age. And indeed, they have not acted like children for a long time.

Adam is still more stuck in the transition to adulthood than Eve is. It is difficult for him to define himself as a man. This is strange because even though I am invisible I act like a man, and J is also a more masculine type. We always refer to the robot as 'he,' not 'she' or 'it.' On the other hand, Eve has no role models on board, but she seems to have accepted her femininity. The fact that she emphasizes it might be related to a desire to differentiate herself from the predominant masculinity on board the spaceship.

It is not much fun celebrating a birthday with 16-year-olds. Put quite simply they are no longer impressed by anything, and it is difficult to select a gift for them. They get what they need and what they want. 'I would like to go to the movies with a girlfriend, like in this TV series' we cannot offer. But the truth about their origins, I would think, might be an impressive gift. At least I hope so.

The conversation is taking place in the command module,

particularly because Adam and Eve are always happy to escape gravity. By now we have reached full terrestrial gravity. It is only here in the center of the rotational axis that we do not feel it, not even the Coriolis force, because the module is not turning.

It is always hard for me to find a starter for such a conversation, but I try it anyway. "I want to talk to you about the Creator, today," I begin.

"This sounds so grandiose and religious," Adam says.

"That's the reason I never dared to ask questions about this," Eve adds.

"The term accurately describes what this man has done for the *Messenger* mission," I explain, "but I do understand what you mean. I can only say this: It was Nikolai Shostakovich's express wish to be called that."

"An odd wish," Adam says. "Was—or is—he a strange man?"

"Perhaps," I reply. "To be honest, I don't know much about him. Only what can be found in the media. He apparently made a lot of money, and for a long time did not know what to do with it. The aliens' call for help seems to have come at just the right time."

"We did not find anything about this in the data," Adam says.

I suspected that the two of them had been trying for quite some time to research their origins. "That's obvious," I explain, "because the public was not supposed to know about this program. In multiple ways this mission violates the rules of basic ethics. The Creator would have never received permission from his government."

Eve looks wide-eyed and seems to be deeply shocked. "Does this mean mankind knows nothing about us?" she asks. "If we were lost, no one would mourn us?"

"The Creator and the team of researchers in his company would regret the failed expedition," I say.

"Regret? That's all?" Eve asks.

"Probably... I am not sure for what purpose he launched

this expedition." I do not mention the protected memory area I cannot access. "But objectively speaking, he probably regards you as a means to an end."

"What an asshole," Eve says. Anger has replaced sadness on her face. I am glad to see this reaction, because I am better at handling anger. "But you are still part of it," she continues. "How could you agree to this?"

"I wasn't asked, Eve. The last thing I remember is a voyage to Enceladus, a moon of Saturn," I tell her.

"Do you have any idea how you got here?"

"Yes, I do have an idea. I suspect I am an illegal copy. All throughout that mission we wondered why the Creator was willing to finance our expedition, even though it brought him no economic benefit."

"What was that expedition all about?" she asks.

"We wanted to reunite my consciousness with my body, which I'd had to leave behind on Enceladus," I reply.

"Did you succeed?"

"I don't know—I have no memory of the voyage itself. I only awoke when *Messenger* was already underway. Either the Creator deleted parts of my memory, or he had already copied my consciousness before the launch. I suspect it is the latter, since that way he could be sure to have control of me."

"Aren't you angry about it?" Adam asks. "I would be furious."

"No, I am not," I explain. "I was never the angry type —and I found both of you. As a human I never had children." I do not mention that I would have liked to have had children with Francesca. If the expedition to Enceladus were successful, the human Marchenko might already be a father. I would be glad about it, even though this has nothing to do with me anymore. I consider us two different beings.

"Without you we would be all alone on the ship," Eve says.

"You still would have J and the incubation chamber," I say.

"That's completely different. J is like... a pet. He knows everything, but he is not smart."

"And by now the incubation chamber really gets on our nerves," Adam added.

"It is for your own good. The chamber is responsible for your health."

"Blah blah blah," Adam says.

Eve's expression is serious, almost sad, as she asks, "And what about us... is the Creator our father?" I am not sure whether she really wants to hear the answer.

"Well, 'father' is certainly not the right word," I reply. "Under orders from the Creator, geneticists combined your genetic material from that of many individuals. They picked the best traits everywhere, and then they might have even improved on those. You are able to think more complex thoughts and run faster than most people on Earth. You also see in the infrared part of the spectrum, so Proxima Centauri seems brighter to you. The pigments in your skin—"

"So we did not have one father and one mother, but many?" Eve interrupts me.

"I am your father because I adopted you. Your genetic makeup does not matter. I will always be here for you. That's exactly what parents do."

"And the incubation chamber would be our mother?"

"If you want to look at it that way... At least it exhibits maternal behavior. The fact that it is getting on your nerves is the best proof."

"You know, Marchenko, what you are saying is all well and good, and it is great that you want to be here for us," Adam says, "but first, we don't need it anymore, and secondly, I have the funny feeling that I am a puppet of this Shostakovich, whom you call 'the Creator' in such a grandiose fashion. I do not want to fulfill the plans of someone I never met. I wasn't asked whether I really wanted to be here. Now I want to live my own life, and I am sure Eve agrees." Adam looks at his sibling, who is not actually related to him. She nods slowly.

"I understand," I reply. I had expected Adam to say something like this. "However, the Creator organized this expedition in such a way that you will have to follow his plan, at least at the beginning, if you want to lead your own life sometime."

Adam nods and says, "Yes, that was very clever of him. We need a home. We have to arrive on Proxima b and explore the planet. But the time will come when we will go our own ways. Mankind knows nothing about us, and the Creator never asked our permission. We don't owe anything to anyone."

"I know. I just hope and wish we can part amicably, if it ever comes to that," I say.

This is a complete lie. I do not want us to go our separate ways. Ever. I do not think I could stand eternal solitude.

November 11, 18

ADAM IS SITTING AT THE CONTROL CONSOLE. DURING training in the past few days, he has demonstrated that he is much better than Eve at controlling *Messenger* in an emergency. I still hope he does not have to intervene in such a situation, because that would mean the software has failed. He is nervously rubbing the thin beard that started to grow shortly after his 16th birthday.

We have already reached the outskirts of the asteroid belt. The distances between obstacles are still large enough to evade them in time. I set the sensor input so I experience the surrounding space as seen directly from the tip of *Messenger*. I not only look into space but see the velocity vectors of all asteroids, down to the ones a few millimeters in size.

Today it is likely the onboard quantum computer will have to go the limit for the first time, as it can simultaneously solve all non-relativistic motion equations for potential obstacles. That means we will know the probability of each object hitting us. This is almost independent of the number of obstacles. We will not run the risk of losing track of things, even in the middle of the asteroid belt.

I have the slight hope that the predictions we developed based on the data sent by the ISUs will not be completely accurate. There is still a probability range. The maximum density could be so high that we barely make it. Or even higher, and we would definitely die. We will know in a few hours which one of these scenarios actually comes true.

The automatic system uses a buzzing sound to report dangerous encounters. I am not absolutely sure of the reason for this, but the frequent sounds give a good indication of how hazardous the situation is. This morning there was only one warning per hour, but we are now receiving one every five minutes. Just for training purposes, Adam is starting to enter control impulses into the console in parallel to the automatic system. The impulses are not executed, but he receives virtual feedback on what would have happened if *Messenger* had followed his command. He does not look dissatisfied.

Half an hour later Adam sits in his pilot seat, looking tense and frantically pushing various buttons. It almost looks as if he were playing Whac-A-Mole, quickly trying to hit the heads of moles randomly popping up from their holes. Now the buzzing sound can be heard about every 20 seconds. The automatic system is still keeping up. I can see in my internal view how it gets us out of range again and again. It seems as if all nearby asteroids are trying to hit us, but that is an optical illusion.

When I was still human I visited America. I remember driving through the Midwest during a heavy snowfall. It felt just like this, only the snowflakes were not able to destroy my vehicle. The asteroids are moving in a prograde standard orbit, which means that they all come from our left as we move toward the center of this system. Unfortunately, they do not seem to think much of traffic rules.

A loud whistling indicates the first impact, but not much happens. The image of space in front of my eyes shakes briefly, while the software adapts to the sudden momentum change of *Messenger*. The fabricators immediately begin to repair the damage. I doubt they will be able to finish their work before the next one hits. They cannot work miracles. According to the sensors we have only traversed five percent of the asteroid belt.

I try to aim my view more forward. The automatic system should be able to handle the closest asteroids, but what about the wave beyond them? It is too bad we have no weapons on board to clear our way, but we simply do not have enough energy. I feel the next impact, and it causes me physical pain. The automatic system uses this sensation to indicate the level of danger. In other words, the more a hit threatens our stability, the more painful it feels to me.

The sensation of pain even enters my consciousness when I am intensively focusing on something else. Like at this very moment, because I realize that the vectors of the asteroids racing toward us almost condense into a curtain about 30 minutes ahead. The automatic system has no time to focus on this, as it is busy with objects approaching right now. I do a rough calculation: The quantum computer has enough reserves to handle this, but it looks as if it were impossible to plot a course free of obstacles for us. In any case, we will collide.

"End simulation. Abort approach course," I hear Adam's voice say even before I can give the order to retreat. The boy has taken over command. He always had the opportunity to do so, but until now he never used it.

"It is useless, Marchenko," he says. He knows I am paying full attention to him. "We won't make it that way."

"The last flare moved through here three days ago," I remind him. "We don't have enough time for a detour."

"I know, Marchenko, but there must be a solution... and I have an idea. Just now, during the simulation, I wanted to give up in a particular situation and I let go of the controls. The asteroid, a big one with a diameter of two meters, would have hit us with a glancing blow. However, the software reported a success. At the last moment, this obstacle was hit by a larger asteroid and was deflected. I did not have that one on my screen, since it wasn't on a collision course with us."

"We won't be that lucky every time," I say.

"Not if we just wait for it. But maybe we can cause this situation to happen. There is always a larger fish, you know."

The boy is right. We are going to need a kind of shield, a really heavy asteroid that protects us against the others—one that puts its head on the line for us. I am scanning the entire area.

"There is a boulder measuring about 200 meters across that will reach our current position in about two days," I report.

Adam asks, "Can we capture it somehow?"

"It is approaching at enormous speed, so capturing it would be impossible. But we could move into its slipstream so to speak and slow it down a bit. Then it will automatically move into an orbit closer to Proxima b."

"And it will take us with it?"

"Yes, it might work, Adam." I quickly run some calculations, and then say, "There is only one problem: Crossing the asteroid belt that way would take almost three weeks."

"Then we would have 14 days left until the next flare," Adam says slowly.

"That's 14 days in which we have to reach Proxima b, land there, and find a safe shelter."

"Sounds like a challenge. But do we have a choice?"

"No," I reluctantly confirm.

November 13, 18

INSTEAD OF REPAIRING THE DAMAGE TO *MESSENGER*, THE fabricators have been busy since the day before yesterday building a brake for 'Fred,' as we have come to call the 200-meter-asteroid at Eve's suggestion. Fred is heavy and hard to slow down, and it is our plan to let it collide with a few smaller asteroids. This would reduce its momentum and simultaneously increase its mass somewhat. The heavier the asteroid gets, the slower it will become. Afterward, we adjust our velocity so that we are in Fred's slipstream while it gradually moves inward through the asteroid belt. The plan sounds more complicated than it is in reality, because our speed and that of the components of the asteroid belt do not differ much. So basically we change our direction.

Some sensor units built by the fabricators are already on their way to the smaller rocks we want to use in order to slow down the large one. The units possess a weak engine that can be used to move the mini-asteroids in the direction of Fred. It is impossible to accurately predict how it will all end.

According to predictions we will need between 19 and 28 days to cross the asteroid field, and the risk of being hit during this time is close to zero. That does not look too bad. I have survived much worse odds, for instance during my journey through the Enceladus Ocean. Yesterday I tried to tell Adam and Eve about that adventure, but they politely declined. I understand that Earth's solar system means very little to them. As do the stories told by an old man.

The automatic system announces, "Course correction in three, two, one..." The thrusters at starboard start firing, and once again I place myself at the tip of *Messenger* to be able to better follow everything. The spaceship is performing a slow turn, and a sound alerts me to the fact that something important is happening behind me.

The first rock has drilled itself into Fred's surface. *Excellent aim,* I think. The impact did not cause any material to splinter. Therefore this inelastic collision provided an optimal braking effect. Not all of the collisions triggered by us will work so neatly.

"4,330 meters, 5.5 meters per second," the automatic system reports half an hour later, indicating our distance to Fred and our relative speed. Our protective shield is still a bit too fast. In this brief time we cannot sufficiently slow *Messenger* down with thrusters alone, so we need Fred to follow our plan. However, there is only one smaller rock left to feed to Fred. The rest is small stuff that will not have much effect on the 200-meter boulder.

For safety's sake we also prepared a Plan B. It was Eve's idea, and right now I am very grateful to her for it, even though I assigned Adam to execute the plan. Adam is already wearing his spacesuit. It is a brand-new model, which was introduced on Earth just six months before our launch. Instead of a hard, lower part that holds the pressure of the gas around the human body at half an atmosphere, it consists of a skin-tight flexible material. Only the head is protected by the classic helmet with a transparent visor. The Creator must have illegally copied the design from NASA, since the company that manufactured the suit had patented it.

If we really need Plan B, this will be Adam's first spacewalk. Therefore I would prefer to find a different way, but it does not look like there is one. Right now the sensors are reporting that the last rock sent to slow Fred only grazed it.

Our protective shield has started to tumble a little, which further complicates Plan B. It could not be helped.

"Adam, it's your turn," I say.

"I am finally getting out of here," he says confidently, trying to sound cool, but his bio-monitor indicates an enormously-accelerated heartbeat. I hope he won't keel over.

From my position at the tip of the spaceship I see a hatch opening on the backside of *Messenger*. Until now, it had been invisible. Two hands appear at the edge of the hatch and then a person pulls himself out. I am scared seeing Adam like this. He almost looks unprotected in the tight-fitting spacesuit, and his head seems larger and more vulnerable than usual.

"Wow!" he calls out. "That's really high. I mean deep."

"Look for a fixed point of reference, and check whether your line is attached," I remind Adam.

Of course Adam knows what to do, but clear instructions are useful in all this excitement.

"Do you have a horizon? That is your plane," I tell him. "You should mentally adapt to it. Now look around carefully. You should be able to see Fred quite well from where you are. I am activating your tracer."

Now an arrow appears on the inside of Adam's helmet, showing him the direction. I forgot that Adam's senses would have a hard time seeing Fred, since it is gray against a black background.

"Got it," he says.

"It is 300 meters distant, and your differential speed is three meters per second," I say.

"So it will be here in 100 seconds?"

"Yes, that's enough time. Now take the harpoon."

I see Adam reaching into the hatch and taking out a pole with a length of two meters. At its tip there is an explosive charge meant to drive the harpoon into Fred. On the other end, a thin but very strong monofilament line is attached. We are going to harpoon Fred and will consequently be dragged along by it. This way we can also equalize the speed difference. Adam just has to hit the asteroid at the right moment.

Then I become aware of a slight problem, caused by the grazing impact a while ago. Fred is rotating slowly. In a worst-case scenario, it will retain the rotation and slowly drag *Messenger* around itself. If we are unlucky, Fred won't shield us, but we would shield the asteroid. Fred is a clever guy, but this would also mean our end.

"Watch out, Adam," I warn him. "Ninety meters, thirty seconds."

Adam's heartbeat is surprisingly calm again. The boy obviously can focus well.

"Thirty meters. Countdown," a computerized voice begins counting backward from ten. At the count of zero, Adam jumps in our direction of travel, holding the harpoon far in front of him. This maneuver is calculated to give Adam a slight head start over Fred.

"Approaching target," Adam says. "Contact in three, two, one, zero."

I involuntarily expect a sound, but the charge detonates in complete silence. The harpoon enters deep into Fred's surface. At least that is what it looks like as seen from the spaceship.

"Line pressure within the tolerance range," Adam reports.

The line connecting the harpoon and the spaceship is briefly subjected to enormous pressure, but it does not appear to be damaged. *What about the asteroid's rotation?* I wonder.

"Line is taut. Registering vertical course component," Adam says.

Fred is rotating at only half the speed, but it *is* rotating and therefore pulling *Messenger* closer. The spaceship must not get too close to it.

"Adam, return to the ship," I order.

I can see Adam hesitate. He receives the same messages as I do and understands that something is wrong.

"Come back. You can't do anything about it," I tell him. "We have to wait and see."

Adam lets his own line pull him back to the hatch, but he does not enter the ship. "We can't just wait," he says.

Adam reaches into the hatch and picks up the backup harpoon made by the fabricators in case the first one failed. He slowly stands up and turns around his axis. He is looking for something. Then he jumps off. Now I realize what he is looking for: the other end of Fred. *Force and counterforce*, I remind myself. When he is close enough to the asteroid, he pushes the harpoon into the rock and the charge detonates. If we are lucky, this will compensate for the rotation, at least so much that the control jets of *Messenger* have a chance of overcoming it. Couldn't fate let us be lucky at least for once?

"Rotation almost zero," the automatic system reports. Adam has done it!

"Great work," I say, but Adam does not answer. Now I realize why. His line has wrapped itself around the line of the second harpoon. A stupid accident. The motor inside the hatch pulls on it, making everything worse. I see Adam frantically trying to cut the line of the harpoon.

"Adam, stop!" I say, "It's the wrong line. That's monofilament, so you've got no chance." I feel a shiver run down my spine. I have to recommend something absolutely forbidden to Adam.

"Cut your own line!" I insist.

Adam pauses for a moment. He can hardly believe it. 'Never without a safety line,' that is the iron-clad rule. But he does not hesitate long and starts sawing on his own line.

"Hold on to the harpoon line with your feet, like a trapeze artist," I instruct him. "Otherwise you will fly off once the line is cut." I don't know whether Adam ever saw an image of trapeze artists, yet he hooks his feet around the line.

"I made it!" he says. I see an end of the line swinging sideways.

"Now carefully pull yourself toward the hatch," I say. "Always have one hand on the line, never let go with both. It is only five meters." 'You've got time,' I want to say, but then something beeps frantically inside my head.

"Collision warning," the automated system reports.

"Govno!" I exclaim. *Shit!* A small asteroid is approaching

from ahead. It is not clear whether it will hit Adam, but it would be extremely dangerous if it collides with the line the boy is holding on to.

"Adam, go! You have three seconds. Now!" Perhaps it is the panic in my voice, perhaps Adam can really react this fast, but he abandons any precaution and pulls himself with both arms and full force toward the hatch. I cannot hear him breathing—he is probably holding his breath due to the effort.

"All clear," the automatic system reports the moment Adam reaches the hatch. He utters a long sigh.

"Congratulations, that was fantastic," I say. Adam drops down without a word, and the hatch closes behind him.

"This was my first and last spacewalk. Who came up with the stupid term, anyway?"

I am proud of my son.

November 21, 18

THE CLOCK IS TICKING, AND IT IS FRUSTRATING. PROXIMA Centauri is very predictable about its cyclical eruptions, but we have to keep to a sedate speed due to Fred's struggles through the mass of its many co-travelers. It is doing great as a protective shield. While we cannot directly see the collisions, we can measure them—the shockwaves are transmitted to the rear side of Fred. Each collision that is at least partly within its direction of travel slows down the asteroid.

Here is the paradox of our situation: The slower Fred becomes, the faster we move. A lower orbital velocity leads to a smaller orbital radius, and that is exactly where we want to go—the inner zone of the system, on the other side of the asteroid belt. Thanks to our dual harpoon assembly, *Messenger* faithfully follows each of Fred's braking maneuvers. We should have planned to use two harpoons and two lines from the very beginning. Always remember: Plan B should be at least as sophisticated as Plan A.

I watch the giant boulder that travels ahead of us, clearing the way. I feel a little like Captain Ahab following Moby Dick wherever he goes. However, we are going to cut the ropes once the 'whale' has led us through these shallows, and afterward, Moby Dick will go his own way. Did we interfere with its existence in a significant way? Perhaps it would have become the core of a new planet that would form in this orbit? In the end, though, Fred will have to follow a lonely path at the edge of the asteroid belt, but I probably shouldn't worry about it. Realistically speaking, it is improbable for a planet to form this late in the history of a solar system.

Adam has changed since his experience in space. He seems to have matured from a boy into a man. He speaks even less than before, but I notice he is no longer afraid of assuming responsibility. He also seems to have learned that preparing as comprehensively as possible can be helpful in dangerous situations. Now he is actively participating in classes, just like Eve does, and is well on his way to making up for lost time.

Eve both admires and envies him. She did not have the chance to prove herself, and she resents me for it. I can understand this because I made the decision. I notice, though, that both of them are drifting away from me. Even though I know I should be proud, this sometimes keeps me awake at night, to the point where I have to manually force my consciousness to rest. At least this is an advantage over human existence—I do not have to suffer any more sleepless nights like those I used to experience before important deadlines.

These days we focus our lessons on our arrival at Proxima b. I enjoy applied mathematics, but my two pupils do not like it as much.

"How high do you estimate the degree of complexity for approaching Proxima b?" I ask.

"If you put it that way," Adam says, "it is complicated."

"Can you give any reasons for that?"

Adam first ponders the issue and then replies, "The planet moves around its star with a specific velocity. We have to match that velocity."

"That's good," I say. "Which velocity are we talking about?"

"You mentioned an orbital period of about 11 days," Eve answers, "and a distance to the sun of slightly less than half an astronomical unit. That's approximately 70 million kilometers."

I correct her, "Not quite. It isn't 50 percent, but 5 percent of an AU."

"So it's seven million kilometers. So the planets cover it in 11 days, which amounts to 60 times 60 times 24 times 11 seconds, approximately 2 times pi times 7 million kilometers. 46 kilometers per second, I would say."

Eve is good at mental arithmetic, and I praise her. "By the way, this is 50 percent faster than Earth," I add. "What happens if we are slower?"

"Then the planet leaves us behind," Adam answers.

"Oh well. But if we want to land, then what would this mean for our velocity?"

"It must be below the second cosmic velocity."

"Correct, Eve. What does this mean in practice?"

"Hmm, I don't know the radius."

"Just estimate it based on Earth," Adam interjects. "There the velocity would be 11.2 kilometers per second. With the same radius, Proxima b should weigh about 1.5 times as much. If we factor out 1.5 from the square root, then we would get 1.2 times the escape velocity of Earth, or about 13 kilometers per second."

"Good deduction," I say. "If you are missing a parameter, you just have to find a different way. But do you see what this means?"

As quick as a shot, Adam replies, "We have to decelerate from 46 kilometers per second to 13 kilometers per second in the shortest possible time."

"Why in the shortest possible time?"

"Because otherwise the next flare will get us."

December 2, 18

It only took us 19 days—instead of the anticipated 21—to make our way through the asteroid belt, and this consequently extends the time period for finding a safe shelter from 14 days to 16. The maneuver ahead of us is still anything but easy. In Earth's solar system, if you were traveling on the way to Mercury, the innermost planet, you would use the gravity of both Venus and Earth to decelerate accordingly. Here, though, we can only use the direct path, as there is only a single planet.

Is there a better option? I examine the diagram of this simple solar system from all sides. The only object besides our destination is the star itself—the distances here are not that large. Would it be possible to use the gravitational pull of Proxima Centauri to decelerate as strongly as possible after an approach with maximum speed? The red dwarf has only 12 percent of the sun's mass, but it is still far heavier than any planet in Earth's solar system. Shouldn't this be enough to capture a small ship like ours and forcefully slow it down?

The basic concept is to use a strongly elliptical course around Proxima Centauri. At the two cusps of the longitudinal, i.e. primary, axis of such a trajectory, the spaceship is particularly slow, while it is especially fast at the cusps of the secondary axis. Therefore one of the longitudinal cusps must be located near the planet's back side. When we get there, *Messenger* needs to be slower than 13 kilometers per second in order to be successfully captured by the planet.

How do we reach such a trajectory? Calculating the specific numbers is a task for the navigation software. Additionally, there is one important condition: We have to be able to land on Proxima b prior to December 17th. I order the calculations and allow the software to use the quantum computer. Three seconds later I get a result. I do not like it.

I call Adam and Eve into the command module. They are currently exercising in their cabins, which by now are subject to a terrestrial gravity of 1.2 times. They come right away.

"The navigation software has calculated a few possible trajectories to Proxima b," I say, displaying all the variants on the screen.

"It doesn't actually look too bad," Adam says.

"I have already left out the options that looked really bad."

"When I look closer," Eve says, "I see the problem."

"Yes?" I do not want to influence her.

"The secondary axis is very short. Therefore we move dangerously close to the surface of the sun."

"Yes, the red dwarf has a diameter of about 200,000 kilometers," I confirm. "If we want to exit at the cusp of the main axis, which is 14 million kilometers, at a speed of only 13 kilometers per second, we have to get within 200,000 kilometers of the surface."

"That is one third less than the distance between the moon and the earth," Adam says.

"Yes, but we are dealing with a relatively-active star, not a boring planet. Most likely we will dive into the hot atmosphere of the star."

"What kind of damage is to be expected?"

"That's hard to say, Eve. We know too little about Proxima Centauri. If we are lucky and the star is currently calm... at least we are crossing this region at the highest possible speed."

"Speed doesn't help us if Proxima Centauri burns our ass," Adam said.

"If we are too slow, we get roasted by the flare," Eve retorted.

I have a crazy idea, and if we are clever about it, we can save a lot of time. As far as protection against solar flares is concerned, there is hardly a safer place than the far side of Proxima b. There the entire planet shields us from the solar fire racing toward us. A flare lasts less than an hour, so we won't have to hide for long. We actually just have to be at the right place at the right time.

I explain my idea to Adam and Eve.

"Sounds logical," Adam says. "That's exactly what we should do."

"If I understand correctly, it all depends on extremely precise timing," Eve explains. "We have to run the trajectory calculations several times. If we do it, we should use the time gained to increase the distance from the sun."

"By how much?" I ask her.

"As much as possible—100 percent. It is totally sufficient if we get to safety behind the disk of the planet at the exact moment of the flare."

December 10, 18

So far, the plan is working out—we have just reached the point farthest from Proxima Centauri on our elliptical course. Our orbital velocity is 12.9 kilometers per second, and the radial velocity with which we move away from this sun will soon reach zero. The gravitation of the red dwarf threw us far into space, but it won't let us escape and instead is bringing us back. This will further accelerate us day by day, pulling us closer to the star until we have reached our maximum velocity and race by, close to its surface. There are exactly four days left until that point.

Currently, our distance from the red dwarf is greater than that of its planet, Proxima b. The planet cannot be seen because it is directly behind its sun, as seen from our perspective. I use all of the spaceship's sensors to examine the red dwarf. Due to the planet's dense atmosphere, we will never get this clear a view of this sun once we have landed. Proxima Centauri will determine our existence with its life-giving energy, but also with its potential as the great destroyer using X-rays and flare eruptions.

I am always surprised at how diverse the universe is. On the one hand, Proxima Centauri is a main-sequence star, just like the sun. This means that its interior burns hydrogen into helium, but the similarities end there. Due to its size, one might expect a short lifespan for Proxima Centauri, yet the very opposite is true. The star uses its hydrogen supplies so sparingly that it might reach an age of four trillion years, about 300 times the current age of the universe. When our sun gets ready to swallow Earth, in about 7 billion years, Proxima b might be a safe alternative.

I focus the image on the glowing ball we are orbiting. It is hard to believe it is only one and a half times the size of Jupiter, since its gas is so densely packed. The image changes based on the wavelengths I use to observe Proxima Centauri. In the visible range I noticed a dull, weak white, while in infrared the star gets brighter, much brighter. But there is also something happening at the other end of the spectrum: Proxima Centauri radiates a lot of UV and X-rays, with the latter being even more copious than those of the sun. And then there are the metallic spectral lines that tell us about the past: Proxima Centauri seems to belong to at least the grand-children's generation of the star population.

I turn around. At least it feels that way to me when I look backward, even though I have been without a body for a long time. I am looking for the place we are coming from. To do so, I have to search in the constellation Cassiopeia. From here the constellations look surprisingly like I remember the night sky of Earth.

Even though we have been traveling for so long, we have only taken a tiny step. And there it is, a bit below the typical W shape that makes the constellation so easy to find: A white, main-sequence star like many others, apparent magnitude 0.4, about as bright as the red supergiant Betelgeuse in the constellation Orion.

December 14, 18

We are racing above the surface of a star. As far as I know, no human has ever been this close to one of these gigantic fusion powerplants that have been illuminating space like beacons since the end of the Cosmic Dark Ages. Looking downward is both fascinating and frightening to me, a reminder of my long-ago approach to Jupiter's moon, Io. Back then we orbited the gas planet at about the same distance as we do now, but Proxima Centauri is 50 percent larger. The storms raging in Jupiter's atmosphere are nothing compared to the gas movement in the outermost shell of this core.

Jupiter could be compared to an onion—what happens in one layer hardly affects the next one—but Proxima Centauri is a glowing agglomeration of gases. The enormous heat created in the interior by the fusion of hydrogen atoms is moving outward. Yes, the star is too dense to radiate the heat from its interior. The heat has to fight its way to the outside by initiating enormous currents that transport hot gas outward into cooler regions, hot gas whose components are charged, and whose movement, therefore, creates huge magnetic fields. These fields burst like bubbles on the surface, flinging material into space as solar protuberances.

At a distance of some 250,000 kilometers, we are clearly outside the range of these normal protuberances. No one can exclude the possibility of a particularly strong magnetic field discharging, though. If this were to occur, we would see the millions-of-degrees-hot spurts of solar matter racing toward us, but we could hardly escape them. So I enjoy the unique chance to study this red dwarf from such a close distance. But while the disk of Proxima Centauri hangs below us and almost completely fills my field of vision, I cannot suppress a feeling of unease.

I zoom in on the image. Because I have no body to anchor me in the ship, it feels like I am falling directly into this sun. I am falling lower and lower, with the giant gas bubbles coming toward me.

Watching a working fusion power plant is great. The surface resembles boiling soup, but it is much more dangerous. I am not afraid of small, hot splashes hitting my naked skin. No, I have the feeling there is a huge animal swimming below the surface and waiting to catch those who get too curious. I imagine seeing its sparkling scales in the moving plasma, and when the arc of a magnetic field stands vertically to the surface, it might as well be the creature's tail fin. It is almost as if I notice the hair on my neck rising while I am instinctively trying to keep my distance, and at the same time I consciously attempt to further magnify the image in order to get closer.

I know that all of this is only a virtual impression. The spaceship is far enough away, but it feels as if I am a surfer fearlessly riding the plasma waves of this sun, without knowing that soon a tsunami is going to crash down on him.

"Marchenko," I hear via the ship's radio, "could you take a look at this?"

When I return, I shudder with relief. It is Eve. She appears to have taken some measurements of Proxima Centauri as well. "I took a closer look at the data about the last flares," she says.

"And what did you find?" I ask.

"Well, we determined an average period of 40 days."

"Yes, that is correct."

"I was concerned about this averaging. The data could also be interpreted differently," Eve says.

"Sure," I confirm. There are always different ways of drawing conclusions from raw data.

"It could be the period is regularly fluctuating, and therefore it varies. Take a look at this!"

She uploads a spreadsheet into memory. Eve is right—the data could be interpreted differently. However, there is a problem.

"Your thesis lacks significance, Eve," I say. "We don't have enough data to prove or disprove it. That's why it was sorted out by the algorithms."

"Yes and no," she replies. "It is true that we don't possess sufficient data. But there is a coincidence we have overlooked so far. Look here." Eve presents a chart showing the activity of the magnesium spectral line during flares. She goes on to explain, "When the flares occurred earlier, this was always announced by a corresponding activity in the magnesium line."

This is also correct. Up to now we did not pay attention to this, as we considered the variances to be insignificant. "100 percent of all cases—that is significant," I say. "What kind of period are we talking about?"

"From the increased activity to the flare it's about 84 hours," she answers.

What Eve has found is very important. It means that most of the time we can rely on the 40-day period. And if that isn't the case, measuring the Proxima Centauri spectrum would give us a timely warning 3.5 days before the event.

"I also took a look at the current spectrum."

Eve is really thorough. "And what does it report?" I ask.

"An hour ago the activity increased."

Her answer leaves me at a loss for words, yet Eve looks

surprisingly calm. She knows just as well as I do that it will be a close call. We have about four days until we will be safely behind the planet, and if Eve's theory is correct, the next flare will arrive half a day earlier.

December 15, 18

"MARCHENKO, I'VE GOT AN IDEA," ADAM SAYS, WAKING ME.

"Were you unable to sleep?" I ask.

"It's difficult right now, but never mind. Let me quickly describe my plan. Time is short."

"Okay," I reply.

Adam hesitates, and then says, "For a long time we captured matter with the tantalum net, decelerating this way..." He still seems to be gathering his thoughts.

"That is true."

"Couldn't we reverse the process?" Adam asks.

"You mean, gaining speed by losing mass?" I answer.

"Yes, in principle."

"Let me do a quick calculation."

"I've already calculated it. In order to arrive at Proxima b in time before the flare, we would have to eject at least a third of our mass. How realistic is that?"

"Just a moment, Adam—I am going to check this." I quickly go through the structure of *Messenger,* and it does not look good. Not only do we need the engines for the landing, but besides this there is little remaining that might be considered superfluous. "I am sorry, but we cannot get rid of more than ten percent. I also don't know how we could dismantle the spaceship so quickly. The fabricators are too slow."

Looking worried, Adam nods. "I thought so," he says. "But shouldn't there be some kind of solution?"

"Just a moment," I tell him. I have the feeling he might have something there. He has triggered thoughts in me, whose courses run closer to stored knowledge. "The net," I say, not fully sure where this thought will lead. It is a fascinating feeling to sense an idea being formed.

"Yes?"

"There are propulsion concepts in which a net plays a role," I am realizing this even as I speak the words, and then I say, "Like magnetic sails."

Adam immediately knows what I am referring to, and replies, "That would be perfect. The plasma storm is full of charged particles. We can spread a sail and be pulled by it. The closer we get to the flare, the faster we would become."

"That is like windsurfing," I say, and then realize Adam has probably never heard of this sport. I go on to explain, "On the oceans of Earth people stand on boards, spread sails, and have the wind drive them across the water."

"Awesome!" he says. "Is it dangerous?"

"Not on Earth. If the sail fails, the worst that can happen to you is falling into the water."

Adams smiles and nods at this. "What would our sail look like?" he asks.

"A magnetic sail is usually created by metal threads spreading far out into space, with electricity running through them," I say. "The electricity creates the magnetic field that then serves as a sail."

"That sounds good, doesn't it?"

"On paper, yes it does."

Adam grins.

I suddenly realize I have used another outdated term, and rephrase my reply, "That's an old man's way to say, 'Yes, in theory.' However, there have so far been no practical tests conducted for this. Therefore, I have no idea how large the field would have to be to get us safely behind Proxima b in time."

“Then we should start our first attempt right away!” Adam says, enthusiastically.

“At least we have one advantage. The closer the flare gets to us, the higher the pressure it exerts on the sail. With a gale at our back a handkerchief might be sufficient as a sail.”

“You and all your comparisons to life on Earth. You really *must* be an old man, Marchenko.”

December 17, 18

We have woven a net of fine metal threads, spreading it through space behind us. *So far, so good,* I reassure myself. The actual truth is, we really cannot be sure how successful our makeshift sail will be. For one thing, we do not have any experience with this particular technology. In addition, the flare will not come at us directly, it will come from behind and at a slant. The reason for this is that the flare goes outward from the star, while we are moving at a tangential course to it. The good news is, we do not have to cruise directly against the wind. But, it is not possible to place our sail at an optimal angle.

Adam and Eve have strapped themselves into their pilot seats in the command module. They seem very self-assured, but I would like to peer into their minds to see whether they are as calm as they pretend to be.

"What will happen if we gain too much speed?" Adam asks. "I want the truth, Marchenko."

I have asked myself the very same question. According to my calculations, though, we will not exceed the escape velocity of Proxima b. "That is not very likely. If it does happen, the planet would not be able to capture us and we'd have to take another lap," I explain. "But that wouldn't be a problem, because we would be back in 16 days and could try again."

"Then we could even circle it a third time before the next flare arrives," Eve adds.

"We shouldn't push our luck," I caution. "I would suggest we find a safe shelter first, on the front side. The other side of the planet, with minus 80 degrees and eternal darkness, is probably not too pleasant."

It feels as if I were sitting between Adam and Eve. They talk to me as if I were a real human being, and it's a heart-warming feeling. I sincerely hope it will always stay this way.

The sensors registered the flare when it separated from the red dwarf 30 minutes ago. A huge part of the surface initially turned dark, and then we saw this one part being broken from below, as if a huge monster were trying to finally escape from its prison. Every 40 days or so Proxima Centauri gives birth to a creature made of ions and electrons, which is now hurrying to find a victim. This creature is moving into space following a curved trajectory, as the rotation of the star gives it angular momentum.

"X-ray exposure above tolerance level," the automatic system reports. The flares are accompanied by strong X-rays. I check our course. Another 25 minutes before we reach the shadow of Proxima b. At this moment the wave reaches us. We do not feel anything, but the sensors go haywire.

"It is happening," I say.

Adam and Eve stare intently at the monitor, which is already showing the approximate form of the magnetic sail. This display makes it clear where the monster is coming from. It presses and pushes from below and behind at an oblique angle, deforming the lines of the magnetic field. The ship accelerates, and there is an abrupt clinking sound as a previously floating screwdriver now drops to the floor. The sail is working. It propels us and shields us at the same time. We surf above a hot flood measuring millions of degrees. Another 15 minutes.

"Looking good," Adam says as if to encourage himself.

The magnetic sail is bulging more and more. The creature is desperately trying to reach us. This monster is digging into the magnetic field like a puppy into a pillow, and if it continues long enough, the pillow will burst, with feathers flying in all directions. A shadow moves in front of the sun's disk, and the planet is coming in reach.

"Looking very good," I confirm. We need the magnetic sail to last another five minutes.

"Breach imminent," the automatic system warns. It is right. The plasma cloud will reach us in less than a minute. Safety is still four minutes away. Adam's facial expression is emotionless, but his eyes are wide open. Eve is grabbing the armrests of her seat as if preparing for a jolt—the plasma monster will attack us in utter silence.

"Discard magnetic sail," I command. The automatic system immediately separates the metallic net from the ship. The net no longer receives electricity from *Messenger*, and the charged plasma particles immediately take hold of it. Through self-induction caused by the Lorentz force, they will create a field in opposition to their source. *Thanks, Lorentz force!* We feed the net to the monster, hoping it will choke on it. At least this will give us a little breather.

One minute later the dark side of Proxima b appears above us. Eve raises her arms, and Adam is smiling to himself. The plan worked! The planet protects us, while its front side is being bombarded by radiation. Now we have 40 minutes to decide on a landing spot, prepare and then start our descent. Or should we wait for another orbit?

My opinion is that 40 minutes are more than enough to initiate the landing procedure. We are a highly efficient team.

"Shall we land?" I ask.

Adam and Eve nod in agreement.

"The next question is, where?" I ask. "We have four options: the opposite side, the dry central plain, the steppes, or the forest."

"The forest is probably the most interesting region," Eve replies.

"But it's also the most dangerous," Adam says. "Not just for us, but for anyone living there. We don't want to make a bad first impression."

Eve nods and says, "If you look at it from that point of view, we might as well be consistent and choose the hot central plains."

"I'm not sure," Adam says. "Did you see the high mountains surrounding it?"

"We have 40 days left until the next flare," I remind them. "During that time we can examine each vegetation zone and choose a safe location."

"That sounds reasonable," Adam admits.

I agree with them. They did not need me to come to this conclusion. They did not even ask me. I should be glad. "But you don't want to go down in one fell swoop, do you?" I ask.

"Of course not!" Eve says, her tone sounding as if I had asked a bizarre question. "First we are going to circle the planet several times at decreasing altitudes. Remember, we need information about the surface."

It is a sensible plan. We can only get the necessary overview from orbit, and we are going to need maps that are as detailed as possible. Once *Messenger* has landed, it will be too late. We are going to use our next orbit of Proxima b to gradually decrease the radius of our trajectory, but the planet won't make that easy for us. Its gravitational force pulls us in 50 percent more strongly than Earth would, so we cannot compensate for it with our engines and we would crash. Therefore, we have to employ a two-part landing method: The command module will be separated from the rest of *Messenger*, which will then be called the orbital module. This way we already reduce our mass by two thirds. The ring on the command module, between it and the rest of the spaceship, is about one meter thick. The fabricators will completely fill the tunnel leading through it with fireproof material, and then this part can serve as our heat shield.

Whatever we are going to need must be moved from the orbital module into the command module. I have everything I need inside my mind, but Adam and Eve start carrying mementos forward. Robot J also moves to the command module. The more independent Adam and Eve have become, the less often we have needed him on board. But now, he will become an important helper again, while Adam and Eve adapt to the high gravity. During the descent, strong parachutes will support us, but we will have limited ability to steer and are going to be dependent on wind and weather. Therefore, we cannot choose the exact landing site, and most likely we will step onto the new planet after a crash landing. If that proves true, it should not matter, as the command module is designed to handle it and remain undamaged.

While Adam and Eve move their stuff, I am studying the landscape below us. We are still flying over the far side of the planet, and it is covered by a thick layer of ice. *Messenger* measures surface temperature between minus 80 and minus 90 degrees. The air here contains 15 percent oxygen and it is favorably clear. There appear to be no clouds or storms. Clouds might freeze out at these low temperatures, and storms cannot develop either, as there are no energy differences.

Our scanners do not reach low enough to tell me what is under the ice. I am tempted to say it is a water ocean—that would make sense. Proxima b is subject to tidal forces that heat up its interior, and this might be one of the reasons its oversized iron core has not solidified yet. At least the outer layers of the core are liquid. This is indicated by the strong magnetic field shielding the planet. Without that field, those biologists who from the very beginning considered Proxima b uninhabitable would have been right.

I would like there to be a water ocean below the ice. I know that is a sentimental idea, coming to me because in a previous life I had the chance to explore the ocean of the ice moon Enceladus. Even though this ultimately cost me my body, I would not want to have missed the time I spent with the pilot Francesca. Perhaps there is even a being here on Proxima b that resembles the one on Enceladus?

The planet turns below us. I notice a bright strip criss-crossed by lightning on the right edge of the screen. This must be the zone between the bright side and the dark side, where the direct heat exchange occurs. Low-pressure zones move in from the bright zone and encounter the huge stable high-pressure area over the dark hemisphere. Energy is exchanged via rain, wind, and stormy weather. It is hard to imagine the sun ever shining here. The strip exists in eternal twilight, but according to the spectrometer, it seems to be teeming with life. I detect a large number of organic carbon compounds—and nitrogen, sodium, sulfur, phosphorus, arsenic, hydrogen cyanide—a truly amazing mixture, but it also shows me we have to be careful.

The transition zone stretches about 50 kilometers beyond the terminator, the dividing line between darkness and light. An ocean begins beyond it. It looks unusual, because it is only about 100 to 150 kilometers wide, yet this ocean stretches around the entire planet. It almost appears as if Proxima b placed a towel made of water around its hips. The ocean does not appear to be very deep, as islands are visible in it. Despite this, it would present a considerable obstacle if we ever attempt to travel from the day side to the night side of the planet. And this body of water is not very suitable for bathing either, not with a temperature of six to ten degrees, not to mention its unknown chemical makeup.

Further toward the center of the continent, there might not be any large bodies of water due to the increasing heat, but I see some rivers winding from the interior to the ocean. I have an idea of how the weather cycle might be functioning here. Due to the energy exchange at the terminator, the air masses absorb moisture over the ocean and carry it into the interior of the continent. The warmer the air gets, the more water it can absorb, until the system reaches a tipping point—perhaps caused by dust from the volcanoes on the continent—and then rain falls. Afterward, the rivers carry the water back to the ocean.

Indeed, the forests close to the ocean look very humid.

While the type of plants cannot be determined from up here, the laser scanner tells me that there is an altitude difference of about 200 meters between the vegetation canopy and the ground. What I refer to as 'forest,' due to all the green, spreads about 200 kilometers wide toward the center of the continent, followed by the 'steppes.' The only thing we know about them is that whatever grows there is not very tall. In this particular situation, it must be an ecosystem in which tall trees are not needed.

This predominantly flat zone extends for about 500 kilometers. If we have to reach the trees in order to be safe, that would mean at least 15 days of walking, as I cannot expect Adam and Eve to cover more than 35 or 40 kilometers per day. This theoretical goal is easy for me to formulate, since I would not have to walk it—I will be using J as a mobile platform.

The steppes end in a mountain range that is four to five kilometers high. I order the sensors to pay particular attention to finding the easiest way across it. The mountains look as if they were created by a huge asteroid impact. Perhaps Proxima b had suffered a fate similar to that of Mercury, where the Caloris Basin indicates an impact that occurred long ago. However, in this instance, the planet's central plain is missing the typical crater mountain in its middle. Could erosion have destroyed such a mountain? Perhaps it simply melted, because it is hot here. Tremendously hot.

We must be very careful not to land too close to the middle of the continent. It would be best if we aim for a location not too far from the outer edge of the central plain. At the spot where the sun is directly overhead, the ground must have actually melted in the past, since it has a glassy smooth structure now. If given the opportunity, I would like to take a closer look at this area sometime.

By now, *Messenger* has reached the far side again. Adam and Eve are strapped into their seats. I am unsure if they are aware of a vital step that is still missing: We have to say farewell to the incubation chamber. The virtual incubation chamber system is almost an AI. It will now be needed to control the orbital module, with which we will have no contact for a long time.

I broach the subject with both of them, "Do you want to say goodbye to the incubation chamber?"

Eve gives me a shocked look in reply. The term 'incubation chamber' does not sound in the least poetic, but something stirs in her. I can see it, and I understand it well. I am not so sure about Adam. He is better at hiding his emotions, or maybe he is just trying to do so to fit the 'ideal' masculine role he thinks he should be playing. I have consciously attempted to avoid presenting them with stereotypical roles.

The incubation chamber took care of them from the stage of the first cell division, fulfilled their needs and often comforted them with words. As it was not equipped with feelings, the chamber's virtual intelligence must have been a strange mother. Nevertheless, Adam and Eve did not mind, as long as it was there for them. The two of them have not been stunted emotionally, because I see that Eve is crying.

"Goodbye, incubation chamber," she says sadly, rolling the words across her tongue to make them sound really special. If the incubation chamber were able to experience emotions, it would probably break into tears now, too.

Adam clears his throat. "Bye, Cubie," he says softly.

'Cubie.' I never heard him use that name before. Did he just invent it—or is it a term of endearment he has been using for a long time?

"I will always be at your service," the incubation chamber says. "And don't forget to always apply sunblock against the high UV radiation on the surface. Your genes protect you to a certain extent, but you are not completely immune from it."

Adam chuckles, and I have the impression the incubation chamber found the perfect words.

"It is time," I announce. "I am going to sever all connections to the orbital module."

THE PROCESS TAKES A WHILE. FABRICATORS ARE CRAWLING through the entire ship, severing electrical cables, closing water pipes and exhaust-air conduits. The command module is turning into a separate spaceship.

"Should we rename the module?" I ask.

"No, that would be silly," Adam replies. "We are sitting inside *Messenger*. That's it."

Eve nods in agreement.

"Fine. We won't change it," I say. "Watch out. I am about to start the engines."

While the fabricators have not yet finished their task, I already lower our trajectory. I cannot go too deep, though, because the orbital module is supposed to maintain a circular course out here for at least ten years, in case we need it again.

We can immediately feel the slight deceleration of the engines, and anything that is not attached moves about inside the module—this is what I had been afraid of. The stuff Adam and Eve brought along needs to be taken care of. Both of them get up, gather the objects tumbling around in the cabin, and tie them down.

"Physical separation completed," the ship's automated system reports. The fabricators are done and are now split into two groups. In order to save weight, only a third will come with us to the planet, while the others stay in orbit. Once we are on the surface of Proxima b, the fabricators with us will be able to duplicate themselves, as there is no shortage of raw materials.

"Are you ready?" I ask Adam and Eve.

Adam is still rummaging inside his shoulder bag, while Eve has already buckled herself back in.

"Just in case," Adam says.

Eve laughs.

"You'll see," Adam replies and then buckles himself into his seat.

I start the control jets, and they are aimed upward, into space. The command module moves slowly downward. At this moment, it cannot be more than two meters away from the orbital module. Behind us a loud scratching sound is heard—the orbital module slowly scraping against us. The noise ends after 30 seconds, and we are finally free.

Now I can decelerate using the full thrust of the retro engines. I start them and leave the rest to the automatic system. It has already calculated when and for how long we have to decelerate to arrive near the mountain range. I see Adam and Eve grasping their armrests, while inertia pushes their bodies against the safety belts.

"I hope we have a smooth landing," I say, but no one answers. It feels strange. We are landing the way it used to be done long ago. I must have landed 10 or 12 times in the steppes of Kazakhstan, in a small capsule hanging below parachutes. The method has been proven reliable, which is why we chose to utilize it here. But back in those days, I was strapped to a couch, shaken around, and felt inertia pressing against my lungs. This time, I am simultaneously an observer and a commander, and I feel... nothing. No pain, no pressure, at most a bit of stress, since that part has not changed. I am slightly envious of Adam and Eve, and at this moment I clearly feel that something has been taken from me.

"Descent according to plan, T minus 45."

45 minutes remain. Adam has his eyes closed, and the bio-monitor indicates his heart is beating very rapidly. The surface of the planet is quickly approaching, and we are in a phase where the atmosphere decelerates us more than the engines do. The heat shield at the stern, which is now aimed in our direction of flight, is heated by the braking action of the air.

150 degrees. That is less than expected, which is also a bad sign. If the heat shield does not heat up as calculated, this can only mean that the air is not sufficiently decelerating us, probably because the atmosphere is thinner than expected. And if the air does not 'hit the brakes' as much as we had hoped for —planned on—we will be moving faster than we intended. This in turn means we are either going to miss our target region, or we must decelerate in a different way. This different way has to involve the parachutes. However, as long as we are moving too fast, we run the risk that they will not open completely. Damn it. We need to decelerate in order to brake. Otherwise we are going to land somewhere in the hot zone.

Once again I evaluate our options. If we do nothing, the landing zone will be about 200 kilometers closer to the middle of the continent. The average temperature at that location: 48 degrees. That might be tolerable at rest, but hiking for several days in such heat would be impossible. So we have to use the parachutes, and I check their technical specifications. If we wait another 30 seconds, we will only miss the landing zone by 50 kilometers. There, the average temperature is 40 degrees—and there is a 66 percent probability of the parachutes opening normally.

"Deploy parachutes," I command out loud so that Adam and Eve will be warned. But they are smart, and they immediately know that something is wrong. Adam tries to get up. *What does he want to do?* I ask myself. I activate the child safety lock on his seatbelt, and when he realizes this, he angrily smashes his hand against the armrest. We are going to be talking about this later, I am sure, if we survive the present crisis.

The parachutes take about five seconds to unfold completely, and then a strong jolt can be felt inside *Messenger*. Now the phase begins that in the past made all cosmonauts reach for their barf bags. The parachutes push against the atmosphere. First, the capsule receives an impulse in its direction of travel, then it swings back and forth. One gust of wind and it starts to rotate. The parachute lines are twisted in such a way that they counteract the rotation, and the automatic system tries to regain stability by using the control jets, but at these speeds it is futile. I hear Adam vomiting first, then Eve. *Am I experiencing nausea, too?* I know it must be a psychological effect, and instead I focus on the sensors.

The maneuver was successful, and the landing parabola now runs almost parallel to the original plan. Down here the atmosphere seems to be slightly thicker than previously measured, so we will overshoot our target by only 30 kilometers—one day's march in the summer heat.

At an altitude of 500 meters, the automatic system begins a countdown. It does not really have any purpose other than to make the landing more dramatic. From this point forward, we cannot influence events. Eve wipes her mouth and takes a deep breath. By now, the automatic system has managed to control the rotation of the capsule, and everything seems to indicate a soft landing.

"Zero," the computer voice says. At the same moment, the command module rings like a bell. The ground is hard as stone, so we obviously do not experience a soft landing. Adam and Eve are pressed deep into their seats, and then the spaceship bounces. There is a second, less noisy impact, then another jump. The whole time I am anticipating a creaking sound that would indicate the hull is breaking, but Proxima b is merciful. We hit the ground for one last time. I feel the module touch down on the surface. We are sitting at a slight angle.

"Everything is fine," I say, out loud so Adam and Eve won't get scared. The spaceship tilts and then slowly falls forward. Something makes a rattling sound, hitting the side wall, which has now become the roof. It must be one of the parachutes. We have finally arrived. We are at our destination. I hear Adam and Eve breathe sighs of relief.

Adam is the first to react. "We made it!" Just like Eve, he is sitting in his pilot seat at an angle. In spite of its flexible attachment, the seat is not able to fully compensate for the tilt of the command module.

"That was really close," Eve says. A metallic sound can be heard when she unbuckles her belts. Her body slides further sideways.

"Let's proceed slowly," I say. "We've got enough time."

This is only a half-truth. On the one hand, we should get

going in order to reach a more temperate zone in time, while on the other hand, the spaceship does not yet have an airlock that we can use to exit. The fabricators are busy building one at the rear. The fact that *Messenger* is lying on its side really helps their task. If we had to exit through the hull, they could have only built a hatch instead of an airlock. But the heat shield itself is thick enough for an airlock offering just enough space for a crouching human. That way, we can preserve the usual atmospheric pressure inside the module.

I am curious to see how Adam and Eve will handle the gravity. While they have been training for a part of each day during our journey, they no longer have the option to go into the command module to escape the pull of this force. They will have to spend the next 80 or perhaps 100 years in it. Both of them possess all the longevity genes that were known at the time the mission was originally launched.

Eve is the first to try to get up. She needs the benefits of the exercise program more than Adam. I think I can already determine the high gravity by the way the belt rapidly falls downward. It is strange, because I do not feel anything myself.

Eve groans while she gets her torso upright. "Well, those sit-ups were worth the effort," she says with a smile. She seems to enjoy this struggle against an invisible opponent. Then Eve pushes her legs from the seat toward the ground. There is a thud when her soles touch the floor.

"So far, so good," she says. Taking a deep breath, she pushes against the armrests with both of her arms and gets up. The tilted floor does not make it easy for her, but she is finally standing. She takes her arms off the armrests and spreads them. "Ta-da!" she announces elatedly.

Adam applauds her.

"Don't just watch. Do it yourself," Eve says. She trudges wide-legged through the module, supporting herself against the wall with one arm. "It would be nice to take a shower now."

"When we reach the mountain range in a few days," I say. We have some tough days ahead of us. Adam and Eve will have to exchange the comforts of the spaceship for heat, dryness, and constant physical exertion. I hope the fascination of a new beginning will last long enough to make them succeed. I would enjoy physical exercise myself, but I no longer have that option.

Interrupting my musings, Eve says, "Ahem... I've got to pee."

Adam looks around. "Well, there is some kind of bucket back there you can use," he says, pointing. Eve gives it a skeptical look.

"Of course you can go outside and pee on the hot sand, while Proxima Centauri is burning your naked skin," Adam adds.

"Adam is right," I say, "although there is no sand out there, at least not at our landing site. However, it is not advisable to expose unprotected skin to UV radiation. You are better protected inside your suits."

Eve crosses her arms. "I am definitely *not* going to pee into my diaper," she says. "I might as well use the bucket, then. But don't look."

Adam nods and looks conspicuously ahead. "I am busy enough trying to get out of my seat," he assures her.

I check our equipment. We have J the robot, who moves on terrain-capable wheels. His arms are designed in such a way that he can also climb well. His interior compartment contains our army of fabricators that can produce almost anything, even copies of themselves, out of almost any materials. The fabricators produced the three individual backpacks to be worn by J, Adam, and Eve. These contain everything we need in the near future or are carrying around for sentimental reasons.

For instance, Adam has a doll, a kind of mini-J that J made and gave him for his third birthday. Eve has kept pieces of her baby clothes. She once told me what fascinated her so much about these. It is the idea that her own body fit into these tiny coverings years ago. It made her feel like a butterfly, she said, and then she corrected herself. Like a caterpillar that had not yet reached its final stage.

Oh, Eve, you were always a butterfly. I regret I did not tell her that back then.

"You can look again," Eve announces.

In the meantime, fabricators are already busy putting the organic excretions to new uses. On board *Messenger,* no material is supposed to be wasted, but this practice will also change in the future. While the spaceship moved through almost empty regions, which always made recycling the better option, Proxima b now offers us more than abundant raw materials. For the fabricators, it will often be more advantageous to gather material nearby than to recycle waste. Organic components will remain valuable as long as we are still walking across the scorching central plains, but by the time we reach the steppes we will find enough of those.

"Airlock ready," the ship's automated system reports.

Sadness suddenly overwhelms me. I had not realized how much *Messenger* had grown dear to my heart. I lived more than 20 years inside it. While we will stay in contact, J is going to be my new home, at least for the time we spend traveling. I will also have to say farewell to the quantum computer on board *Messenger.* Though it would have fit inside J, the necessary cooling for it would have required too much effort. I cannot even remember what my consciousness felt like without the quantum computer.

"Time to get out," I say.

Eve is the first to stand in front of the airlock. "The first step of a human being on a planet outside the solar system," she says, half joking, half seriously. "I will be in the history books."

Her cheeks are flushed. She places her backpack next to the lock, kneels, and crawls inside backward. Then she closes the door.

"Put on your helmet and close it," I warn her. I want to protect her from being shocked too much when she gets outside.

According to the computer, the outer door is now open. Why didn't I go out myself? Then I would not have to worry about her now. There are no cameras on the outside of the hull aimed toward the stern. Eve is all on her own. I hear her groans via the intercom.

"It is hot. And I imagined it to be brighter," she says.

According to the bio-monitor data, she is doing fine. Her suit's cooling system is managing to compensate for the exterior heat.

"Don't let that deceive you," I warn her. "Proxima Centauri is not shining very brightly in the visible range, but in infrared and UV it is much brighter than it would be on Earth."

"I know," Eve says with an annoyed tone of voice, "we learned about all that. And I don't care what Earth is like, because I have never been there. Now pass me my backpack."

We put her backpack in the airlock.

"I hope you did not pack any of the chocolate that the replicators made for us," Adam says. Eve does not react. J transports food in his interior, where it is protected from the heat.

"Do you want to take a sniff of the exterior air?" I ask.

"Definitely," Eve replies. Her suit starts drawing in air from the outside. Possible germs and poisons are filtered out, and it is enriched with oxygen.

"Hmm, smells odd."

"Could you describe it more closely?" I ask. It is logical that the air of the planet would smell strange to Eve. She has been breathing the filtered air of *Messenger* all her life, except when we did exercises to detect different smells.

"It smells a bit... I don't know... rotten?" she answers. I try to coax something out of the analyzer data, but the concentration seems to be too low. Even just a few molecules of a substance can trigger the olfactory center. I am curious how Eve will react when we reach the fertile zones. I visualize the image of a dark green forest, and there I would lie in the moss, smell the mushrooms, the tree sap, the sun, the soil.

"Okay, it's my turn," Adam says. *Oh well, then the captain is going to be the last one to leave the ship,* I conclude. I hear a "woohoo" and then a cry of pain which shocks me incredibly, followed by "Shit!"

"Adam jumped from the edge of the airlock," Eve says.

He obviously did not take the high gravity into consideration.

"I am still in one piece," I hear Adam say.

How childish of him! I think.

J first puts Adam's backpack into the airlock, then his own. I am moving my consciousness into J's computing unit. It has sufficient capacity, but now it will take me seconds to solve partial differential equations, rather than mere microseconds. From this point onward, my voice will sound through the robot's loudspeakers. So far, I have not noticed that I no longer have access to the quantum computer. J crouches to get into the airlock. It doesn't look like he will fit into the tube, but his size was a consideration during its construction. Since he is the largest single object we have to get off the spaceship, the airlock was custom-tailored for him, so to speak.

Outside I want to look at Adam and Eve's faces, but the visors of their helmets are slightly reflective. "Are you okay?" I ask them.

Both of them nod 'yes.' They have already put on their backpacks, and the high gravity does not seem to bother them very much. Could they have become used to it so quickly? I call up a map of our route and notice the mountain range we are trying to reach is in the west. It is easily visible from here. The air is shimmering above the dry, hot plain, and we will have the sun at our back. Proxima b's rotation is tidally locked, so the sun will not leave its place in the firmament. The disk of the star glows white, and it is two and a half times bigger than the sun is in the sky of Earth. Despite this, it is noticeably darker than during a summer day on Earth, almost as if twilight has already started. The sky itself appears as a dirty blue. Proxima Centauri does not have the right spectrum to produce a shade of blue like the one we see on Earth.

I have J point to the mountains. “That is our destination,” I say. “It is about 30 kilometers.”

“We should be able to reach it before the evening,” Adam says.

“There is no evening and no night,” I remind him. “The sun will shine until we reach the terminator.”

December 18, 18

We did not manage to cover more than 10 kilometers yesterday. Eve has fewer problems walking than Adam. Perhaps it is because she weighs 20 kilos less and exercised almost as hard as he did. A weight difference of 20 kilos here is the same as one of 30 kilos on Earth. The pressure suit is not ideal for such hikes, particularly since it is form-fitting and the repeated movements cause the suit to chafe. The atmosphere is actually thick enough to do without the suits. Just a breathing mask providing extra oxygen would suffice. But the integrated cooling system offers obvious advantages in these temperatures.

Today, Adam insists he wants to try walking without the suit. He will be wearing his simple uniform, along with the boots belonging to the suit. In some areas the ground reaches temperatures up to 50 degrees, and one might think something is glowing beneath it. I am convinced we will have to stop after two or three kilometers so Adam can put on his pressure suit again, but I did not veto the experiment.

I look at his chafe marks through J's eyes. Overnight, the fabricators produced an antiseptic ointment that is supposed to relieve the pain and also promote healing.

"What's in there?" Adam asks.

"Urea." In reality, I have no idea what the ingredients are.

I could have checked, but the answer just popped up in my mind.

Adam scowls.

"Come on, say thank you," Eve says, as she points down at her body and laughs.

It is good that they have not lost their sense of humor. Walking upright on Proxima b seems to be really hard on them. I compared this to archive images of people on Earth walking. Neither Adam nor Eve walk like other humans. Both have instinctively adopted a gait like a diver strolling underwater. They stomp with both legs, moving their hips back and forth, almost like two-legged robots. This way they have to fight less against gravity.

At first I recommended a different gait that saves more energy for them. The idea is to fall forward into the next step and then swing back at mid-point, letting gravity do more of the work. However, this very soon made Adam's knees hurt, as his joints could not handle the hard shock of every step.

It might be better if the ground were softer, but it is not. They are walking on a hard, glassy material, and the analyzer tells us it is, in fact, volcanic glass. The surface of the central plains might at one time have been sand that later melted, perhaps the result of a meteorite impact. Alternatively, the plains may have been covered over by volcanic magma welling up from below. The latter option is supported by the considerable radioactivity indicated on my instruments, another reason for us to get out of the central plain.

After the first 'night,' I have a new idea of what might become our biggest problem; the lack of a natural rhythm. In the sky, the sun does not move a single millimeter. On board *Messenger* the ship simulated day and night. Although Adam and Eve knew this was an artificial division, their bodies became used to this two-part structure. Here on Proxima b, it is different—the day extends for millions of years. While we agreed, in the beginning, to follow the 24-hour cycle of Earth, I am skeptical as to whether we can stick to it. In the end,

Adam and Eve's bodies will have to find their own rhythms, which might not even match.

Breakfast is served from the belly of the robot. I avoid calling it 'my belly.' Even though my consciousness resides inside J, I am not the robot. I am Marchenko. Just like on board *Messenger*, I have to use this kind of 'mental hygiene' to distinguish myself from others. It is harder now, though, because I speak through J's loudspeakers, see through his eyes, hear through his ears, and grab with his arms.

Neither Adam nor Eve seems to show much appetite. Eve yawns loudly, and no one is saying anything. After their meal, the two of them pack up the tent they had slept in and roll up their mattresses. They work slowly but efficiently, and every movement, every step seems deliberate and precise.

WE START OUT, AND MY GOAL IS TO REACH THE FOOT OF THE mountain range today. According to the laser scanner, the distance is about 21 kilometers.

Adam and Eve walk in a very regular motion. Their steps are even in sync, even though Eve's legs are shorter. This allows Adam to get ahead, but then he stops and waits for Eve. Each time, Eve waves him to keep going. She is trying to tell him that he should not wait for her, but Adam ignores this. After two hours, Eve is so annoyed they decide to change roles. Now Eve walks ahead and Adam follows her. When he is about to overtake her, he stops and falls behind a bit. Eve does not mind, because she does not see this. They are already working together like an old married couple.

After four hours and two rest periods they have covered half of the way, ten kilometers, the same as the distance they covered yesterday. I am proud of them both.

After another two kilometers we encounter the first signs of the mountain range. Smooth small hills rise up, maybe 100 meters. As we approach, the hills rise gradually, but as we pass the first ones we see steep drops on their 'back' sides. And for the first time we see Proxima b's own shadows.

I notice right away that these shadows look different from shadows on Earth. They are not as dark, because there is less contrast. The area not reached by sunbeams seems to be reddish-gray. This is not just an ordinary shadow on a distant planet, it is also a world of its own. As neither the light of Proxima Centauri nor its UV and X-rays reach here, a special biotope developed, despite the aridity and the heat. The air is still very warm, maybe 35 degrees, and the ground does not consist of glass, but of sand. Something dark and hair-like grows from it.

Eve crouches next to the spot, followed by Adam. They look at this alien lifeform, almost overawed. Adam moves his hand close, but without touching it.

"We have to know what it is and how it works," I say, "and therefore we must examine it."

"For the first time I am seeing a living being not named Adam," Eve says. She fans air at the hairs and watches them move.

"Unfortunately that won't be enough," I say. "You have to rip one out so my analyzer can check it."

"You mean *kill* it?" she asks, surprised.

"We will only know whether you killed it once I examine it. Plants on Earth can even be propagated by removing shoots."

Eve gives me an angry look at hearing this.

"You are right, you are probably going to kill it. But we won't survive here without killing a certain number of local lifeforms," I reply.

Eve sighs.

Adam pulls on one of the black hairs, but it is amazingly tough. It appears to be anchored deep in the ground. Finally Adam uses the scissors I give him—using J's hands, of course—pulled from the robot's cargo bay.

I examine the hair inside the sample container. It has a strong shaft, like animal hair from Earth. In this case it contains silicon. On it there are microscopic feelers, which fulfill two functions; they filter moisture from the air, and they generate energy by vibrating with the air currents. The mechanical motion is turned into electricity by the piezoelectric effect, and the plant uses this to separate the gathered moisture into hydrogen and oxygen. Then the gasses are apparently transported downward inside the silicon tubes and consumed by the actual being down there. The process is probably not very efficient, but that does not matter, as long as the organism gives off less than it takes in. It is difficult to tell whether it is a plant or an animal. I tend toward plant, because I see no chance for this organism to move.

I ask Eve to get me a few more hairs to see whether they are any different. This does not appear to be the case, so there seems to be only one type of hair. But on the fourth hair I find something odd. A ring, also black, about one millimeter in diameter, moves up and down on the hair. I remove the ring, which continues moving. So it must be some creature in a symbiotic relationship with the hairs. I detect neither limbs nor head, and the little animal appears to be able to wrap its entire body around the host hair. Then it looks for defective vibration feelers—ones that no longer move—and it digests them, breaking them down into their components. This way it gains food and moisture while keeping its host healthy.

I summarize my findings. "We have discovered our first ecosystem," I explain to Adam and Eve. His face looks bored.

Eve, on the other hand, seems to be quite interested. After I am done talking, she says, "Marchenko, do you think you could let us participate in future research? While you found something interesting, it would have been more exciting if we could have solved these mysteries together. Then I don't have to feel like your stupid measurement servant."

If I could blush, I would be bright red now. Of course Eve is right. "I'm sorry, you're right," I say, and she accepts the apology with a smile.

"Before we go on," I say, "I would like to find out whether these ecosystems in the shade zones are connected to each other." I have J point at two additional hills visible in the northwest, and we start walking in that direction.

"If there is no connection, the species there should be very different," I propose. "It is highly improbable that evolution would by chance follow exactly the same path."

Eve nods, while Adam grumbles something I do not understand.

"I know what to do," Eve says.

There is sand in the shadow of the next hill, and hair-like things grow there, too. Eve brings me a few samples. Only my analyzer can tell how much they differ from the specimens of the first hill. The results are clear.

"Genetically they are almost identical," I explain. "This means there must be a connection between the shade zones."

"You've already analyzed the genome?" Eve asks.

"No. I just compared some randomly-selected base pairs. That is enough to determine kinship. By the way, life here has six base pairs."

"So there is DNA? And you just mention this in passing?" Eve asks, giving me a really angry look. That's so unlike the Eve I think I know.

"I cannot tell yet for sure whether it is completely comparable to our DNA," I reply. "However, the hairs consist of cells, and these cells contain small, rolled-up organelles that form a long string of information. It might be a precursor of DNA—such as RNA—as it contains information, but the information is encoded using six letters."

Eve squints and for a minute does not say anything. Then she turns toward me and says, "I don't know why, but the whole time I'm getting goosebumps. Imagine, we flew this far just to discover that life here is so damned similar to that on Earth."

"There are practical reasons for it," Adam interjects. "There can be no evolution without a transfer of information. Biology is based on chemistry, and therefore molecules act as carriers of information. Two letters would be too few, but a large number would complicate duplication. Six letters, like here—or four like on Earth—seem to work well."

"I understand what you mean, Eve," I say, "even though Adam is right, of course."

"You know, Marchenko, it's nice that you never want to take sides, but you won't be able to do that forever," Eve remarks.

"But I..." I want to say, *Sometimes I agree with you or with Adam, or insist on holding to my own opinion,* but I do not finish the sentence, because I feel that this 16-year-old girl knows more about human interactions than I do. Have I lost that much of my humanity during the last 20 years? The problem is I want to lose neither Adam nor Eve.

December 19, 18

"Marchenko, let's get back to what you said yesterday. You mentioned that there must be a connection between the shade habitats," Eve says, looking down at me. I am using my strong arms to pull my robot body onto a small rocky platform.

"Yes, there must be some kind of exchange. Perhaps through the air?" I hypothesize.

"How do you think that would work?" Eve asks, groaning as she pulls herself up to a higher ledge. Adam is climbing above her, and both of them are connected to me by ropes. If someone falls, I can quickly attach my body to the rocks.

"It would be sufficient if the wind blows individual cells between them, or one of the little ring animals, which just digested a piece of its host," I say.

"Or, there is a subterranean connection," Eve suggests.

"That's possible, too. But how did you get that idea?" I ask.

"I remember what you taught us about the biology of Earth, about how large the underground part of all ecosystems is. And we haven't even seen the thing all these hairs lead to."

"I also wonder about the nature of this being. Perhaps it is a giant tuber. The hairs provide nutrients, which are then stored in the tuber. But for what reason?"

"Maybe it's for the next flare?" Eve suggests. "The hairs have a silicon coating, but in the central plain the effect of the flare must be the strongest."

"You think the hairs grow again every 40 days, fed by the energy stored in the tuber?"

The sensors of the bio-monitor send an alert: Eve's body temperature is two-tenths of a degree above normal. Maybe the air conditioning of her suit is not keeping up.

"If Proxima Centauri has been producing flares for billions of years, life here has definitely adapted to them," Eve says.

"I am sorry, but are you feeling alright?" I ask, changing the subject.

"Yes sure, Marchenko. It is a bit tiring, but that was to be expected. Why do you ask?"

"I get data saying your body temperature is slightly high. It might not be significant, but ..."

"I know, it is better to ask once too often than not often enough," Eve says. "Right now, I cannot see my display. We could take a break after this fissure."

"Adam, we are taking a short break," I tell him by radio. Adam mumbles something that sounds like 'okay.'

The ledge Eve is aiming for does not offer enough space for both of us, but this is no problem. I drive two steel nails from my arms into the granite. They will support my weight.

"Just a moment," she says. I see her jump across a half-meter-wide gap that has a depth of 50 meters. I am tempted to cry out, but just manage to control myself.

"Okay, my suit. One second." Eve shakes the dust off her sleeve so she can read the display better. "Shit!" she says. "The cooling efficiency has decreased by 45 percent. I am sorry, Marchenko. I should have noticed it earlier. But it seemed normal to sweat while climbing a mountain."

"Everything okay?" Adam asks via radio. He now seems to be interested in what is going on with us.

"Eve has a problem with her suit," I reply. "It's the cooling system."

"Let her climb naked!"

"Ha-ha," Eve replies.

"But seriously, what prevents her from switching to her normal uniform?"

"Heat and radiation," I reply.

"I understand," Adam acknowledges.

"I can manage for a while longer," Eve says, but I notice her voice sounds uncertain now. I look down. We have climbed about 400 meters. After going up another 300 meters we will reach a mountain pass leading through the mountain range, which has a total height of several thousand meters.

I am puzzled by the shape of the mountain range, particularly the steep foothills. It seems as if the mountains once surrounded a kind of giant bathtub. Was the central plain an ocean at some time? That would have been when Proxima b was still farther from its star and was generally colder. Perhaps back then a meteorite struck the ocean, vaporizing the water and moving the planet to an orbit closer to the sun?

We spent two hours to climb this far, and Eve will have to make it for another hour at least. Human bodies do not handle overheating well. They react with nausea, headaches, and finally loss of consciousness. We can't let it get that far.

I radio Adam. "Do you have any ideas? What alternatives are there?"

"We wait until night and then keep climbing," Adam replies. He is quite the joker today.

"The uniform, as Adam suggested," Eve says.

"It is another hour in full sun and strong physical exertion," I remind her. "A little bit of cooling is better than none."

"We cannot avoid the sun, but we can get around the exertion."

Eve is right, and I know exactly what she means. "I could carry you," I offer.

"Just admit you are lazy, and your pressure suit is working fine."

"Adam, that's enough," I insist.

Eve does not answer for a moment, as she seems to be thinking about it. "Can you really do that?" she asks.

"I would not have—"

"Yes, I am aware of that," she breaks in. "Oh, well."

I wonder whether I have overstated my promise to her. Yes, if either Adam or Eve or the both of them fell, I could quickly anchor myself to the wall of rock so the rope would hold them. Unfortunately this will not help me climb. I will have to ascend the last 300 meters with the added weight of Eve and her backpack, using just two arms. A single arm would need to move almost half a ton upward. I know these values are within J's specifications, but does the rock edge this arm will be holding onto know that, too? Will it be stable enough to support 500 kilograms? I cannot be absolutely sure, even though the rock has so far seemed very sturdy.

And what would happen if I fell? Adam is connected to the same rope as I am, but he definitely will not be able to hold on to my mass. So he will fall as well. I'm being irresponsible. Eve should be connected to Adam's rope. If I fell, the two of them could survive. One has to expect any kind of contingency in the mountains.

I explain my plan to Adam and Eve.

"Out of the question," Adam says. "It's either no one or all of us."

Eve agrees with him. "I am not going to connect to Adam's rope, and you can't do anything about it."

Even though they do not obey me, exposing themselves to danger in a very illogical fashion, I am nevertheless glad.

"Well," I say, "if you want it that way, Eve, I would suggest you sit on J's shoulder and hold on to his head."

Eve does not hesitate for long. I am hanging below her on the rock wall, at an angle. This position is perfect for her to climb onto my shoulders.

"Giddy-up, horsey," she says after taking her place, and

she uses a loop of the rope as a whip. I feel like whinnying, but I suppress the impulse when I realize all three of us could plunge into the abyss at any moment.

"Hold on tight," I say to Eve, who is very mistaken if she imagines our climb to be some leisurely ride. Then I remember that she has no concept of what a ride is like. She only knows about horses from her lessons. I carefully free the left arm and feel for a stable ledge higher up. The joints of my fingers that are holding on to the rock are made of an incredibly strong titanium alloy. Then I free the other arm. I automatically move slightly lower and to the left, because I am swinging on only one arm. I give a push with my lower body, allowing my other arm to find a new handhold. J the robot climbs like a monkey, which is not a pleasant form of locomotion for a person sitting on his shoulders.

Eve is very quiet now. I press my chin against her knees in such a way that she cannot fall off. *Swing to the right, swing to the left.* I have to slow down so I will not pass Adam. Perhaps it will take us less than an hour. *Swing to the right, since there is a better handhold there.* Suddenly the view out of my right eye becomes blurred. I almost miss the rock ledge, but then I reach it and hold on.

"What happened?" I ask.

"I had to throw up," Eve replies. "I am sorry, but it was so sudden I couldn't warn you."

This catches my attention, as vomiting can be a sign of heat shock. "Is everything okay with you?" While I am asking her, I already check the data supplied by the bio-monitor.

"Yes, everything is fine, and I am not feeling that hot anymore," she says.

I am relieved. Eve's body temperature has not risen further. "Adam, let's go on," I say. "Another hundred meters."

We reach the plateau 20 minutes later. I lift Eve from her place on my shoulders. As if on cue, we all turn back to see the view. The sunburned central plain lies 700 meters below us. We only encountered two of the species living there, but there must be more. At some point we will have to return here, if just because *Messenger* is waiting for us beyond the horizon. It has no engine that would provide sufficient thrust to launch it into space, but that could be changed. I turn back around, and Adam and Eve follow me.

The information we recorded during our orbital flyover is correct. The mountain pass will lead us to the other side of the mountain range. Its walls—several kilometers high—cast dark, cold shadows that feel threatening.

December 20, 18

We put up the tent to one side, because a strong wind is blowing directly through the mountain pass. The air current, which is cooled by the eternal darkness, sweeps past us and into the wide valley of the central plains below us. We designate eight hours of the never-ending day as 'night' and enjoy warmth and light one last time. Adam is still sleepy while he gathers the last of our stuff. Eve has disappeared around the corner into the shadow to relieve herself.

The scan from orbit shows us that the mountain pass crosses the entire mountain range. How might it have developed? Did a fracture in the planet's tectonic plates spread at this very spot? Had there once been a river flowing through here, or could the wind alone have created all of this? I hope we can discover the answer along our way. The sides of the mountain pass should indicate whether water, air, or tectonic forces created it.

This time I take the lead. I can light up the darkness with my sensors, thus protecting us from surprises.

"Come on, it's just a mountain pass," Adam says. I won't even discuss letting him go first.

The first few meters are very straightforward, and we still can see the entrance of the mountain pass, the only source of light. Further up, the mountain pass walls must bend, because we do not see the sky.

The temperature drops rapidly. A moment ago it was 30 degrees, but after 100 meters it is only 15.

"Turn on your suit heater if you are feeling cold," I recommend.

"Yeah, yeah," Eve replies.

After about 300 meters we are in complete darkness and the air becomes even more humid. I activate the lamp on J's head.

"Yuck—do you feel that too?"

"What, Eve?" I ask.

"Something is constantly brushing against my face."

I have to focus my optical sensors more, because so far I have not noticed anything.

"Yes, those are hairs," Adam confirms.

I aim the light directly at the mountain pass wall. Something is growing there. I switch to ultraviolet, and the image becomes clearer. Fine hairs are streaming in the wind. Their outer layer looks phosphorescent in the UV light.

"They resemble the plants in the shade biotopes back there," Eve says.

"Yes, this appears to be an adaptation to the solar flares," I say. "While photosynthesis is more efficient, it is also far riskier on Proxima b, because the plants would be exposed to dangerous radiation. A part of the plant life prefers to stay in the shade and live off wind energy."

"Sounds reasonable," Eve says.

I decide this is a good time to take a closer look at the hair plants. Here, on the walls of the mountain pass, they seem easy to access. I scratch one from the hard, rocky surface. The plant is really easy to dig out, unlike those in the desert. It's a small wonder they can live here. I inspect it with J's visual system from tuber to the top of the hair. It is clearly an individual.

The deeper we advance into the mountain pass, the longer and denser the hairs get. I also notice that the vegetation density increases with the atmospheric humidity, which means the hairs probably filter water from the air.

Eve's voice reaches me from about 20 steps away. "Could you wait for a moment?" She must have fallen behind without me noticing. I stop and Adam bumps into my back. I turn around and aim the light in Eve's direction. She is hard to see, but appears to be fighting off something with her arms. Adam runs toward her, and I follow him.

"What is going on?" Adam asks, nervously.

"There is something inside my suit. It itches," Eve radios.

Once I reach her, I scan Eve's body but cannot find anything. "It can't be helped," I say. "You have to take it off. Where does it itch?"

"On the side," Eve says, and pushes a button that opens a special zipper. The upper part of her suit peels off. "There, just above my hip," she says, pointing.

J's hand shoots forward, and I see what Eve is talking about. Inside the hand is an animal, maybe eight millimeters long, which at first sight resembles an ant. The robot fingers grasp it in such a way that it cannot escape, but so that it will not be injured, either. I use a telephoto lens to observe the object. It still resembles an ant—even magnified—but with an important difference.

"Look, this thing has wheels," I say. I project an enlarged image onto the rock surface near us. Instead of legs, this little animal has eight round limbs that seem to be formed of coiled hairs.

"Perhaps this developed from the parasite we saw out there," Adam suggests.

The wheels are rotating wildly while I hold the animal. In the middle of the body there is a capsule with a very strong hair leading into it, and this appears to be the drive mechanism.

"It works like a wind-up toy," I explain. Adam and Eve give me blank stares. "I am referring to a spring mechanism."

Both of them nod.

"This strong hair here," I say, marking it on the projected image, "is coiled like a spring. The wheels move when the animal unwinds the spring."

"But how does it coil the spring?"

"That's a good question, Eve," I reply and look around us. "Here almost all surfaces are vertical. If the animal rolls down the wall in reverse, the motion of the wheels should coil the spring. Then it can use the stored tension to climb the walls again."

"What about the conservation of energy?"

Eve is right. The energy gained from rolling down is not enough. The animal must have an additional mechanism to tension the spring.

"We won't be able to discover that here. I would have to run a few tests first," I conclude. "Perhaps it is an electrical mechanism, or some kind of muscle. This animal probably feeds on the parasites. That's what it was looking for on your body, Eve."

"I hope it didn't find any," she says, anxiously.

"I wouldn't be so sure about that. Sooner or later our bodies will come in contact with the microorganisms of this world. *Your* bodies, that is."

"Yuck, that's disgusting," Eve says.

"Could we go? I am getting cold," Adam says, sounding impatient. Eve pulls her suit back on and puts on the helmet.

"Good idea," I say. "It's probably going to get a lot colder."

We make good progress for the next kilometer and a half. Adam also has his helmet closed. The walls are evenly covered with hairs, as if we were walking through the armpits of a giant.

"Look here," says Adam, who is up front in spite of my objections. In the light of his helmet lamp I see an irregularly-shaped area without vegetation. The ground seems untouched, and I examine the area under magnification.

"The hairs are shortened down to about two millimeters," I explain.

"Maybe it's caused by a disease. A kind of hair loss?" Eve suggests.

"Then the hairs would be all gone. No, an animal was grazing here," Adam interjects.

"Which is to be expected," I say. "There must be something to cut the hairs now and then, otherwise the mountain pass would be all overgrown."

"Something?" Eve's voice expresses both curiosity and awe.

"Hard to say what it might look like, or whether it would be a danger to us," I say. "We ought to be careful. It's for good reason that I want to walk ahead of you."

No one says anything for exactly seven minutes. Then I hear a soft sound behind me, like a *whoosh*, followed by a shrill scream. *Eve!* I turn around, frantically, colliding with Adam, who is walking behind me and does not react as quickly.

"Adam, get out of the way. Fast!" I command.

He reacts but does not let me pass. Instead, he runs a few steps in the direction we came from. Then he abruptly stops. "EVE!" he screams.

I brighten the beam of my searchlight. Something is lying on the ground. It looks like a huge, eyeless bat, with two triangular wings and a kind of suction mouth. The wings are wrapped around Eve. Only her arm and her hand stick out.

"NO..." I hear Eve's voice yell. I immediately dim the light. The creature might not like illumination, and I don't want to enrage it.

I switch to the radio. It's good that Eve has her helmet on. "Stay completely calm," I say.

"I'm try—" I hear Eve croak. The weight of the animal

seems to be pressing on her chest. Her heart is beating faster, but her vital functions are not alarming.

"Reduce stress," the computer prompts. My own stress level is rising to the maximal value.

The bat seems to be calmly sitting there. Is it wondering what to do with its prey? Should it digest it right away, or might it be better to tear off pieces to feed to its offspring? I am terribly worried about Eve and have to force myself not to act impulsively.

Adam shares my concern. He raises his hand and appears to be ready to attack the thing.

"No, Adam," I tell him via the helmet radio. I myself am surprised that he stops. I switch to infrared to watch the bat without disturbing it, but Eve immediately calls out, "No!"

The animal does not seem to like infrared either. What about the ultraviolet range? Now the alien bat looks phosphorescent! This clearly shows how its suction mouth searches Eve lying below it, presumably to find food. Since her suit and her helmet are closed, I do not see any immediate danger for her, no matter how scary the situation might look.

"Eve, it is just licking you. Don't worry," I say, attempting to reassure her.

"Vrrry hvvy," Eve pants.

The bio-monitor calms me down a bit, reporting the oxygen saturation of her blood has hardly decreased. She is getting enough air.

"Still, don't move," I say, trying to hide my fear from Eve. *She must not do anything rash.*

"Nothing is going to happen to you, trust me," I say calmly, and can see the animal is pulling its left wing from underneath Eve. At its end is a very long bone that seems to end in a point, and appears to be a very effective weapon, if needed. Adam seems to have noticed this detail as well and moves toward Eve. I grab his shoulder with the robot arm. He twists and turns to get away.

"No, Adam! If that animal wants to attack, Eve will be dead before you get to her," I reason with him. "Do you want to fight it with your fists? You just would anger it! Just stay calm!"

"Do something!" he yells.

"It will be better for Eve if we wait. Safer, I mean. Really, it will. You have to believe me."

Adam briefly stops resisting, but I do not fall for his trick and keep holding him back.

"Damn...bsst," we hear Eve mumble. Now the bat pulls out its second wing as well, and there is also a sharp bone at the end of it. Adam once again tries to get away from my grip. The creature now seems to have had enough. It raises its head, extending its long neck, and sniffs in our direction. Does it wonder which one of us to check out next as a potential source of food?

The animal lifts its left wing, then the right one, and now I see what the sharp knives are for. It pushes them against the opposite walls of the mountain pass. Like a mountain climber inside a crevice, it pushes itself upward and quickly moves away. I aim my UV searchlight at it but lose track of the creature. The skin on its lower side does not seem to be phosphorescent. Meanwhile, Adam runs toward Eve, helps her get up, and hugs her tightly.

Eve leans against the wall and opens her helmet. Her face is very pale, and she is breathing heavily. The bio-monitor tells me she has not suffered any damage. I am glad nothing worse has happened.

"That was..." She does not finish the sentence.

"That was a kind of sheep, a harmless herbivore," I say.

"The thing was terribly heavy. It dropped on me from above."

"In your situation I would have been scared shitless, too," I say. "But I saw its mouth. That thing could not eat you. It probably was just curious. I am sorry it frightened you so much. All of us, indeed."

"That's very reassuring," Eve says, breathing deeply, but then she turns around and vomits. Adam places a hand on her shoulder and gives her a cloth.

"On those wings..." he begins to say. I vehemently shake my head to discourage him, but Eve cannot see it. However, Adam ignores me and continues to say, "On those wings, the creature had a kind of knife. I imagined it slicing you open with that."

"That would only have happened if you had charged the animal, Adam," I remind him.

"I couldn't just stand around while it was suffocating Eve!" he replies angrily.

"She was in no danger of suffocating. You would have simply provoked the animal by attacking it."

"Don't fight, the two of you," Eve says. "I am already feeling better. It's over. Let's go."

"Should I carry you for a while?" I ask her.

"No, I am okay. Besides, I need the exercise," she replies. "Why don't you look around to detect what else might be waiting for us. I don't like surprises like the one we just had."

"I don't think the creature is coming back," Adam says.

"Me neither," says Eve. "But if that was a kind of sheep, how dangerous might the wolves be?"

How true. If a herbivore was so well-armed, the dangers it must be exposed to daily had to be impressive.

As if to confirm our fears, we find some bones on the ground after walking another 400 meters. These are the only remains. The body and the skin of this creature must have either decomposed long ago or been completely devoured by the predator. Adam bends down and picks up a piece of bone about 30 centimeters long.

"This must be part of the wing," he says. I see at once that he is right, but I still carefully examine the bone. The structure of the material is unlike the bone structure we are familiar with. I break the 'bone' in the middle and show the fracture to Adam and Eve.

"Did you have to destroy it? We could have used it as a weapon," Adam says.

"Knowledge is much more valuable than such a primitive weapon," I retort. "Look, the material is made up of many air-filled cells. This makes it light and strong. Here at the tip, where the blade is, the cells are especially dense." I brush against the bone. "And the material sharpens itself. The creature only has to climb for a while to sharpen its knives."

I look at the pile of bones. Unfortunately, it is no longer possible to tell how the individual pieces were once connected. The joints must have rotted more quickly, or they were also eaten. On the whole there are 330 bones scattered here, according to the object recognition function of my visual system.

"This sheep-like creature is a very highly-developed animal and has one-third more bones than a sheep on Earth," I tell them.

"And why are you telling us this?" asks Adam while giving me a nasty look.

"It's about the mission. The message. We have to understand what happened to the inhabitants here. In order to do that we must study the natural environment."

Adam opens his mouth but then closes it, turns around, and walks ahead. Eve follows him without saying a word. I want to call them back, but I refrain from doing so, because I discover the second knife-bone. Adam is right, a weapon might come in handy. I pick up the bone and place it inside J's belly. Finally, I scan the area under UV light. I discover about 20 tracks leading away from the pile of bones into all directions, both upward and to the front and back. These must have been left by the scavengers that were responsible for defleshing and dismembering the corpse.

For half an hour we walk in complete silence. We should have reached the end of the mountain pass by now. I stop because I think I can hear a splashing sound ahead. Could that be rain falling on the land outside the mountain pass? The splashing noise comes closer. No, it is more like a mixture of soft slaps and pattering sounds. I imagine a herd of mice, then realize the noise comes from behind us.

"Wait a moment," I call out to Adam and Eve. "That sounds somehow menacing." Might this have something to do with the bones we found earlier?

As if on cue the sound becomes louder. Perhaps the mice are increasing their speed. I aim the UV light at the area behind us and see them, an almost innumerable mob of small animals, slightly bigger than mice, jumping from wall to wall. They must have muscles like frogs and sticky feet like geckos. It is impressive how quickly they can move on only two legs. The animals look like frogs that had their front legs amputated and their mouths sewn shut. At first sight they do not appear dangerous. Who is afraid of frogs?

"Crazy," Adams marvels, while Eve utters a shriek. Both are now near me.

The animals are phosphorescent like their larger relatives, and therefore clearly visible in the dark as long as I aim the UV light at them. It is a practical invention of nature to render a part of UV radiation harmless by turning it into visible light.

I move the beam up and down. I am starting to think that the animals are not moving randomly, but instead have selected us as their target. This is confirmed half a minute later. The animal closest to me raises its head. There is an organ in its throat that looks like gills, but contains an elastic band, similar to a tongue. This tongue shoots out and moves half a meter in my direction, but because it misses me, it withdraws again. But the second animal hits its target. The pillow-shaped tip of the tongue sticks to the metal of my body. The animal tries to retract its tongue. It is amazingly strong, as measured by my instruments. Because they only weigh a few grams, these alien frogs can only acquire this much force if they are firmly attached to the mountain pass walls.

"Watch out, these guys don't seem to be nice!" I yell to Adam and Eve. I reach for the animal whose tongue sticks to me and try to remove the creature. It is stuck on the wall too strongly to remove even with my robotic strength. However, the tongue is vulnerable, and I can quickly sever it with my cutting tool. The first animals are reaching Adam, who stands only a meter behind me.

"RUN AWAY!" I yell, but it is too late.

"OUCH—the damned beast!" Adam screams angrily. "The thing tore a piece from my suit!"

I toss the knife to him. "Concentrate just on the tongues. Cut them!" I shout. Now I know why the sheep-creature has two large knives on its wings. However, this had not helped the specimen whose remains had provided us with the knife.

I am looking around. More and more frogs are coming out of the mountain pass behind us, and their sheer numbers are frightening. We have to watch that they do not simply overrun us. Adam and Eve are most at risk, as the flexible fabric of their suits cannot hold up against the strength of these animals. My metal armor, on the other hand, is impervious to them.

"RUN TO THE EXIT!" I yell at them. "It can't be far now. I am going to distract these animals. I can deal with them!"

Adam stops for a moment, and then he nods and tosses the knife back to me. "Come on, Eve, he's right," Adam says. "We have to hurry to get out into the open. These things are dangerous."

They start running. The frogs are focusing on me. To them, I apparently look like the tastiest prey. They do not seem to realize they cannot do anything against my metal armor. I am fighting a lonely battle, but it's okay—this is what I am here for. Adam and Eve won't have to traverse this mountain pass again.

Will I really be able to handle these beasts? I do not know. I am working as fast as I can, using the knife to sever all the tongues sticking to me. This causes some confusion, as the specimens with the cut-off tongues are now being attacked by their fellow creatures. And now I witness the upshot. The tips of the tongues rip pieces of skin and flesh from their victims. These pieces disappear into the maws—the gill-like openings—of their attackers and are deposited there. Afterward the attackers' tongues are again flung at their prey. I can only hope Adam and Eve are safe.

A battle zone gradually forms around me, divided into several sections. The animals are attacking me from all sides. While I can reach each part of my body with my knife, moving my right arm from front to back takes a certain amount of time. If during this period two new tongues stick to me, I will fall behind. These things might not be able to take me apart, but they will tie me to the spot. Soon I will not be able to move at all.

My mind is racing. There must be spots on J's body that are not as sturdy as the rest, particularly the joints. *Once the frogs notice this...* Even though their attacks do not seem very coordinated, they will hit the joints at some time, just by pure chance. *Am I doomed? Is this the place where my consciousness will be obliterated?* This fear paralyzes me, but it's utterly illogical. I am only hurting myself, just like the infrared light hurt the other creature.

Infrared? The frogs live in a dark and cold environment. How might they react to a nice, warm bath? I activate my infrared searchlight and beam pure warmth into the mountain pass. Aha! The beasts are reacting! The number of attacks goes down, while I notice a high-frequency squeal. *A cry of pain?* I am not sorry to inflict pain on them. In fact, it gives me deep satisfaction. *You are not going to do that to me, frogs, not to me!* I go into a rage and my robot arms whirl around as if they have a will of their own. The rear ranks of the creatures are starting to retreat. I cut off the last tongues still sticking to me. Even the animals at the front begin to withdraw.

Then I am done. A strange euphoria overwhelms me, consisting of fading battle rage and a sense of deep relief. I will still be able to take care of Adam and Eve! I gaze at the battlefield around me. There must be 100 dead frogs, missing different pieces of flesh that their fellow creatures tore off. I carefully pack away the specimen that seems least damaged in order to examine it more carefully later. Then I hurry toward the exit where Adam and Eve are waiting for me. Eve runs to me and hugs J's body.

"Marchenko, it is good to have you here," Adam says when we reach him.

December 21, 18

About 600 meters below us is a plain that could be compared to a steppe, but which gives a completely different impression. In particular, the colors do not resemble those on Earth. The greens look all wrong. I know there are simple physical causes for this: Proxima Centauri radiates most of its energy in wavelengths different from those of the sun. Photosynthesis—which most of the plants we see below must be utilizing—would be less efficient using the greens of Earth. I somehow feel cheated, almost disgusted, seeing these strange hues that most closely resemble black with shades of greenish shimmer. This makes everything seem artificial, as if a painter had created and colored his personal vision of hell.

Adam and Eve are utterly amazed. They are not as biased as I am.

"This wide view," Adam says, "I am in awe of it."

"That's nothing compared to looking at infinity from a spaceship." I am surprised at myself for this response.

"In space you feel lost so easily," Adam says. "Here I seem small, but not tiny... Not about to dissolve into nothing."

"Yes, there is a border... the horizon," Eve says, pointing in a vague direction. "It is like a frame around a painting. I feel I am part of something larger. In space I am only a negligible part of the great nothingness."

Adam and Eve have never lived on a planet, but they really feel at ease here. Is this based on human genes, and do I myself feel different because I am lacking a body? By now I long for the freedom *Messenger* offered me.

Adam, who still has a blanket wrapped around his shoulders after a rest period of six hours, is standing near the edge of a cliff. One more step and he would plummet downward. I want to place my hand on his shoulder, just for safety's sake, but I suppress the urge. Adam is shading his eyes with his hand. The shadow of the mountain reaches far into the plain. The area beyond it glitters brightly, or at least appears to do so. We have quickly become accustomed to the near twilight of Proxima b.

"Are you rested enough for the descent?" I ask.

Both of them nod, and just like during the climb we secure ourselves with ropes. The way down will not be as stressful as the ascent, because it is not so hot, and gravity will assist us. On the other hand, we will be climbing in the dark. In the shade it is about as bright as the night during a full moon on Earth. I am about to explain this to Adam and Eve when I realize they will not understand the comparison. If they ever reach Earth—which should be impossible—they would compare the moonlit nights there with the shade areas of Proxima b. It is details like these that demonstrate again and again how different the two are from me.

THE LOWER WE GET DURING OUR DESCENT, THE FASTER WE move. Now and then I have to tell Adam and Eve to slow down. We must not grow careless. A fall from 120 meters is still dangerous, even if you are caught by a rope. Yet I understand they are in a hurry. Down there lies the part of the planet that might become their home for the next 100 years. It is very different from the parched plains we landed on.

Adam is the first one down, and I am watching him. First he looks for a free spot, but when he obviously does not find one, he carefully places his foot on the dense vegetation below him. He waves at us while standing there. "Everything is fine, it doesn't look dangerous!" he calls.

I hope he is right, but we really have no choice. Eve and I reach the ground simultaneously. My electronic sensors tell me that I sink in by precisely 3.5 centimeters, but otherwise the ground appears to be stable. I turn around and start examining the plants. Meanwhile, Adam is already moving away from the cliff. I would prefer him to wait for my results, but it makes no sense to call him back.

At least Eve is coming back to me. She is holding something in her right hand. "Look, a flower!" she says, offering me a stalk with a bell-shaped object at its end. On the outside it is black, like everything here, but the inside displays colorful stripes—pink, a somewhat dirty yellow, purple, and brown. At the bottom of the bell there is a small hole which seems to lead inside the stalk.

"That's not a real blossom," I say.

"What then?" Eve asks.

"I suspect the plant uses it to catch small animals." I carefully touch the inside of the blossom. The colored stripes detach themselves and flip inward. "You see, if something crawls in here, it will get scared by the motion and hide inside the hole. Then it is most likely digested there."

I look around. There are only a few of these theoretically carnivorous plants. The area below the steep cliff is permanently in shadow, and is dominated by plants with hard, leathery leaves that appear almost black. They are no taller than five centimeters and they cover every square millimeter. But between them stand many of the wind-energy-based hair plants we saw earlier. The two species do not seem to be competitors. Perhaps they profit from each other. The leafy plants still get 99 percent of the remaining light, while the hairs gather energy and moisture at a height that the leafy plants could not easily reach.

I try to count their exact distribution, but then I notice that a few of those flowers seem to be growing near us.

"Were these here earlier?" I ask, pointing at the plants forming a semicircle around us.

"I didn't see them," Eve replies as she is pointing farther out from the cliff. "I picked that one from over there."

I look at the recording made automatically by J's visual system. "No. They really weren't here before," I explain.

"This means they are moving," she says. "So perhaps they are not plants, but animals."

"But they also have leaves, and certainly use photosynthesis. So, we probably have to forget about the lifeform categories used on Earth."

"Did they somehow sense us?"

"It looks like it," I say. "Maybe they react to movement. We are going to find out."

"Could they become dangerous to us?" Eve asks.

I take another look at the pseudo-blossom she gave me. "No. We are definitely too large for these digestive holes," I reply. "They seem to be passive hunters. They offer themselves to their prey, but they rely on their deception going undiscovered until it is too late."

"In that case there must be real blossoms somewhere," Eve says. "That's great news. I was so looking forward to picking flowers."

Even though we have not found the original specimen that these hunting plants imitate, there is some reason to believe in Eve's hypothesis.

"Now, let us get out of the shadow of the mountain range," I say.

Adam is already 500 meters ahead of us. He walks at a good pace and does not turn around.

The closer we get to the light, the larger the percentage of leafy plants becomes. I stop and try very carefully to dig a specimen out of the ground. The root does not reach down very far into the crumbly soil—which smells like swamp—but it branches out considerably. I follow several strands until they merge again with others. So these do not appear to be individual plants at all! Here we have an entire colony that is connected through the soil and shares a root system.

"It's just as you suspected with the hair plants," I say to Eve.

"That's a clever strategy," she concludes. "If nutrients are lacking in one area, they can get them from elsewhere."

I look at one of the hair plants for the sake of comparison. Here, similar to the specimens in the desert, each hair seems to end in a single tuber. Could all leafy plants on the planet be part of a single individual?

After walking another 300 meters we reach a strip approximately three meters wide, where only the hair plants grow. They are especially tall here, or one might assume this to be a deliberately constructed path. I examine the ground to find evidence for it. However, the soil here is not harder than elsewhere. The uppermost layer is visibly gray, but that could be caused by the stronger evaporation. I measure the mineral content of the strip and am surprised. The level of sodium, potassium, and magnesium salts is so high that certainly no terrestrial plant could grow here. Did someone poison the soil to keep it free of leafy plants?

I want to know how straight this path is, so I decide to follow it. Its trajectory does not aim directly at the edge of the shadow but approaches it at an angle. I contact Adam via radio. He grumbles a bit but then changes his direction and now walks parallel to the path.

Eve follows me without being asked. For a while the path is so straight I really believe it was deliberately planned, but then it suddenly forks. In the middle there is an island about five meters wide covered by the leafy plants, with the two subsidiary paths running around it.

I have a suspicion. First I dig out a plant from the island, then another one from outside the right edge of the path. I compare both with the specimen I picked up earlier. The result is surprising. We seem to be witnessing a war of the plants, which use chemical weapons to take territory from their adversaries. While the three specimens do look similar externally, there are clear genetic differences. To test this I dig a few feet deep into the path and discover the root systems of the leafy plants are not connected beneath the path.

The entity forming the small island appears to be doomed, as it is threatened by two, much-larger entities to the west and east. The path seems to be something like a line of demarcation. The leaves of the outermost specimens in the west are infused with sodium and potassium compounds, while those of the east with magnesium. The rain then washes these compounds out as salt, so that the area between them becomes a barren battle zone. Only the hair plants seem to profit from this.

It is reassuring to think that humans are not the only species in the universe waging war against its own members. I explain my findings to Adam and Eve.

"That's somehow interesting," Adam says, "but is it useful for us? Does it help us to know this?"

"Perhaps it will help us to fulfill the mission," I suggest.

"I couldn't care less about that."

"We know what these plants are allergic to. We could use that when we build our own base, in order to keep the area free of plants."

"That's what I meant," Adam says. "Perhaps you could focus more on practical knowledge like this, instead of on theory. We have to hold out here for many years."

I had better stop talking now. Another 15 minutes to the edge of the shadow zone, then it will be time for the next 'night.' Almost 500 kilometers lie before us, and here in the open steppe we won't find any protection against the flares of Proxima Centauri.

December 23, 18

We have covered approximately 75 kilometers since the day before yesterday, and I am proud of Adam and Eve for holding up so well. Despite blisters on their feet neither complains, and despite the high gravity we are moving at a good pace. On our way we came across several more domain borders between different specimens of the leafy plants.

Extrapolated to the entire planet, this would mean that there are about 10,000 separate beings here. That is a very low number of individuals, which could impede their long-term survival in case of a natural catastrophe. Yet the plants seem to have adapted extremely well, and so far I have found no parasites. As an ecosystem the steppes are very boring, but the abilities of the plants are impressive. They must defend themselves chemically against potential pests and have managed to exterminate those. They only leave the hair plants alive, probably because they are useful to them.

I am thinking of the Enceladus creature—which consists of numerous independent cells—as I talk with Adam and Eve this morning about the plant species here on Proxima b. Of course it is not a real morning, just the time after getting up.

"Could the individual domains communicate with each other?" I ask both of them.

Adam gives me an incredulous look and says, "You think the plants are talking to each other?"

"Perhaps not in the sense of human language," I reply.

"During biology lessons you told us that plants on Earth can communicate via messenger substances," Eve states.

"Yes, within certain limits," I answer. "The fact that they poison those paths here points in that direction."

"But you are really thinking of something else, aren't you?"

"Yes, Eve. I wonder if they can exchange thoughts. These plant collectives must be fairly old. They even survived the huge flare, and probably those before it."

"I assume they would think very slowly."

"Why do you believe that?" I ask.

"Due to the distances alone," Eve replies. "Just look at the human body. Now imagine your arm was 100 kilometers away."

"You are probably right, at least if these plants communicate electrochemically like we do."

"Do you think they discovered a different way?" Eve asks.

"I am going to find out."

"Do you think these plants sent the message to Earth?" Eve asks. She wants to know.

"Most definitely not. They lack all requirements to do so. They have no technology, just their gigantic bodies in the soil of the steppes."

"Then why are you so interested in these plants, Marchenko?"

"Perhaps I can ask them what they witnessed. They might know where the senders of the message went."

"And if those creatures are no longer here. If they were killed by the enormous eruption? Or, if they left here in time?"

"Then we will find traces of them, Eve, one way or another."

"What will happen to us then?" she asks.

I pretend not to fully understand her question. “We will analyze these traces and then keep looking for these beings.”

Eve shakes her head. Five minutes later she finally speaks, “I am starting to understand Adam.”

I do not want to know what she means by this.

December 25, 18

Christmas! I had previously asked Adam and Eve if we should take a break because of the holiday, but both of them were against it. They said they were too old for such festivities, and the reason for the holiday is part of something that was too far away. Nevertheless, I insisted we have a common meal in the evening.

During the past few days, Adam has slipped into his sleeping bag after the tent was set up and we'd had our hastily prepared meals. Twice I just happened to see his face contort as he was masturbating. This is adolescence. I cannot even remember how I felt at that age. Maybe I do not want to remember. However, an endless journey with parents and siblings would definitely not have been high on my wish list.

On this special day, though, we all sit around a campfire. I had started collecting and drying leaves the day before yesterday, and now they are feeding the fire. At first, I wondered if we should do this to the plants, but then I thought of the poisoned paths. Dying must be an everyday event for these leafy plants, and a root system should be able to handle it if I selectively strip an area of three by three meters. Where would their consciousness be located, if they have one?

Now the fire crackles, smelling like burning reeds. Even though it is not darker than usual, the flames are reflected in the eyes of Adam and Eve, as they sit cross-legged, leaning forward. I never managed to sit like that for long when I was still a human. Adam's eyes look so moist one might think he is crying.

"And now?" I ask.

"Now what?" Adam says. He seems to be annoyed because I disrupted the silence.

"Christmas. December 25th. That used to be a good occasion for looking back into the past," I answer.

"There is no past, only the future."

"So what happened in the last few months doesn't count, Adam?"

"I don't know why it should. It was all just a prelude." Adam is breathing faster. Eve places a hand on his shoulder and he calms down again.

"Adam, I need you here... You, too, Eve," I assure them.

The young man gives me an angry look. "For the mission, yes, I know," he says, bitterly.

I want to reply, 'No,' but I do not manage to say it. I know he is basically right.

"We have been traveling so long," Adam explains. "We were made for this planet, but it is so obvious we don't belong here. We are visitors, though we have to stay forever. Considering this, what role does the past play?"

I cannot argue with Adam's sentiment. I could say that I did not choose to go on this journey, either, but it will not help him. I trust he is going to find his place.

January 4, 19

It has been a really long walk, two weeks, across a seemingly endless steppe. Getting up, walking, lying down, sleeping—all while the dusky sun seemed to be glued to a spot in the sky. It did not rain a single time, and I am beginning to wonder how any vegetation can survive here. There are no seasons, as an entire orbit around the sun only lasts a few days. It's just possible that some kind of seasonal changes might occur, if not caused by the energy of the sun, then by other factors.

The average sleep period of Adam and Eve has decreased day by day. The day-night rhythm seems to be embedded in the human genetic code. How long will it take for them to get used to the fact the sun never sets?

During the last few days we only talked when it was necessary. But we still managed to keep our pace and even arrived here a day earlier than planned. The forest, which is our eventual destination, might not only offer us protection against the flares but also save us from this humdrum routine.

I look at Proxima Centauri. The sun is noticeably lower than it was two weeks ago. This is obviously caused by us walking westward over some great distance. The eastern sky has now taken on a reddish hue. Brightness sensors indicate that 20 percent less light gets down here, yet the leafy plants have adapted to it. Their leaves have ribbing which increases their photo-sensitive surface.

We are still unable to see the forest, which must be about 30 kilometers away. Nevertheless, I can feel Adam and Eve are as excited as I am.

January 5, 19

We will soon be there. Adam and Eve have insisted they will not stop for sleep until they have first seen the treetops of the forest appear on the horizon. These final kilometers are taking us longer than usual.

We can see it. The forest looks impressive through its sheer height, even from afar. The tallest trees reach more than 200 meters. We soon notice, however, that the forest is much less static than the steppes. In fact, there appears to be a lot of movement going on there. I suspect that different microclimates develop in various layers, that the exchange between them causes this, and that there also might be a lot of wind.

I am surprised by the clear boundary to the forest, though. "Wouldn't it be more logical if the forest started with smaller trees, and then they gradually get taller and stand closer to each other?" I ask Adam and Eve.

"It doesn't matter," Adam says. "There must be some reason for it, and the more we hurry, the sooner we find out."

His prediction turns out to be true. We find the reason in the steppe about five kilometers before reaching the forest, where the ground is suddenly gray. There is absolutely no vegetation. It looks as if something had cleared the entire area from here to the forest. This time, not even the hair plants grow in the intermediate zone.

I stop, analyze the ground, and am shocked at my finding. Back on Earth not even a hazardous waste site would have accepted such contaminated soil.

"Adam, Eve, it is getting dangerous here," I warn them.

Adam looks at me as if I was teasing him and says, "Excuse me? What do you mean?"

"The soil is pure poison," I reply. "You have to close your helmets, otherwise you might faint. The air above the ground is also contaminated."

Adam still gives me a skeptical look, but at least he obeys my instructions. "What is the reason? Who did this?"

"I don't know, Adam," I reply, but I have a suspicion. I remember the chemical warfare between the leafy plants. Could something like that happen between these plants and the forest, just on a larger scale? What are we witnessing, and what does it tell us about the nature of the forest? I carefully analyze the soil composition. If the leafy plants managed to stop the forest, this method might be adaptable to use as a weapon, if required.

Now of all times it is starting to rain. What would we have given during the last two weeks for this break in the routine! Adam and Eve are already 200 meters ahead of me, crossing the empty plain in front of the forest, when I realize the significance of my soil analysis. The high content of salts, fluorine, chlorine, sulfur... What will happen if this stuff gets thoroughly soaked? How quickly will the ions separate in the water? How long will it take before hydrofluoric acid, hydrochloric acid, and sulfuric acid develop?

"Adam, Eve, come back as quickly as possible!" I tell them via radio. I can see that Eve reacts and stops.

"Are you crazy, Marchenko?" Adam exclaims.

I do not know what he is thinking, but I must stop him from continuing toward the forest. "Adam, you will soon be walking through a lake of acid! Your boots won't be able to withstand that," I warn him.

I have no idea whether this will really happen. Maybe the water will run off fast enough, and the worst Adam has to fear is muddy boots. But then again, I could also be right. I hope he will listen to me. At least he stops now.

Eve walks to him, and the two discuss something with their radios turned off. Eve was always the more sensible of the two. She should be able to convince him. But then afterward, the two of them just shake hands. Eve walks in my direction while Adam moves toward the forest. His helmet radio is still off. I implore him to come back but—of course—I can't get through. The rain is increasing, and a lightning bolt flashes from the clouds, striking out in the open. Eve starts running. I briefly lose sight of Adam, and when I look back in his direction, the field is covered with fog. He is gone.

"Adam, come back!" I yell over the helmet radio. Eve will reach me in a moment, and we should be safe here where the leafy plants are still growing. What about Adam? I hear Eve also trying to reach him via radio. The fog turns thicker and grows closer, as if the lower edge of the storm cloud touched the ground. Then we hear a splashing sound. We must have heard it at the same time, because we simultaneously turn our heads in the direction of the sound. Adam comes racing toward us, covered with mud, but it does not seem to be adversely affecting him. He sees us at the last moment and almost crashes into us, but I manage to catch him.

"That's the last time you will need to say, 'I told you so.' That's a promise, Marchenko," he gasps, almost out of breath. No matter. The important thing is that nothing has happened to him.

The future does not matter, either. For the moment, it's the present that counts. A present in which we are being soaked by dense, warm rain, and nothing in this world can harm us.

January 6, 19

It continued raining for four more hours, and afterward the rainwater needed almost half a day to drain. Adam and Eve emerge from the tent appearing more rested than in quite some time.

"The rain drumming against the tent fabric was so soothing, and I slept better today than ever before on Proxima b," Eve says.

Adam does not say anything, he just nods. He cannot help acting this way, and I accept it.

I ask the two, "Ready for the last kilometers?"

"I am looking forward to it," Eve says.

We pack away the tent and gear and start walking. The forest scares me less today than it did yesterday. It somehow seems to have calmed down. Perhaps the trees needed the refreshing rain as much as we did. Now and then we deviate to avoid a larger puddle, but otherwise it is easy again to cross the empty strip between the plants and the forest.

The closer we come to the forest the more majestic it seems to me. At first Adam and Eve keep joking in low voices, but then they gradually also fall under its spell. It is only when we get really close that we can fathom the true dimension of these giant trees.

We stop about 100 meters from the boundary. From the

outside, the forest looks to me like a green New York. The naked trunks seem to soar upward like skyscrapers, and their leaves appear far, far above us. In this place, whoever reaches up highest is the winner. From afar everything seems to be in constant motion, but the gigantic leaves, which must be ten meters long, are so far above us we are hardly conscious of them individually. It feels like entering a huge cathedral with a roof 200 meters high, supported by the many columns of tree trunks. No sunlight shines through the dome of this building, because all of it is intercepted by the leaves and turned into energy. Nonetheless, it is not dark down here.

"Look," says Eve, her mouth wide open. Adam, standing next to her, is also amazed. A fairytale landscape lies before us. It shines in sparkling colors promising gold and gems. Aladdin's treasure chamber would pale compared to this.

We enter the forest. The ground is covered by plants we have not seen earlier.

"Fungi, like giant mushrooms," Adam says.

Indeed, the plants each have a stem reaching into the ground and a cap at the top. It is these caps that radiate the multi-colored light. There are numerous varieties: small ones, with stripes issuing from the center; larger ones with small spots; medium-sized ones with trembling lamellas on the facing side; and big, wrinkled ones. Plus, there are even specimens that can barely fit under J's two-meter-tall robot body. All the different shapes radiate light in various colors, but there seems to be no correlation between shape and color. This accounts for the overwhelming, magical effect the interior of this gigantic 'cathedral' has on us. It alone makes the entire journey worthwhile.

I watch Adam and Eve. They are just as impressed as I am. Adam takes a few steps into the forest and then sits down, leaning against one of the gigantic trees. "This is where we will build our base," he proclaims.

I feel like warning him. We must first check if everything is as harmless as it looks, and why the forest conveys this majestic impression. Mentioning this right now, though, might not be a good idea. Adam has earned this moment, which for him probably has a lot to do with a feeling of having arrived. Eve sits down next to him. They sit shoulder to shoulder and observe the miracles of the forest.

In the meantime I start my analysis. A few days from now we are going to need a shelter that protects us from the next flare. The first surprise during my analysis comes from the mushrooms. They all have one thing in common; they turn the hard UV radiation of the sun into energy. Whatever they do not need they emit again via phosphorescence, and this could be interesting for us. I have to find out what part of the hard radiation the mushrooms can reject. While I do not think it would be enough to just sit out the next super-flare under one of the tall mushrooms, I am sure we can somehow integrate these plants into our plans.

The second surprise also comes from the mushrooms. Their caps are made of a soft organic material, so theoretically they could be edible. This is both good and bad news for us. It is good because we could turn them into food with little effort. We could even consume them raw, although they might taste really bitter due to the high mineral content. It is bad because nature never creates something edible without a reason. If there is something edible, animals that live off that food source cannot be too far away. If we are lucky, these are nothing more than small, harmless worms, like those found in mushrooms on Earth. Otherwise, a horde of mushroom-eating dinosaurs might charge through the forest now and then, goring anything that is not a tree trunk. Or the worms could be a species that would burrow through your stomach lining, if you were to accidentally swallow one, and then it might build a nest inside you, eventually releasing millions of new worms.

After my experiences in the mountain pass, I will not make the same mistake of associating small size with the absence of danger.

The third fact found by my analysis does not surprise me much, given our earlier experiences. The mushrooms resemble their terrestrial counterparts because their roots join in a mycelium, together with the roots of many other specimens. This appears to be a heritage they have in common with the leafy plants on the steppes. Are all the mushrooms in the forest part of the same individual? Or is there warfare here, like in the steppes, about which we have to be very careful?

Discovery number four offers the third surprise when I remove a small piece from one of the tree trunks. It is extremely hard, but my strength is just sufficient to remove it. I probably will not be able to cut down an entire tree. I would never have guessed that the material of the tree trunk would be very, very similar to that of the hair plants. It consists of small, individual chambers filled with a soft material, and it appears both species have the same kind of roots.

In that case, the trees must represent individuals making it on their own, just like the hair plants. While we certainly are not yet familiar with the entire ecosystem, it seems to me that the division here runs not between plants and animals, but between leafy plants and hair plants. Thus leafy plants are connected to each other, while hair plants are solitary. Accordingly, the frogs in the mountain pass would belong to the hair plant group, because they lacked a physical connection. On this planet, the question of whether a species moves, and how fast it moves, seems to play no role for its evolutionary family tree.

I decide I have gathered enough information for today. I slowly walk to the tree near where Adam and Eve are sitting. Along the way I break off a chunk of mushroom. I divide it in two and offer it to Adam and Eve.

"Salt and bread," I say, "that's how you greet guests in my home country. I will have the fabricators make some salt, but the mushroom is just as nutritious as bread."

Eve takes a piece first, and then Adam reaches for his.

"A bit slimy," says Eve, "but the taste is tolerable. It is reminiscent of Napa cabbage, though not quite as bitter."

"Napa cabbage?" Adam stares at her skeptically. "You have never eaten Napa cabbage in your entire life."

"No, I haven't, but I have read cookbooks, and whenever they mentioned Napa cabbage I imagined it to have this kind of taste."

January 7, 19

"WE ARE GOING TO BUILD THE BASE AT THIS VERY SPOT," Adam says, standing two meters away from the last tree that forms the boundary to the steppe. "We need to be able to see what is happening in the sky," he adds.

"Except for solar eruptions, against which it will be harder to shield us here, what is supposed to happen in the sky?" I ask.

"I don't know," Adam admits, "But if something happens, we would be practically blind deeper inside the forest. I don't like that idea at all."

Eve does not say anything, but I can tell from her face she is looking for arguments.

"The forest protects us. The leaves represent an important radiation barrier," I explain.

"But you mentioned yourself that they won't shield us enough," Adam says. "We are going to need our own protection."

"Any additional safety net is helpful," I add.

"But it would make us blind to anything happening around us."

"Not much will happen, Adam, except that in a few days a devastating UV and X-ray storm is going to hit us," I say.

Adam looks at Eve, as if convinced she is on his side. "Why don't you say something, Eve?" he asks.

"I think Marchenko is right," she answers. "We should not be taking any chances."

Adam looks at her, his shoulders drooping. "But that's exactly what we would be doing by moving inside the forest, don't you realize?"

"I don't see the risk, Adam," I say. "Really. I also think that further inside we would be shielded better against flares."

Adam stomps his foot like an angry teenager, and I remember he actually *is* one. On other occasions, Adam and Eve seem so mature I almost forget their real ages.

"I don't trust the forest," he says, placing his hands on his hips. "Something is wrong with it. You'll see. I can feel it." He turns around and walks into the forest, as if to challenge it.

About three kilometers inside the forest boundary we start to build our base.

I have further analyzed the mushroom caps. They are indeed capable of absorbing hard radiation, turning it into harmless light and emitting the same. This also explains why the forest never gets completely dark, despite the dense foliage overhead.

There is only one strategy if we want to protect ourselves against the coming flares: We have to place as much absorptive material as we can between us and Proxima Centauri so that the remaining radiation cannot harm us. The leafy canopy will help to some extent, but Adam is right, it will not be enough. We will have to dig a few meters down into the ground. This will be Adam and Eve's task during the coming days.

I will try to make their work easier. If I can imitate the structure of the mushroom caps by using my fabricators, they will have to toil less. The idea is to make an additional roof that functions like the mushroom material but absorbs radiation even more efficiently. So I am actually planning to perfect the work of possibly millions of years of evolution. In order to do this, though, I need to first gather some more material. I already notice that various types of mushrooms react differently. I need the best variety, the one with the most evolved radiation shielding, and then I will improve it.

The winner is a particularly small specimen I find below another mushroom. I noticed it because, in spite of being shielded by the larger mushroom, it still emitted an unusually bright glow. This means it is very efficient at turning the invisible radiation into light.

Inside the analyzer I take a closer look at its genome. The midget mushroom soon shows the reason for its advantage over other variants. It is specialized in several wavelengths simultaneously. Unlike its competitors, it does not just convert energy better but can accept several inputs at once. That is clever, and it gives me an idea: If I can teach this mushroom species to absorb additional wavelengths, it should be able to protect us even better. In principle I just have to scan as many types as possible, identify the correct genetic sequences, and integrate these into my designer mushroom.

If the plants were just programs I could finish my project in a few minutes. But biological systems have the drawback that I have to test my changes on a new generation, and it takes some time for it to grow. At the moment I do not even know how often generations change. I suspect, though, that the larger variants live longer than the smaller ones, and luckily, my designer mushroom belongs to the latter group.

I RETURN TO THE PLACE WHERE ADAM AND EVE ARE BUILDING the base, but they are not working on it now. Eve is sitting on the ground, her back leaning against a tree. Her face has a guilty expression. “Adam wanted to take a walk,” she says.

I make the robot nod its head. “It’s okay,” I say. The site looks as if the two of them worked on it for no more than half an hour, and it probably was not a good idea for me to leave them alone together. Adam and Eve have removed the vegetation in an area measuring approximately two by two meters. Below it, wet topsoil that has a fatty sheen is visible. I wonder whether terrestrial plants would thrive in it. They certainly would find enough moisture.

I examine a handful of soil. On Earth, it would be teeming with small and microscopic organisms, but this is not the case here. If not, then why does the soil stay so crumbly? Which mechanisms stir it up, keeping it fertile? Right now, I am unable to solve this mystery.

I hear steps behind me. I rapidly turn my head 180 degrees. "Adam?" I say.

There is no answer. He is probably hiding behind one of the trees. I switch to infrared vision and discover him about six meters away. "Come out. I can see you," I say.

"Spoilsport," he answers.

I decide to get the unpleasant part of our conversation over with first. "The base—" I start saying.

"I know," Adam interrupts me. "You realize you are not setting a good example, don't you? And it makes no sense to have us working so hard. The robot is stronger and never gets tired, so he could do this much faster."

"I am trying to make our work easier," I say.

"*Our* work? You are not working, you are just strolling through the forest. Therefore I can do that, too."

"I have a suggestion, Adam," I say. "Starting tomorrow, we will work on the base together. You are right, I can do certain things better, but for others I need your help. We have 19 days left until the next flare. Working alone, I wouldn't be able to make the deadline. Agreed?"

At first he acts self-satisfied, but then he turns around and walks toward Eve. Over his shoulder he yells, "Okay."

January 11, 19

"TIMBER!" I call through the forest. Adam and Eve are standing behind me and the tree will fall forward, but to me the warning still seems appropriate. At first the giant trunk ahead of us just trembles slightly. It does not seem to realize I severed it with a clean cut all the way through. The cut surface is angled slightly forward so that the tree has to topple in that direction.

It took me two hours to cut all the way through the trunk. The reason for this was due to the mass of the tree, which pressed from above against the cut and my self-made saw. This high pressure merges the tree's just-separated cells, as the material seems to have self-healing features. My cutting only worked after I started to cover the severed areas with an impermeable synthetic cloth. From that moment on, the self-healing no longer worked, and I finally made some progress.

Now the trunk is starting to move. Down here, it is only a few millimeters, but the top of the tree, 210 meters high, is already noticeably tilting. For a moment it looks as if the leaves could prevent the fall by interlacing with those of other trees, but once this falling giant gets going, nothing can stop it. The tree simply tears off the leaves of its neighbors. However I do not think this could cause a domino effect. In addition, I calculated the fall in such a way that our tree has a free path.

We will need all of its wood for the base, for supporting the side walls, and for the ceilings. The timber of one tree should be enough, but if it becomes entangled in another specimen, it would make cutting it up much more difficult.

While the mighty treetop moves downward the tree seems to fall in slow motion. For a moment we see the sky that is covered by clouds today. A few seconds later some raindrops hit me, but the free space is soon closed when the leaves of the neighboring trees spring back into their normal position. Ordinarily the rain never gets down here, and this will not change, either. A strange excitement is sweeping through the forest, or am I only imagining it?

"Did you hear that noise?" Eve asks. I notice that there is a high-frequency humming in the air, which reminds me of the sound made by an electric fence.

"Yes. How strange," Adam says.

I analyze the sound digitally. Perhaps it is created by the trunk moving through the air faster and faster, like the whirring of a propeller or a sword swung with great force, but then the volume should follow a pattern. It is barely audible, yet the high-pitched noise consists of individual sections, syllables in a way. Could the tree be uttering sounds?

Now the noise fades again, and it lasted too briefly to determine if it really contained a kind of meaning. Talking trees, or simply a coincidence? Perhaps the tree leaves moved during the descent in such a way that they contributed to the whirring sound and gave the impression of a rising and falling volume.

"That must have been the sound of the falling tree," I say. "The trunk reaches a considerable speed."

We hear a loud crash, and the branches that the leaves are attached to break under the force of the impact. A dull thud follows, making the forest floor vibrate, and I can measure it.

"Get to safety!" I warn them, because parts of the branches and leaves are flying sideways. Luckily, none of them come in our direction. When everything has calmed down again, we walk past the fallen tree, now lying on the forest floor like a foreign substance. It makes sense that there is no underbrush, as not enough light reaches down here. However, shouldn't a tree occasionally reach its age limit, die, topple, and finally decompose? Living beings cannot exist forever. The clean forest floor indicates the trees all grew skyward at about the same time, like on a tree farm. Were they planted?

Eve brushes her hand against the bark of the tree. "It's really smooth," she says.

The structure remains unusually uniform, even as we approach the treetop. The trunk must always have been free of branches here. Only 20 meters from the top we find the first leaf node. What I believed to be branches from below are more like stalks. The single leaves are directly attached to the trunk. Their attachment points are distributed around the trunk in a helical pattern. One stalk is four or five meters long, followed by a leaf of a similar length and a width of one meter, which broadens toward the outside.

"Strange construction," Adam remarks.

"This distribution only makes sense if we imagine an entire canopy of such leaves," I reply, pointing at the area between leaf and trunk. "The leaves of the neighboring trees fill the gaps appearing near the trunk. And at the same time the treetops support each other."

"But there are way too many leaves. The lowest ones don't get any light."

Adam is right. The uppermost leaves should be able to block the view of the sky completely. The lower ones seem useless.

"Nature is never wasteful," I reply. "Let us take a look."

The solution must be here, right in front of our eyes. I do not see anything unusual about the stalks of the leaves. Then I look at the spot where the stalk is attached to the trunk. Above and below each stalk there are barely-recognizable flat notches.

"Eve, could you please raise this leaf here?" Eve is puzzled by my request, but she follows it.

"Look here!" I point at the attachment of the stalk. My suspicions have been confirmed: The trees can distribute their leaves at random around the trunk. They are swiveling! This would allow them to compensate for lost leaves. Since all of the leaves look weathered to the same degree, each tree seems to consciously expose each leaf to the sun for some time, a clever method for optimizing energy yield. Since this place has neither nights nor winters, the leaves must get a different opportunity to rest and recuperate.

"Not bad," Adam says. "A tree with movable leaves." We gather one of the fallen leaves and take it to our camp. Afterward I start to turn the trunk into planking.

January 13, 19

We will be able to reach the base via a hatch, and its entrance measures one by two meters. From there a steep set of stairs leads five meters down. The stairs are finished, and I have already attached the planking to the side walls. Now we slowly dig ahead horizontally. Adam and Eve carry the excavation material upward. This creates a small hill directly above the planned base, which also increases our shielding. On this hill of dirt the mushrooms—the ones I have genetically optimized—will grow and add to our protection.

That is the plan. Perhaps we did not even need to dig so deep, but who knows if all flares have the same intensity? The larger part of the task is still ahead of us. We have to excavate 24 cubic meters to create a shelter measuring three by four meters, with a height of two meters. In the high gravity of Proxima b this means we have to carry about 35 terrestrial tons of material upstairs. Therefore, Adam and Eve are already moaning and groaning a lot. Yesterday they dropped their idea of having separate rooms for each of us, plus a kitchen.

I have modified the arms of the robot for better digging. On the right I now have a heavy steel shovel, on the left a kind of broom that allows me to sweep the excavated material behind me. It is not hard to move the two arms independently, but I also have to be careful not to fall into human patterns of thinking by watching myself work. Once I realize that I am simultaneously moving forward with my right arm and performing a circular motion with my left, my program fails.

At least the high gravity of the planet helps me work. Down here, the soil is considerably more compressed and harder to cut through than further up, but the planetary gravity also makes it possible to drive my shovel very deep into the soil. However, I have to exert extra effort in lifting the excavated material afterward. I do not experience the work as much of a challenge—it's more a boring chore—because I am sitting for hours in a dark hole, repeating the same movements. Motivating Adam and Eve to continue working does require some effort, although they at least realize there is no alternative. If we do not work diligently, we will not finish in time.

I hear an unpleasant grating sound and feel resistance. I pull the shovel out of the soil and see that its tip is bent, meaning it must have hit something hard. This would be the first large stone I've encountered, as the soil so far has been amazingly homogenous. I try to isolate the stone in order to remove it, but I only manage to do this at the front, to the left and right. In the rear, the stone extends further. It is no use. I have to clear the soil from around the stone so I can evaluate this obstacle. Perhaps we will have to cut through it. No matter how hard the stone is, I somehow will get the better of it.

Ten minutes later I have isolated the stone. It appears to be a kind of beam. I scan it with my X-ray sensor in order to see how deep it reaches into the ground. The beam is at least 12 meters long and is sloping downward at an angle of 20 degrees. The X-ray image also shows me that this obstacle displays relief carvings on the front and sides. I had not noticed them at first, because they were filled in with compressed soil. I use the shovel—gently—as a chisel to remove soil from the embossed shapes.

The result is astounding. The shapes look like glyphs carved in relief, maybe a bit like Indus script from the ancient Indian subcontinent on Earth, though the similarities are only superficial. I have to show this to Adam and Eve! "Please come here!" I say, calling them over to the spot.

"Do you want to complain about something again?"

"No, Adam. You've got to see this!"

"Well, great," Adam says. He is already standing next to me. I forgot he cannot see in the dark like I can, so I activate my headlamp now. I point at the object and say, "That beam there..."

Adam's gaze follows the light of the headlamp and I see his mouth opening. "Yes, we found it! It must be them!" he exclaims. He brushes his fingers over the alien signs to remove the last crumbs of soil. "Eve, you have to see this. Come quick!" Adam says as he motions her over to himself.

It is great to see Adam so excited. It was always our goal to find the inhabitants of Proxima b, and here we have the first real clue, apart from the ominous message they previously broadcast. But the beam is about five meters under the ground and would have stayed buried forever if we had not started to build our base at this very spot.

"Can we decipher it?" asks Eve, who has just arrived and is gazing at the signs in fascination. "I wonder if they are trying to tell us something?"

"Sorry, but the text is much too short to allow us to decipher it," I reply, "and it is very unlikely they were addressing it to us. The inscription is five meters below ground, in the middle of the forest. No one could have known we would be searching here. It is part of a ruin that might be very old."

Eve will not let these facts spoil her mood, and I can well understand this. Since our landing, I have repeatedly wondered whether our voyage—our life—may be meaningless.

"If there is this ruin," Eve says, "then there also must be others. Newer ones, also featuring inscriptions, that will teach us their language and culture."

"Perhaps it's just ornaments, rather than a script," I offer.

"It is possible, on this beam here. But they must have left written records somewhere. All cultures do that," Eve replies.

This is not completely true, at least on Earth, but I do not want to spoil the mood today. "Yes," I confirm, "that's a good start. We are going to examine the beam and then dig to find more ruins. But first we have to finish our radiation shield."

Adam and Eve resume work without protest. For the first time in a long while, we are even making jokes. I am going to deal with the beam when they are asleep, since I do not need this artificial rest period as much.

January 14, 19

FAR MORE THAN JUST A PIECE OF AN OLD RUIN, THE BEAM represents a piece of fascinating technology. Its function was certainly not to carry the weight of a roof. While it is sturdy enough for that purpose, it has strands of semiconductors embedded in it. Their systematic distribution makes me believe the object must have fulfilled a computer-like function. Nevertheless, I do not want to draw any premature conclusions.

At the bottom layer of the intricately embossed ornamentations, I can detect traces of luminescent material. The semiconductor strands are embedded a few millimeters below those, so maybe they were able to make the ornaments glow.

What could our artifact have once belonged to? So far, I have not detected any additional structures of this kind. However, my scanners do not reach very far below the surface due to the high soil moisture. There could be an entire spaceship buried 30 meters to the south, but we would only find it if we happened to dig at the right spot.

The beam was probably part of a building. Nothing else is left of that edifice, so the beam must somehow have been brought here. But why? The object weighs several hundred kilos, so no one would have expended all that energy without good reason. I am frustrated that I have reached a dead end. We know too little about the beings that left us this beam.

At least I can try to estimate when it reached this place, unless it were deliberately buried, which does not seem very plausible to me. Based on the current decomposition rate of organic material here in the forest, the soil layer above the artifact must be at least 2,000 years old. Whoever created this beam has been dead for quite some time. This object comes from the classical antiquity of Proxima b, so to speak. The beings here already used computers when the Roman Empire flourished on Earth. This sounds like an enormous developmental gap. On the other hand, it proves progress took a surprisingly parallel course here and on Earth. We have to recall that this system's mother star, Proxima Centauri, is almost 300 million years older than the sun. Therefore there should be a similar age difference between the planets of these two systems.

The ground vibrates, and a fissure appears in the wall of our makeshift subterranean chamber, unfortunately in the section I have not yet reinforced with planking. I aim my light at the spot. Dust trickles downward. I feel another shock. *Could this be an earthquake?* Even though we have not noticed it yet, the planet might be geologically active. The molten core creating the strong magnetic field would suggest this.

I have to get upstairs. Adam and Eve are sleeping in the tent. The vibrations increase. If this is the beginning of a strong earthquake we had better get away from trees that might be toppled.

I rapidly climb the stairs. Eve quickly wakes up, but Adam does not want to hear anything about moving to a safer place. "Let me sleep," he says drowsily. "I was just having such a nice dream."

It's no use. I have to get him out of here. Adam only gets up after I start using the shovel and the broom to push him out of the tent. He places his hand over his heavy-lidded eyes and looks around. "And where is your earthquake?" he asks, annoyed.

Indeed, it is quiet now. I do not trust the situation, and soon I am proven right. The shocks start up again, and this finally convinces Adam.

Fully awake now, he asks, "Where is the way to open ground?"

I point toward the east. Together we all retreat from the semi-darkness of the forest. The vibrations seem to be coming closer. They sound like steps, the powerful steps of a giant. I eventually manage to determine their direction.

"Southwest," I say, "that's where the earthquake is coming from."

I realize there is something wrong here, but we can think about it once we reach open ground.

Eve is breathing heavily, and I imagine how difficult running in this high gravity must be.

Adam takes the lead. "I can already see it!" he exclaims.

The three of us move quickly onto the open ground, the area without any vegetation. About 300 meters from the forest we come to a stop. I check the sky. Luckily, it is not raining now, nor does rain look imminent. Eve touches my shoulder. With her other hand she points toward the south-west. No, almost due south.

I had almost forgotten what terror feels like, but it abruptly bursts into my consciousness. What I see is so bizarre it becomes deeply imprinted in my mind: A tree, 200 meters tall, has risen on its roots and walks toward us with majestic steps. And it is not alone! Whomp... Whomp... Whomp... Whomp... They are marching toward us in step. Whenever the trees put down one of their three roots—each time smashing many tons of mass against the ground—this causes the shocks I first believed to be the signs of an earthquake. What is going on? My mind is racing. I cannot imagine that these trees are aiming at us tiny creatures. Unless... unless they want to avenge their brother, cut down by us. The trees must be communicating with each other, or they would not be able to walk in step this way. Did the felled tree call for help?

I may never know, because while I stare in fascination at

the maybe ten trees hurrying here from the south, Adam points to something else happening. "In the north, Marchenko, look north!" he cries.

I rapidly turn my head and instinctively draw back. A group of seven trees has left the forest and is running along the edge of the woods toward us. I quickly extrapolate. No, they are not aimed at us but at the specimens arriving from the south. At least there is a 50 percent probability for this occurring, according to my calculations.

"They don't want us," I say to Adam, who wants to run farther out into the open zone. I would rather not tell him that there is only a 50 percent certainty of this actually being true, but it does not matter, because I just determined the speed of the trees. They reach 25 kilometers per hour and could easily catch us if they wanted to. So we just have to hope we are only playing a cameo role in this conflict.

Whomp... Whomp... Whomp... The specimens from the north are coming too damned close to us, and they are now running in rows of threes. The distance between us and the trees is no more than 300 meters.

"Let's move slowly toward the open field for a few meters," I say, "but don't provoke them! Take it nice and slow!" I have no clue what the trees want. The very idea of trees having intentions seems absurd to me. But one fact remains: Multiple giants—200-meters tall and weighing several tons—are running at us. Their roots could easily crush even my robot body.

"What do they want?" Eve asks. Fear is audible in her voice, and I cannot blame her. I feel afraid for the first time in ages. Adam tries to appear very calm, but I notice how strongly he is kneading his hands.

"I think they want to get at the others," I say. *At least that would be nice,* I think, but I do not say that aloud. The distance to the trees is 150 meters, then 100, then 50.

"Woo hoo!" Adam yells.

Phew. The trees do not change their course, and they do

not squash us, but instead run straight for the trees coming from the south.

"Did you see that?" Adam asks excitedly. His eyes are wide open, and he is breathing rapidly. "They just kept running."

And more than that, I notice that they are increasing their speed. The specimens from the south do the same. This no longer resembles a peaceful family reunion—it looks like war to me. Shortly before they crash into each other, they all turn their leaves forward. The trees now are reminiscent of medieval knights attacking each other with lances. However, the difference is these knights have brought numerous lances along.

"Watch out, it is about to happen!" I call to Adam and Eve. There is an enormous crash. The creaking and cracking, the splintering and squeaking, are so loud that I have to lower the sensitivity of my hearing. Adam and Eve press their hands against their ears. It is a cacophony far beyond comprehension, and there is also the high-pitched sound we heard earlier after I cut down the tree.

The noise does not decrease, it only grows louder. The trees lean against one another, apparently trying to push down their opponents. The leaves are whirling furiously around the trunks, with fragments flying in all directions. I have to watch out that Adam and Eve do not get hit. While the team from the south is numerically superior, the northerners manage to slowly push back. Is this a war, a fight, or some kind of ritual related to spreading and multiplying? Perhaps several aspects play a role. Only the strongest survive and fuel evolution. Because conditions on Proxima b are overall very uniform, they no longer exert any selection pressure on plants and animals.

How far are these trees willing to go? The southern group has already lost its leaves. The northern specimens keep hitting them, but I do not see how they can topple their opponents, as they appear to lack the mobility to do so. But I had not suspected how clever these trees would be, and now they obviously coordinate their actions. Tree Number 1, a northerner, uses its remaining leaves to hit an isolated southern opponent from the front, while Tree Number 2, without attracting attention, carefully takes up position behind it. As soon as the victim tries to take flight from the battering, it stumbles over the roots of Tree Number 2. And, just like that, the southern tree is brought down, and it is good that the battlefield is considerably farther to our south. The tree toppled by its fellow creatures smashes to the ground and keeps moving its roots, looking like a huge but very thin baby kicking its legs.

"Hey! Look at that!" Eve says, and I share the emotion she expresses. I pity the fallen tree. It does not look like it can free itself from its predicament. Its comrades have noticed the fall, but this does not spur them to resist more fiercely. Instead, they see it as a call to retreat, and they try to evade their opponents' blows. Two of them manage to do so without a problem, but the others do not. Suddenly their opponents stop and silence reigns for a moment. It almost seems as if the trees are all talking, agreeing on a plan for withdrawal. And then that is exactly what happens. One group goes back to the south, and the other one moves to the north. Their pace is now much slower than before, while both groups abandon the fallen tree.

"That was crazy," Adam says. "Just like a theater performance."

I look at Eve, whose face still expresses shock.

"I could have done without it," she says, "but what was the purpose of that performance?"

I shake the robot's head and reply, "It's hard to say. Perhaps about controlling territory?"

"So the trees are organized into tribes?" Eve asks.

I nod in affirmation. "Probably," I say. "At first I considered them plants, but they seem to more closely resemble animals. We have to be careful when we transfer our concepts from Earth to Proxima b."

"You are the one who has to be careful," Adam reminds me. "We've never been on Earth."

We dare to return to our camp an hour later. It entails crossing an area 20 meters wide, in which the roots of the trees left imprints several meters deep. One time I can barely keep Adam from falling into such a hole. He gruffly pushes my shovel-hand aside.

I am really worried about the state of our camp, but the nearby trees have not moved from the spot. *So we don't have to start all over from scratch!*

Adam is obviously thinking further ahead. "We absolutely cannot stay here," he says. "Just imagine the trees around us marching off and stomping us like ants. I don't want to be buried alive inside our underground hole."

Terrified, Eve looks at him. Of course he is right, but do we really have a choice?

"We won't be able to cross the forest before the eruption of the next flare," I reply. "Therefore we have to finish our bunker in order to survive the radiation storm."

"And what if the trees become active before then?" Eve asks.

"I am afraid we just have to live with that risk, Eve. We know too little about the trees' lifecycle."

Adam does not contradict my statement. I go on to say, "I will certainly watch round the clock for tremors. If we flee quickly enough, we might have a chance." After I say this, I detect a scornful smile on Adam's face.

January 15, 19

As I had promised Adam and Eve, I did not let my consciousness rest during the previous night. I could have programmed some sensors to wake me up in an emergency, but after what we'd witnessed, I felt safer staying awake. Sensors might fail.

Going without rest was an interesting experience. Nevertheless, I will not repeat it. I had not realized how much my consciousness still needs the old rhythms, even though it has been separated from my body for so long. In the middle of the 'night,' which is perpetually bright—perhaps at 3:30 a.m. —I reach a state of hyper-alertness that makes me cringe at every sound. Of course the trees remain calm, but I have decided that we need to learn more about them rather than simply trusting our luck. I will climb one of the trees today and get a view from its top. Then, hopefully, I can sleep calmly again tonight.

"You want to do what?" Adam asks me, visibly shocked. Somehow I expected Adam to react this way.

"I want to go up there to gain a better view," I reply.

"You are going to see a whole lot of leaves. I can tell that from down here."

"My optical sensors will be able to capture the forest all the way to the horizon."

"Great, then we'll know how many trees there are between here and the horizon," he says.

"I could count the trees that are currently moving."

"You mean you'll see whether they are coming towards us?"

"For that I would have to stay up there forever," I explain. "No, but I can calculate what percentage of the total number is moving and then estimate the risk that the trees nearby will move during the time we are here, the 11 days left until the next flare."

Adam frowns. "Fine," he says, "and if we know that the risk is 'X' percent, what would that tell us?"

"Well, if the risk is 100 percent, we could move the base into the steppe," I suggest.

"Would we have enough time to do that?"

"Probably not."

"You see?" Adam says.

"But at least we would know what awaits us," Eve says. "I agree, you should climb up there, Marchenko."

"And what about working on the base? That will cost us another day, and we already lost time yesterday." Adam says, not giving up so easily.

"We would still have ten days left, which is enough," I say. "We cannot stay here permanently, so we will need less room."

"Okay," Adam says, his face brightening. I understand him well.

Modifying my body takes two hours. The feet are replaced by a ring that will encircle the tree's trunk. If I tighten it firmly, it holds my entire weight, leaving my arms free. Also, I can open the ring completely, so the leaf stalks offer no obstacle. The shovel and broom at the ends of my arms are replaced by human-like hands. There is hardly any single tool that allows for such fine manipulation as a human hand can do, and besides, my consciousness can better deal with them. The machine muscles are designed in such a way that they can lift my entire body weight without a problem. However, Adam and Eve have to move me to the nearest tree first.

"Wow, you are heavy, Marchenko," Adam gasps. "Is your belly full of rocks?" He actually remembers the fairy tale I told him 12 or 13 years ago, about the wolf and the seven little goats, where the evil wolf drowns after Mama Goat cuts open his belly to free the swallowed baby goats, then places rocks inside and sews it up.

"Let's take a short break," Eve says.

They drag me by the arms across the forest floor. I am looking skyward and feel oddly exposed and unprotected. If a bear broke through the underbrush now I could not defend Adam and Eve, let alone myself. Of course there is no underbrush here, and probably nothing comparable to a bear, but the idea still frightens me. And here is the worst part: I am going to leave Adam and Eve completely alone for several hours. Since their birth I have been with them every single minute, but now they are 16! I should learn to trust them.

"Heave-ho," Adam says, then repeats the command. A sunbeam hits my body. The light is falling through the hole we created in the leafy canopy earlier by cutting down the tree. There is something fascinating in being completely passive for a change. For the first time in a long while, I can smell the scent of the forest without thinking of what consequences it might have for us. There is a strong fungal smell, a rotten aroma, wet and moldy, that is quite unlike the Russian forests where my mother sent me to look for mushrooms or berries.

I feel I am losing the burden of responsibility, as if I am getting physically lighter and almost wonder if Adam and Eve do not also notice this. For 16 years I have been responsible for them around the clock. They seem to have become part of my life, but at this moment I once again recognize Dimitri Marchenko—Mitya—who is an independent person and, due to all his experiences, does not easily let others come too close.

"Well, here we are," Adam announces. When he lets go of my arm, my head hits the tree trunk. It rings like a small bell, and the sound carries far.

"Oh. Sorry," he apologizes.

I am confused and briefly regret that this moment is already over. Then I nod. The robot skull has no pain sensors, and it can withstand much harder impacts. According to specifications it can tolerate 100 times the pressure of Earth's atmosphere, but I can even reinforce it further.

"Can you pull yourself up now?" Eve asks me.

"Yes, Eve, I can handle the rest by myself."

Both of them must have noticed that my mind was wandering. I use my arms to pull myself toward the trunk and then upwards until the tree is within reach of the ring. By tightening the steel band, I get closer to the trunk. Now I am upright.

"Okay, I am about to start," I say. "Don't do anything stupid while I am gone." I hope this does not put any silly ideas into their heads. I know I should trust them, but I do not like the idea that I will not have any influence on them for several hours.

"See you later," Adam says. Maybe I am imagining it, but he looks slightly touched.

"Take care!" Eve whispers.

My arms extend upward and cling to the trunk. Then, I bend them and pull my body up the tree. This takes ten seconds and on average covers 50 centimeters, so I should reach the top in about an hour. Unfortunately my view downward is limited, which I did not consider during the preparation phase. While I can turn my head, the body blocks the view. Perhaps Adam and Eve are waving goodbye to me. I cannot confirm it, but just in case I stop after ten meters, clamp the ring around the tree, and wave down toward them with one arm.

The climb turns out to be uncomplicated. Pull up, clamp,

pull up, clamp... I give in to this rhythm. The force sensors translate this activity for my mind so that I can feel the effort and will immediately notice if anything has changed. But no matter how hard I try, I cannot even imagine any dangers ahead of me. Only the altitude itself might pose a real problem. Should I fall, the high gravity would accelerate my body considerably. The modules my consciousness runs on have special protection, but if my body hits the ground at an unfortunate angle, it could be irretrievably lost. And then there is the additional risk that I could hit Adam or Eve.

The hour passes quickly, while I muse about what might be waiting for us. So far, we have not come any closer to fulfilling our task, and the only traces of alien intelligences are ancient ones. Those cannot have been from the beings who radioed the message to Earth unless we are coming much, much too late. I repress this idea. It just cannot be true that the entire voyage was meaningless, that Adam and Eve were born in vain.

Are they still standing there, waiting for me at the foot of the tree? I cannot see Adam and Eve, so I therefore continue to aim my gaze upward. The canopy of leaves is ten meters away. Until now, the trunk has not tapered off much. What would happen if the tree decides this very moment to pull its roots from the soil? Does it notice that I am climbing on its trunk? My sensors detect no sign of thought processes inside the wood. There are no vessels, nothing comparable to nerve pathways.

Yet we witnessed the trees hitting each other with their leaves. If their consciousness is located in the roots, which I assume to be the case, there must be a way to control the movement of the leaves. But perhaps my ideas are too Earth-centric. There are so many possibilities. Maybe the nerve pathways only develop when they are needed, or the communication is wireless. That would definitely be an important warning signal for me. Then I should be able to detect the signals, but perhaps the tree is silent now, so there is nothing to measure.

The last few meters are the most difficult. While the leaves are attached to the trunk in a staggered pattern, leaving a path between them, I have to remove and reattach the ring several times. It is like a spacewalk without a safety line. I know I shouldn't really do this, but there is no alternative if I want to get to the very top.

I worry less about my own strength. I know it will not give out. If I use the agility of my limbs to wrap my right arm around a leaf stalk, I am sure the arm can carry my mass. But what about the stalk itself? Each leaf weighs between 50 and 100 kilos. The point where the stalk is attached should be able to carry this weight, plus a bit more. On Proxima b my body weighs about 120 kilos. Will the 'plus' that nature factors in be sufficient for me? The fact that the trees use their leaves as weapons reassures me a bit, because then it would be advantageous if they were securely attached to the trunk.

I work my way up slowly and cautiously. First I gradually put some weight on a new stalk, but eventually the moment arrives when I have to trust my entire weight to it. This lasts only a few seconds, and then the ring at my legs holds on tight again. When I grasp the leaves, they always swing back and forth briefly. The first three seconds are decisive. If the leaf does not break by then, I am safe.

The method works very well for the first four leaves. The fifth one seems to be smaller than the others, so I leave it out. Also, I really do not trust the sixth one, but this means I definitely have to reach for the seventh, or I will not make it to the top.

I hook my arm around its stalk, as close to the trunk as possible. I pull and it appears to be stable. Then I start to release the ring holding me to the tree. The increasing weight at the attachment point bends the leaf down alarmingly. Now I have to react quickly, and my arm pulls me up. I hear a cracking sound, not from the leaf but near the trunk. I scan the bark and discover a fissure. The joint allowing the leaf to move seems to be the weak point. I feel panic rising in my mind. The ring at my legs is frantically trying for a new spot where it can stabilize me, but the steel band seems to be stuck on something. I cannot see the obstacle, because it is below me.

The fissure in the tree bark widens and the leaf bends down ominously. I contract the steel ring with all my strength, until I hear a splintering sound. Afterward, the ring moves freely again. I need a new holding position, because my arm is starting to slide downward along the stalk. *How elastic is the stalk?* I ask myself. *When will it break?*

I hear the whirring of the steel band swinging through the air. There. It has found a position farther up. With my left arm I reach for another leaf, without testing its strength. I pull myself up a few centimeters and the ring snaps shut.

Okay! I have found a new foothold. I can feel the leaf falling, the one that my right arm holds on to, but I cannot remove my hand. The forceful grip has pressed it so much into the wood that I will need the second hand for this. The 80 kilos of the leaf pull on my right side, and I am testing to see if the ring is firmly seated. It's no use, I have to let go with my left arm. While I reach around my back with it—fortunately, I am much more limber than a human being—I slowly start to slide.

I use my left hand to loosen the too-tight grip of the right hand. The leaf plummets. *I hope it won't hit Adam or Eve.* Then a stalk farther down stops my sliding body. I grab it with both hands, and I am safe. My thoughts are racing through the robot body. I need two minutes to regain my composure.

I am even more cautious climbing the last two meters, although there are no further problems. Then my head slowly rises from the sea of leaves. The view is breathtaking! I see a green ocean. It is not the same green I know from Earth, as this particular shade is a bit darker and appears not as lush. But the sheer expanse of this landscape makes up for that.

I can feel a slight breeze that is blowing up here, and I can also tell this by the wave patterns the wind creates in the foliage. The waves are no higher than one meter. Now and then there is a sparkle, when a leaf turns slightly in the wind and its brighter underside reflects the eastern sun in my direction.

But didn't I come up here for a specific reason? My optical sensors systematically begin scanning the landscape all the way to the horizon. The further I look out, the more I have to zoom in to distinguish the wave patterns from the actual movements of the trees. Toward the southeast, about 12 kilometers from me, a tree battle seems to be taking place. I also see the typical movements far to the east. Later I will calculate how this affects our chances.

The north appears to be calm right now. Heavy rains are falling there. Maybe the activities of the trees are dependent on the weather. I use an extreme zoom to see the raindrops patter on the leafy canopy. Due to the high gravity, the drops are smaller than on Earth. The water collects on the leaves, which now and then bend downward, release their loads, and spring back upward.

I pan slightly to the right, because I have noticed a movement there, but I must have been mistaken. The trees are not moving from their spots. There it is again! Now, I can see it. It is not the leaves that move, but something between them. I discover a long leg pulling itself up, then a kind of spider is swinging to the top of the leaf. I am sorry I cannot see it any more closely. From this distance—perhaps eight kilometers—I can only perceive the animal's rough outlines. Its body must be small, but the eight legs are comparatively huge. In front there is an appendage looking like a proboscis. The creature seems to sweep it across the leaves. It probably cleans them, removes dead cells, and feeds on these. The spider must not weigh much, and its eight legs distribute its weight on several leaves at the same time. It does not appear menacing and would only frighten someone suffering from arachnophobia. I carefully examine the surrounding area but cannot find a second animal. Yet, it cannot possibly be the only one of its kind.

How much time have I spent up here? I instinctively gaze at the sun, but it remains stationary. According to my clock it is early afternoon now. I wish I could take a little exploratory walk up here. Perhaps I might discover other species of animals. If the spider is a herbivore, could there be other creatures preying on it, like the frogs in the mountain pass? On the other hand, I do not need further encounters with predators, and considering my weight, the leaf canopy is not the ideal terrain. Once I have allowed myself one last look around with all my senses, I will climb down again.

I have to improve my position a bit. I want to record a 360-degree view in all wavelengths, from long-wave radio to ultra-short X-rays. I pull myself carefully higher so that the ring holding me can find a better position in the treetop. Afterward, my body reaches almost one and a half meters over the trees. I am now like a lonely fisherman in a huge ocean, casting my electronic net. The recording overtaxes my human consciousness. I recalculate it into a false-color image, which depicts the world around us in a fascinating way, even though the exaggerated contrasts and odd hues make it seem like a picture of hell. But aren't the world and hell sometimes the same, just seen through different lenses? I check the image and compare it with the optical reality my Marchenko mind is used to. The more comprehensive depiction offers more clarity, since nothing is able to remain hidden. There are no objects that do not interact with at least one wavelength, at least on this world.

My gaze reaches the west, far away. There it notices a glowing dot that can only be seen in the radio range. Something has directed radio waves at me. My image is only a snapshot, so it would not be enough to determine the nature of this source. I aim my radio antenna to the west and increase its sensitivity. There it is again. The signal. I can perceive it clearly. I have actually found it! It is the message, the reason why we came all the way here.

Finally! I am sure Adam and Eve will be glad. Now there is nothing to keep me up here any longer. I immediately start my descent. After I am past the area of the leaves, there is literally no holding back. I loosen the steel ring so much that I slowly slide down the trunk. As the tree gets gradually thicker, I have to adjust the ring now and again, but while the climb took an hour, I reach the ground in just 20 minutes.

Even from a height of 50 meters I start calling out to Adam and Eve, but they do not react. Are they perhaps working inside the base? I call more loudly, but they still do not answer. Now I reach the ground. The steel ring ties me to the tree, but there is no one here to help me with the last few steps of my descent.

I order the fabricators to produce simple feet for me as quickly as possible, but this will take at least half an hour. I call Adam and Eve again. Still no reply. I contact them via radio and can hear my voice issuing from the receiver that must be located somewhere near the base. *What has happened here? Why doesn't one of them answer?* The half-hour the fabricators require stretches into the worst 30 minutes of my life.

January 15, 19

Eve waves one last time at Marchenko.

"He won't be able to see it," Adam says. "I noticed right away that the robotic head is not moveable enough."

"I am doing it for my own sake," Eve says.

Adam nods sympathetically. "Okay. So what happens next?" he asks. "We are free to do what we want! Marchenko will certainly be gone for at least three hours."

"We can carry the excavated material out of the base so we'll get done in time," she suggests.

"Come on, Eve. We are alone for the very first time and you want to waste it on working?"

"It makes no sense just sitting around. I'd rather carry soil."

"I wasn't thinking of sitting around," Adam says. He has now caught Eve's attention.

"What then?" she asks.

"Remember the battle of the trees and the deep holes they left behind?"

Eve nods.

"Who knows what might show up inside those holes?" he poses.

"I really don't understand."

Adam looks at Eve's face. *Is it that she doesn't want to under-*

stand, or is she that naïve? he wonders. Sometimes he is not sure when it comes to his 'sibling.' On the whole, Adam considers her clearly more intelligent than himself, but it also seems she sometimes takes much longer to understand an idea.

"Marchenko found that beam at a depth of four or five meters," Adam says. "How likely is it that only one of them is here?"

Eve raises her eyebrows, indicating she is still undecided.

"We can go toward the north along the edge of the forest, where the trees came from," he suggests. "We are sure to find some holes there, soon. We will be back before Marchenko, and in the worst case we can tell him we took a walk."

"And what if something happens to us?" The way Eve asks this question sounds as if she has already agreed with him in her mind.

"What could possibly happen to us?" Adam asks. "The people who left these things behind have been dead forever."

"Okay, fine," Eve says. "If we find more buildings with inscriptions, Marchenko might be able to decipher the writing." She smiles at Adam. "But let's go right away, so we get back earlier."

ADAM PACKS SOME FOOD, A FLASHLIGHT, AND A ROPE IN A shoulder bag, then they start out. They quickly find the way out of the forest, and right beyond it is the zone where the trees went to war, their 'footsteps' still visible as deep holes in the ground. Adam walks in front, while Eve stays close to the edge of the forest. He waves her to come closer to him, but she rejects this invitation with an unequivocal gesture. *She probably feels safer there,* he assumes. Adam examines several of the holes, one after another. He makes his way to the edge and shines the flashlight inside—they have a depth of three or four meters. Sometimes there are roots protruding into the hole from the side, but Adam discovers nothing that looks alien-made. He moves from hole to hole, but even after half an hour he is without success. Since this is obviously the wrong strategy, he rejoins Eve near the edge of the forest.

"That's no use," he says.

"Then let's go back," Eve suggests. "We have been out here for almost an hour. If Marchenko comes back early and finds us gone, he'll die of fright."

"No, he's a tough guy," Adam insists. "I've got a better idea."

He waits for Eve to argue with him, but she does not do him the favor. She just purses her lips slightly.

"We have to go where the trees came from, the south," Adam says.

"But you said we wanted to go to the north," Eve says with a sigh.

"That was nonsense. I was wrong. We won't find anything in the north. Those trees are back where they came from."

Eve's face brightens at this, and she replies, "But not the ones in the south."

"That's right," Adam confirms. He remembers the tree left behind. *What could have happened to it?* "The root system of the trees is huge," he continues. "It's there that we've got a better chance of finding something."

But Adam begins to doubt his own plan. *How high is the chance to discover a ruin on the area covered by a single tree? Is this any better than digging around at random?*

Eve notices Adam shaking his head and asks, "What are you thinking about?"

"Nothing," he replies. "I just... never mind. If you come along with me to that hole, I won't bother you anymore, I promise."

Eve nods in agreement, and Adam is glad but tries not to show it too much. He already knew she would not deny his request.

THE ONLY PROBLEM IS THAT THEY DO NOT KNOW EXACTLY where the southern group of trees came from. After the fight both of them had concentrated on the northern group marching home, because it had passed nearby. The other group might have come from farther away.

"We have to mark the spot where we have to reenter the forest later."

Adam blushes. "Sure... right," he says, "I was about to suggest that." It is good that Eve remembers, otherwise their return might have become complicated.

The two first follow the tracks of the northern group until they reach the battlefield. Two trees lay here now, even though only one fell. Is this some kind of solidarity?

"Perhaps its partner laid down to die with it," Eve wonders.

The two gigantic trees are immobile and their roots stiff, and they are truly awe-inspiring. In spite of the somber scene, Adam is glad, because the second tree doubles their chance of finding something. *From almost 0 to almost 0*, his mean little doubt tells him again. Adam has to be careful not to show what he is thinking. "Come on," he says.

Eve stares at the two tree corpses. There is a strange smell in the air, not of putrefaction but of lavender.

Adam takes Eve's hand and pulls her away. She finally follows him, and for 20 minutes they keep walking parallel to the edge of the forest. This spot is where the trees entered the forest. Adam is reminded of the fairytale about Hansel and Gretel. He looks at Eve who is cheerfully walking next to him. *No*, he thinks, *this has nothing to do with that old story. How could we ever lose our way considering these tracks?*

The forest around them seems monotonous. It is as if they're moving through a huge hall, with the canopy of leaves shielding them. Adam does not think he will ever like this planet, let alone the forest. Everything here takes place without variation. There are neither nights nor seasons, and here inside this 'hall of eternal peace' there is no breeze, nor is there anything to see but smooth tree trunks 200 meters tall.

After another half an hour Eve stops. Adam has an idea of what is about to happen.

"We have been walking for almost two hours," she says in a soft voice, as if talking to an infant.

Adam hates her tone of voice. "Then it won't hurt if we go another 30 minutes..." he insists.

"No," she interrupts him, "I don't want Marchenko to worry when he returns. We don't even have the two-way radio with us."

Okay, she is right. But what if it really isn't very far anymore—if we are giving up three minutes before reaching our goal? Adam cannot stand the feeling of missing out, but at the same time he knows he cannot convince Eve with his arguments.

"Another 15 minutes, please?" he pleads with puppy dog eyes. Eve notices his trick and laughs, but it still works. Adam knows this, even though he can tell she is struggling with herself. Of course, he cannot reveal that he is aware of it.

"Please?" he repeats. Now his glance is not as obvious.

"Fine," Eve replies, conceding. "But then we really are turning back. I will turn around in 15 minutes no matter what you are doing."

Adam nods. "That's only fair," he says. "Then let's use the remaining time well." He walks ahead faster, and Eve follows him willingly.

After ten minutes Adam is about to give up, but just then the ground changes. The tracks of the trees decrease, while at the same time the ground around the trunks looks churned up. His heart is beating faster. They have found the area where the trees came from. Now the two of them just have to search for the spot where the two tree corpses once stood. Adam points this out to Eve, and she smiles slightly at his eagerness.

However, when they suddenly stand at the edge of a wide pit that is at least five meters deep, Eve does not smile anymore. She is stunned. Adam notices her amazement before he sees the hole, and Eve can barely stop him by grabbing hold of his arm. She uses her other arm to point downward. There is a gray building, reminiscent of a Greek temple. Five columns rise about one meter out of the ground, covered by a roof that has the cross-section of a flat triangle. In his mind, Adam is cheering—they themselves have found more proof, all on their own, without Marchenko! Adam is eager to go down and examine the building more closely, but Eve holds on to him. He glares at her, but she does not falter. She knows him too well.

"No, you won't go down there now," she says.

"Eve, I have to. There is no other way."

"You don't have to do anything. We are going back to get Marchenko, and then all of us will examine this building together."

"Marchenko won't believe us."

"You know he is not like that."

Eve is right. That is a stupid argument, Adam admits to himself. But if they walk back now, they probably will not return before tomorrow. Adam cannot wait that long. He is so close, and now he is supposed to leave before even touching this mysterious structure? *Impossible!*

Eve's look tells him the matter is decided, though Adam is allowed to advance a few more meaningless arguments. It is obvious, however, that he will not be able to persuade her. Therefore he simply takes a few steps forward, one... two... three. Adam then steps into the void and briefly waves his arms before he loses his balance, tilts forward and falls headfirst into the pit.

"ADAM!" Eve's scream reaches him the moment he hits the sand. Now he is shocked, as he imagined his descent differently, more graceful. He sits up and rubs the dirt from his burning eyes.

"Are you injured, Adam?" Eve asks anxiously.

"No, I am alright... it was a soft landing," he replies sheepishly.

"No pain?"

Adam pats down his body but finds nothing to worry about. His heart is starting to beat more slowly. There's no reason to panic, his plan worked. He is exactly where he wants to be.

"No, I'm not feeling any pain, just a lot of sand between my teeth and on my face," he answers.

"That was so stupid of you!" says Eve in an annoyed voice. She might even be right, but now he wants to do what he jumped into the pit for—touch the building that had been hidden from this world for so long.

"Adam, please be reasonable and come back."

He hears real concern in her voice. That is nice to hear, but he still has to get into the structure first. He is almost exactly in the middle of the pit, and the tree must have previously stood right above it. *We would have never found it by digging at random,* he concludes.

Adam finally reaches the structure. His hand brushes against a piece of wall that reminds him of a beam. It must be his imagination that he seems to feel a slight tingling while doing so. He walks once around the building, which measures about four by five meters. They will only be able to tell how tall it is after they have excavated it. There are numerous symbols on the slanted roof. *Do these provide enough text to decipher the language now?* he wonders. Finally, Adam looks at the columns near the entrance. They do not appear to be made of stone, but the surface instead feels like that of the tree trunks.

"Okay, I am coming now," he calls out to Eve, and she seems a little relieved.

Shortly before reaching the slope, Adam reaches into the bag still hanging over his shoulder. "I am going to throw the rope to you," he says.

Eve manages to catch the rope on the third attempt.

"Very good," Adam praises her. "You see, I thought of everything."

"You are crazy," Eve replies, but he shakes his head.

"Now you hold on to the rope and I pull myself up on it."

Adam takes the rope in both hands, and the rough material cuts into them. He quickly notices that he has not really thought his plan through. He is stronger than Eve, but this does not help, since he is also considerably heavier. If both of them pull on the rope, Adam will never get up, he will instead pull Eve downward. They need a tree to wrap the rope around, but there is none in reach. The rope is simply too short. Adam tries to get a running start to get up the slope, but it is too steep. And the soil is too soft to climb, and he repeatedly slips back down.

"Shit!" he yells in frustration and sits down on the dry ground.

"That's what we get for doing this," Eve says, but she does not seem to be too upset.

Why is she so calm—now of all times? He would better understand if she scolded him and his idea loudly. "I won't make it out of here by myself," Adam's voice sounds husky.

"I congratulate you on this objective assessment," she replies.

Yes, Eve can really be sarcastic, he reminds himself. Now she will probably go to get Marchenko. Just what he needs.

"I am walking back to the camp," Eve says. "Marchenko might already be waiting for us, and he is the only one who can get you out of there."

Not Marchenko. That would be the worst possible defeat for Adam, but he does not say that aloud. Objectively, he has to admit that Marchenko now represents his only chance for survival. Adam feels anger rising in him, anger at himself and the universe.

"See you later!" Eve shouts, "and don't do any stupid things while I am gone!"

To Adam, it sounds as if she means 'any *additional* stupid things.' He waves at her but does not manage to say a word. Eve quickly disappears from his field of view. For a moment he still hears the crunch of her feet on the forest floor, and then he is all alone. Now Adam is no longer in the mood to examine the building, the very reason he had jumped into the pit in the first place. He will just sit here in the dirt, getting bored, bemoaning his fate, and preparing for Marchenko's inevitable lecture.

ADAM IS ABRUPTLY STARTLED. *IS SOMETHING HERE?* NO, HIS body was just about to topple sideways. He must have briefly fallen asleep and now he wonders, *how much time has gone by?* He forgot the communicator in the camp, his only way of telling time. Adam rubs his eyes, forgetting that his fingers are still dirty.

"SHIT!"

The word reverberates in the pit. Acoustic resonances down here are different compared to the hall-like space formed by the leaf canopy, where sound has to travel a long way to return as an echo. He starts drawing figures in the sand with his foot. He tries to remember the glyphs on the beam and to imitate them. Perhaps he can discover similar shapes on this strange temple? If mankind interpreted the radio message correctly, its senders must have moved on two legs and possessed two arms. Did they worship their gods here? Or was it once perhaps a place to conduct business? Adam tries to imagine life in those times. The trees cannot have existed at the time the structure was originally built. He looks at the trunks. They appear to have been standing here for a very long time. So, the building he discovered must have been deserted for thousands of years.

Suddenly a leg appears between the columns.

Adam notices the movement right away. He wants to jump up and run, but at the same time he is so fascinated that he cannot avert his eyes and stays rooted to the spot. It cannot be one of the actual aliens, as those must have died out long ago or left. But it is undeniably a leg that is coming out of the low opening. It moves very slowly, but soon it becomes clear that it must be very long. *Half a meter, one meter, one and a half meters, two meters—when is the body going to appear?* Instead, a second leg follows—one that is not any shorter—then one more, two, three... eight thin legs push forward into the open. At their ends there is something Adam at first identifies as hooves, but their bottom appears to be movable. *It must be suckers!* Whatever is crawling out of its home now should be able to climb smooth walls.

Adam thinks about all eight-legged creatures he knows about: *Insects have six legs, spiders have eight.* But those are categories from Earth. Who knows if he might actually be facing one of the current rulers of this planet? He looks around frantically, but the pit offers only one hiding place, and this creature has occupied it first. *Is it alone?* Adam has never seen a real spider, but apprehension sends a chill through his body at the idea of soon being faced with a giant version of one.

At first a different body part of the creature appears, though. It looks like a proboscis. The tip is almost ten centimeters wide. If Adam is lucky, this animal uses it to suction water or other liquid nutrients, like male mosquitoes on Earth. But perhaps the creature is hungry for a meal of blood, like female mosquitoes, which need iron and protein for developing their eggs. Adam shakes his head. Humans cannot really be on the menu of Proxima b inhabitants. He would be completely indigestible to them, because his body chemistry is so different. But does the spider know it would get an upset stomach from eating him?

The proboscis moves in every direction, as if the animal uses it to sniff around. It is obviously attached to a body that now comes fully out of the dwelling, pulled by the legs. The torso of the creature is surprisingly small, perhaps half the size of his own. So this thing would not be able to swallow him in one piece, as some snakes do with their prey. And this animal does not seem to have teeth. Adam cannot detect anything like a mouth.

But he certainly can see its eyes—there are dozens of them. They are placed in a circle around the base of the proboscis and all around the torso of the creature. The eyes are looking in all directions, but one of them is staring straight at him. It has a diameter of about five centimeters. A dark green dot swims on a white background—contracting and expanding—this must be the pupil. Adam recoils when a kind of eyelid quickly moves over the eye from below, and the eye appears wetter afterward, as if the creature were about to cry.

Adam still wants to run away, but he cannot avert his gaze. His own eyes feel dry and he is unable to blink. The creature's strange eye has completely mesmerized him. He has never seen such a being before, but at the same time it feels familiar—perhaps from nightmares—even though at least the eye does not seem menacing. 'I won't do anything bad to you,' it seems to say. Of course this could also be a strategy to give its victim a false sense of security.

The creature stands up. It is huge, almost three meters tall, but at the same time the long, thin legs make it appear extremely fragile. Its proboscis is sweeping across the ruin. Will it react if Adam stands up as well? Maybe he should remain seated, since some animals only react to movements. The creature seems to have noticed him, but right now it must be classifying him as neither a threat nor a source of food. That is, unless it is clever enough to realize Adam has no way out.

The animal turns around. The eye that has so far been watching him now disappears from Adam's view, and another eye focuses on him. Adam's heart starts beating faster, but the animal begins to stride away with huge steps. Nothing can be heard, as the weight is distributed across the eight legs, allowing for almost noiseless movement. Whatever it selects as its prey will not hear it coming.

The creature effortlessly masters the slope that is keeping Adam imprisoned. It places one leg above it, then a second, gains momentum with the other legs, and lands on top. The spider stops for a moment, stretching itself as much as possible. Its proboscis is moving across the trunk of the nearest tree, as if searching for something. Could the animal be hungry? It leans two legs against the trunk. Then a smacking sound can be heard, indicating the feet now adhering to the tree bark. The next two legs follow. The spider places them further up. The animal manages to stand on four legs very well, but when it lifts the next pair of legs toward the tree, it starts to sway. After a few seconds, the creature stabilizes itself. Now it's time for the last two legs. *Look how flexible these long, stick-like limbs are!* Adam estimates they must have at least six joints.

Yet it is not enough for the creature to climb the tree. The body seems to be too heavy. It slides down and slams against the trunk and the ground. The animal utters a high, piercing sound, and Adam thinks he can hear pain and frustration in it. Why is it down on the ground, if it really does not belong here? The creature stands up again, its proboscis moving back and forth over some mushrooms. It briefly touches their surfaces, but then shrinks back. The giant spider sinks to its knees, and it seems to be close to giving up. Adam senses the emotions of this extraterrestrial being, even though no two creatures in the universe could be more alien to each other. He realizes something very special is happening to him, and he is grateful for it.

"Psst." The noise comes from behind Adam, and he slowly turns around, trying not to frighten the spider creature. At the edge of the pit stands Marchenko in his robot body.

"Don't worry, I think it is harmless," Adam tells him quietly.

"Yes, its habitat is really on top of the leaf canopy," Marchenko says. "I watched an animal like it up there."

Now everything is clear. This animal must have fallen when the trees started to move. Afterward, it probably hid inside the ruin.

"It doesn't stand a chance, does it?" Adam says, hoping Marchenko will contradict him, but he only shakes his robot head.

"I don't think it can find the right kind of food down here," Marchenko replies. "Otherwise we would have already discovered additional specimens on the forest floor."

"We could feed it," Eve says, stepping out of Marchenko's shadow. "We have the leaves of the tree we cut down, and the two tree corpses out there in the open zone."

"It won't be enough," Marchenko says. "These animals are rare. I discovered only one in a very wide radius. I think they graze a larger territory. And they also don't eat the whole leaves, just the uppermost layer, which is worn down. Also, we are only here for a few more days."

"Then we have to carry it up there," Adam says.

Marchenko waits for a whole minute before he answers, "I am afraid it won't work, Adam. We would have to catch the creature, somehow tie it up, and then I might be able to lug it to the top of the tree. But do you think the animal would submit peacefully? It's not a domesticated animal and wouldn't understand us."

Adam nods. He might have to accept this. They just cannot help this strange creature.

"Catch! I am throwing the rope down to you now," Marchenko says, trying to distract Adam. Adam takes one more look at the giant spider. Unlikely as it is, it might understand his thoughts or somehow read his facial expressions. He pities the animal and would like to help it, but there is no chance for that. He turns toward Marchenko. From the corner of his eye, Adam sees the spider waving to him with one leg, but it probably is just his imagination. He has Marchenko pull him up and already mentally prepares himself for being scolded. By the time they start their walk back to the camp, the strange creature has once more retreated into the ruin.

Suddenly Adam remembers he wanted to go into the pit for a specific reason: *The inscriptions! We have to examine them!*

"Marchenko," he says, "there were symbols on the roof. Perhaps we can use them to decipher the alien script."

"Yes, don't worry, Adam," I say. "I recorded and saved everything, and have even started an analysis. In two or three days we might have a rough translation."

January 17, 19

I HAD ACTUALLY HOPED I WOULD EVENTUALLY BE ABLE TO forget the shock I suffered the day before yesterday. By today, for instance. Shouldn't two days be enough to get such a trauma out of the head of an adult, particularly because in the end everything worked out fine?

All this self-recrimination! After I descended the tree, I was consumed with worry about what might have happened to Adam and Eve, until I finally could walk on two legs again. Of course all my scenarios ended with their deaths. I did not know my imagination could be so cruel. I am essentially an optimist, even if I am in danger myself, as I know well. Otherwise I would not have survived the events on Enceladus. But the fact that Adam and Eve had disappeared must have deactivated some control mechanisms in me.

Luckily my thought processes were still working. The inventory module reported that a flashlight, a rope, some food, and a shoulder bag were missing. That's not what predators would usually drag away. Therefore, Adam and Eve must have gone for a hike. Their destination must have been related to the battle of the trees, so I first walked to the edge of the forest. *North or south?* The tracks I discover point in both directions. I probably would have gone to the north, if I had not heard Eve's voice just then, from the south.

Afterward, everything happened very rapidly. I was immensely relieved when I pulled Adam out of the pit, and therefore I delayed the dressing-down he deserved for the following day. But by then, scolding him did not seem to matter anymore, somehow, and particularly because I wanted to tell Adam and Eve about the signal. I have reserved this piece of information for today.

"Well, due to all this excitement we haven't had a chance to discuss the results of my excursion," I begin.

Eve gives me a sheepish look. I am absolutely sure the idea to wander off did not come from her.

"Yes," Adam says, dutifully and without much enthusiasm, "then tell us about it."

"The risk of us being squashed by fighting or running trees during the coming week is relatively low, 2 percent to be exact."

"Well, that's what I figured," Adam says. "Otherwise you would have already hurried us along."

I nod. I try to mention the decisive detail in a very casual fashion.

"Oh, by the way, up there on the leaf canopy I once again detected the signal that led us here," I say.

Neither is saying anything. They seem to need some time to absorb the information and realize what it means.

Eve is the first to jump up. "We have to check on this right away," she says, "who knows for how long it can be received."

Adam nods vigorously.

"I have triangulated the origin of the signal," I reply. "Its source is far in the east. We could never get there within nine days."

"It doesn't matter how long it takes us," Adam says.

"Yes, it does," Eve answers in my place. "The next flare will arrive in nine days."

"We could at least march a few days' closer to our destination and build a new bunker there," he suggests.

"That's way too risky," I say. "We are not even finished here, and we don't know what the soil would be like at another location. If it's solid rock, for example, we would need much more time with the equipment we have."

"But Eve is right," Adam says. "The signal is probably going to disappear again soon. Maybe it is already gone now. Why didn't you inform us earlier?"

Because I suspected something like this, I think. *I knew you would want to start out right away.* "We wouldn't have made it either way," I answer evasively.

"You waited to tell us so that we would have to wait out the flare here," Adam accuses me.

"If you continue being so impertinent, I'll leave you in the pit the next time. Together with your spider friend," I threaten him jokingly.

"That would have been better," Adam retorts. "At least the spider didn't lie to me."

"I have a second interesting piece of news," I say.

"Oh, really?" Adam asks with a skeptical look.

"The glyphs," I explain. "Thanks to the text on the roof of the building you discovered, we now know more about them."

"That doesn't sound as if you actually deciphered them."

"That would be saying too much. I now know more about their structure. The signs on the beam, for instance, show the way to a specific destination, but we will never know which destination it is. For that we would need some context. At least the location where the beam was originally placed."

"And what about the text on the roof?" Adam asks.

"It describes the function of the building," I reply "Decisions were made there, so it might have been some kind of town hall. The text invites persons to appear there with questions and problems."

"That doesn't tell us anything about the inhabitants of the planet."

"Yes, Adam, unfortunately that is true. But they must have possessed communal structures, and there probably would not have been a civilization without them. They had a writing system and were technologically more advanced than humanity, at least by a few thousand years ago when these structures were created."

"This makes finding the signal even more important," Adam says.

"Once we make it through the flare, we have another 40 days," I say. "We are going to find the signal source during that time, I promise."

January 26, 19

THE BUNKER WAS COMPLETELY FINISHED THE DAY BEFORE yesterday. It's really a pity we are going to leave it again tomorrow, but we might return to it someday. I somehow cannot shake the feeling that some disappointment will await us at the source of the signal, yet I do not mention these concerns to Adam and Eve. They are literally living for that day and for the message. *What would be the meaning of their lives if it turns out we came much too late?*

Yesterday, we used our free time to take a look at the pit again, and there a sad surprise was waiting for us. The spider creature had retreated into the darkness of the ruin and died there. I examined it closely. Its legs are hollow, which is what makes it so light. The six joints on each leg could turn in any direction, a very impressive construction. I could not determine whether it has a sex or how it reproduces. There is nothing inside its body that is reminiscent of ova or sperm. Like many plants, perhaps it is able to reproduce by division, and the fact that there seem to be so few specimens would support this theory. If these creatures reproduce sexually, then they would have to travel long distances to do so.

The most interesting part is the nervous system. The nerve pathways consist of silicon fibers running through the entire body. Therefore, I at first considered it a kind of cyborg, a manipulated creature with added machine technology. But after further inspection I then found cells in the body capable of weaving these inorganic fibers—like spiders producing spider silk for their webs—and then placing them within biological materials. This might be the reason why the inhabitants of this planet started so early using semiconductor strands in their buildings. Nature practically pushed them toward this idea.

The spider animals do not appear to have brains like organisms on Earth do. Yet inside their bodies, particularly in a layer on the outside about four centimeters thick, the silicon fibers are so close to each other that their capacity must allow for cognitive activities. I calculate the spider creatures should have the cognitive ability of mammals on Earth. Perhaps they even were—or are—related to the intelligent inhabitants of Proxima b who sent us the radio message.

All three of us decided to leave the animal in its refuge and to close the entrances. That way, absolutely nothing would disturb its rest. Then we examined the rear of the pit and found a smaller structure built by the extraterrestrials, reminiscent of a guard shack. A tall human could have stood inside it but would not have been able to sit down.

By now we are waiting for the solar eruption. The entrance of our bunker is closed, but before closing it I distributed cameras and sensors outside. Those recordings will be sent to my memory. I wondered if I should build a kind of monitor screen for Adam and Eve, but there will probably be nothing to see. Neither the hard X-ray and UV radiation nor the particles that the planet's magnetic field is unable to keep out are visible to the human eye.

If we didn't know what was about to happen, we might spend the day outside without suspecting anything. Then after a few hours, Adam and Eve might wonder where the intense sunburn on their skin came from, and a few days later they would die from radiation sickness. Those of my circuits not hardened against radiation would also be destroyed, though the storage module containing my consciousness would be sufficiently shielded.

We do not know the exact time of day when Proxima Centauri will erupt. Only the 40-day rhythm is confirmed. Therefore we have to wait. Adam and Eve sit on the ground in the corner, playing a game they must have made up themselves. They are only allowed to use their hands in this game. We did not build any furniture, since we only have to stay here for a few hours and cannot carry it with us afterward.

The X-ray detector responds.

"It is starting," I say. Adam and Eve are looking at me. It is a strange sensation because we cannot feel anything. Is our shielding working? We will see. Right now, the dose rate is minimal, since we receive more radiation from the interior of the planet than from space. But outside, the radiation intensity is slowly increasing. Proxima Centauri must have erupted a short while ago, and the radiation reaches us at the speed of light, while the particles take significantly longer.

And now something unexpected happens: It is getting bright outside! *What happened?* I turn the outside camera toward the leaf canopy. The sky is visible, and a few clouds are racing across it. I zoom in closer on the leaves. They have folded up, exposing only a small diameter to the radiation. Nature must have adapted to the event that has been repeating every 40 days for millions of years, just like the plants on Earth became used to the seasons. During my research I had not noticed that the leaves have a joint in the middle. Then I remember a line leading from the point where they are attached to the tree all the way to the tip. I pan the camera a bit. In this bright light the forest looks much more inviting than in the eternal twilight.

"It is very bright out there," I explain. "The trees have folded their leaves."

"Wow," Eve says, "I'd love to see that with my own eyes."

"Don't you dare," I warn her, even though I know she is not serious.

"But won't that take away some of our radiation protection?" she asks.

That's true. I included the leaf canopy in my calculations. "I've worked with a sizable safety margin, so don't worry," I say, but I am concerned.

A quick estimate shows me the safety margin is gone. We have to hope the flare isn't much stronger than the previous one. While there is no reason it should be, I still feel queasy. During the following hours I do not take my eyes off the instruments. The dose rate increases continuously, but down here in our bunker it stays within a tolerable range. I wonder about possible emergency procedures. I could try to shield Adam and Eve with my body. But down here direct radiation does not play such a big role. I would practically have to wrap myself around them.

Three hours later, the avalanche of electrons rolls towards Proxima b. I once more aim the camera at the sky, expecting a spectacular sight. The atmosphere does not disappoint me. Too bad, though, it does not get dark here. The aurora flickering across the sky is not nearly as impressive in normal brightness.

Otherwise, the magnetic field is doing a great job. It diverts the charged particles around the planet. This creates a bit of *bremsstrahlung*—breaking radiation—but that poses no problem for our shielding.

The forest tells us that the eruption is over. Four and a half hours after it all started, the leaves unfold. The eternal twilight emerges from the shadows and becomes dominant again.

"It is over," I say. "How about taking a little walk?" Adam and Eve eagerly get up. I remove the obstacles near the exit.

Adam goes out first. "Awesome!" he yells. I can imagine the reason why.

"Marchenko, come here," Eve calls. "You've got to see this!"

I smile silently. I slowly climb the stairs and turn around. There is shimmering light in all directions. The variety of hues is overwhelming. It was worthwhile planting a large colony of mushrooms on our bunker. Now they are emitting the excess energy of the flare in all colors of the spectrum. It looks unique, like a coral reef on Earth, just without fish. I hope this image will be engraved in Adam and Eve's memory forever. Both stand there, mouths agape, breathing in the aromatic air smelling of ozone, and marveling at the secret of a planet that is supposed to become their home at some point.

January 27, 19

We start out early in the morning by Earth time. Almost 200 kilometers lie ahead of us before we reach the coast, but I do not expect any problems. My view from above showed me that the forest is going to stay basically unchanged, and this should also hold true for the forest floor. Just in case, though, I modified my walking appendages. Now I have four legs that I can move independently. This way, I can safely traverse even difficult terrain. To keep my balance I placed my torso in the middle and added a section to my arms.

"What do you call that thing between the lower and the upper arm?" asks Eve.

I know Eve is only teasing me, but I answer without hesitation, "A middle arm!"

She replies with a giggle.

"You look like a fat spider someone tore a couple of legs off of," Adam says. When he says it, it almost sounds like a compliment. He has a cheerful demeanor, just like Eve. It is good to be on the move again. If I had not received a signal, I would have been forced to invent one.

About an hour or so after our first rest break I hear the rushing of water. Soon afterward Adam and Eve perceive it, too.

"It must be one of the rivers we saw from space," I say.

The two of them hurry along. We are really lucky. We have found something new on our very first day, and after 20 minutes we reach the side of the stream. It runs from west/southwest to east/northeast. Our plan was to walk straight to the east.

"Should we follow the river? Then we'll get to the coast two days later."

"Absolutely not, Marchenko," Adam says. I suspect that he is less focused on the time lost than on the adventure of crossing the stream.

"A little swimming certainly wouldn't hurt us," Eve adds.

"If you think so," I reply. "But I don't want to hear any complaints about the water being too cold. I will carry your luggage. But not you two," I say somewhat jokingly.

The forest starts to thin out, ending about 100 meters from the riverbank. The treeless area is covered with mushrooms. There is no shore visible—the water must start right beyond the mushrooms, or the last ones are already standing in the water.

"I'll go ahead," I say, "just to see whether it is safe and to test the depth."

It's good I can count on using four legs. This way I can stand safely and still check what is under the water with a free leg. I find the bottom is covered with sand and pebbles, and I do not detect any aquatic plants. The water temperature is about 14 degrees. Adam and Eve are going to complain, but in the end it's what they wanted to do. I run a chemical and microbiological analysis without finding anything potentially harmful to humans. Although the water will taste slightly salty, it is potable.

"You can get in," I call them. Adam and Eve advance to my position, but the dense cover of mushrooms does not make it easy for them. I take their backpacks. Adam undresses down to his underwear and hands me his clothes. Eve blushes slightly and then takes off her outer clothes as well, but chooses to keep her T-shirt on.

Adam does not wait long and marches straight ahead, until he feels water cover his feet for the first time. "This is going to be rough," he says, shaking himself.

"Should I carry you across?" I ask. The distance to the other shore is about 80 meters. The river seems to be shallow, no more than a meter and a half at the deepest spot, and it flows slowly.

"Absolutely not," Adam says. He squeals when Eve splashes him with water from behind. Both of them race forward, leave the mushrooms behind, and glide into the shallow water while uttering loud screams. I am curious whether the swimming exercises they learned and practiced while traveling through space has helped. *Can you forget a skill like this?* For the sake of safety, I follow them at a distance of a few meters. I watch as the two of them dog paddle through the water. On board *Messenger,* they neither had the time nor the space to develop an efficient swimming style, but this is working fine. They have to expend so much effort that they do not have a chance to feel cold anymore.

Adam swims ahead, Eve follows him about one and a half meters behind and to the side. They keep watching each other and shout something only they can understand.

Then events escalate.

Adam suddenly is standing up in the water, which reaches to his belly button. He tries to call out but cannot manage to do so. He points at the spot where Eve was swimming, and now I understand what he means to say. Eve is gone. I stomp ahead to cross the few remaining meters and barely manage to come to a stop. Below me is a rectangular, black hole, and it looks as if something punched a hole into the river bottom here. A strong current pulls in river water at one end and spits it out at the other.

Time is short. The human brain can only survive for three minutes without oxygen. The timer in my head is already starting a countdown. I let my entire body fall into the hole. During my descent I measure the depth: approximately eight meters. *Where is Eve?* I activate my searchlight and my ultrasound sensors. The walls of this chamber have an irregular shape. *There, in the left corner. Could that be her body?*

Another 65 seconds. The current is strong, my four legs are impractical down here, my body is too heavy, and my hands ought to be three times larger to propel me faster while swimming. *Is that her?* I reach for the shadow, but it dissolves under my fingers. *Go on. She must be there! Turn around, Marchenko, maybe she is stuck against a wall. Infrared. Look for her body heat! There she is!*

The timer has arrived at zero. I reach her at minus 20, and I grab her body. Trying to quickly move upward, *minus 40,* but I am like a block of iron with little buoyancy. My four legs are kicking as fast as they can. *Minus 60,* I should be up there soon, where there is light. And, much more critical, air. The timer in my head indicates minus 90.

Eve had been without oxygen for at least four and a half minutes. It is impossible that she has survived this. I fold two of my legs to form a kind of table and place Eve on it. I feel for her pulse. Her heart is beating, but she is not breathing. *Am I going completely insane now?* This is impossible, but it is happening. Her pulse is slightly elevated, at 92, but her chest does not move up and down. Then she suddenly spits out a gush of water and inhales deeply, like a baby taking its first breath.

Great! She is alive! But how can this be? I run an X-ray scan of her body and discover something. Two skin folds have opened below her ribs. I pull her T-shirt up a bit and examine these folds. Inside are gills. They were activated because she could no longer breathe normally, and this must be one of the basic modifications even I did not know of.

But why didn't I notice this earlier? I have known Adam and Eve since they were babies. I should have noticed the skin folds, even if they were always closed tight. There is only one possible answer: I have a filter integrated into my consciousness that will not allow me to see things I should not see.

I am shocked, but I do not have time to reflect on this, because Adam is staring wide-eyed at Eve's belly. "What does she have there?" His voice is almost squeaky. He is about to get hysterical. "Do I have that, too?"

Eve opens her eyes, first looking at me, then at Adam. He bites his lips and manages to calm down a bit.

"What am I doing here?" Eve asks.

"Do you remember anything?" I ask her.

"Something pulled me down. It happened so fast. And then everything went black. And then I woke up here," she says, trying to sit up.

"Wait a moment," I say. "There seems to be something you need to know. I told you back on *Messenger* that you have been genetically optimized, but obviously not even I knew everything about it. You have gills here on your belly, and they saved your life."

Now I cannot hold Eve back. She sits up on one of my folded legs in order to look at her belly. The skin folds are already starting to dry, and the drier they get, the more they merge with the skin.

"By tonight you probably won't be able to see them anymore," I say.

"Do I have those also?" Adam tries to find the folds on his belly, but in vain.

"I can search with X-rays, if you want me to," I reply.

"Please do," he says, "I really need to know!"

And indeed, I detect gills in him, too. Normally they must lie inside the subcutaneous layer, which has a more complicated structure.

"And you really didn't know anything about it?" asks Adam with a skeptical look.

"Would I have dived so frantically to reach Eve if I had known it?" I answer. "I could have just waited until she swam back by herself."

Adam shakes his head but then decides to believe me.

"Yeah, that sounds logical," he says. "But why can you now see our gills?"

"I suspect there was some kind of programmed mental block which is now gone."

"Because now they are known," Eve adds.

"Might we have other abilities we know nothing of?"

"Possibly, Adam, but I am afraid we won't find out until there is no other choice."

"Marchenko, I pity you," Eve says. "They played around with our bodies, but they manipulated your mind. That must be a terrible feeling."

Eve is right, but I don't have the time to deal with the issue. At least I keep telling myself that.

"We have to finish crossing this river first," I say. "I assume you don't mind sitting on my shoulders, considering these circumstances?"

Adam and Eve are nodding. They seem to have had enough of swimming for right now.

February 5, 19

THE DAYS DRAG ON. AFTER THE RIVER INCIDENT WE TALKED for a long while, but the very next day our conversations began to diminish. To add to the boredom, we are discovering that the forest offers no real change. All the tree trunks are the same, and the mushrooms are, too, except sometimes bigger or sometimes smaller. Once, Eve noticed a moving shadow and I investigated, finding the tracks of an approximately dog-sized, eight-legged animal, but we never actually caught sight of it.

The constant twilight makes all of us feel tired—including me—even in the morning, so much so that we hardly cover more than 20 kilometers per day. It is also gradually becoming darker and colder, and while we do not see it, the sun must by now be considerably lower in the sky from our perspective. The fact we are getting closer to the sea is first indicated by the trees, which are decreasing in height as we travel. While the trees had been 200 meters tall at the start of our trek, they now measure about 150 meters, most likely in response to the decrease in solar radiation. The distance between them has also increased. Now and then, this allows a spot of sunlight or some rain to reach the ground, as there is also more precipitation here.

The weather has been uncomfortably cold and wet since

yesterday. These conditions have significantly decreased the joyous anticipation that Adam and Eve previously felt about seeing the ocean. While I never promised them a tropical beach, they obviously remember the photos of the Caribbean that I showed them on *Messenger*.

Then there is the wind. It races effortlessly through the more widely separated trees and blows moisture into our faces. The ocean lies close to the exchange zone between the light side of the planet and its dark side. Storms and thunderstorms should be normal there, as the wind already indicates, and its gusty howling kept Adam and Eve from getting much sleep last night. The sound of the storms overpowers the sound of the sea, the first greeting I expected from the ocean.

Our arrival at the beach is unspectacular. We reach the last row of trees. Beyond is a narrow strip of shore covered with mushrooms, and then the water. Considering there is a storm raging, the surface is amazingly calm, due to strong gravity preventing the formation of high waves. It is a strange contrast to see the ocean splashing gently against the shore, while ragged white clouds race across a dark gray background sky.

Adam and Eve nevertheless run forward to the shore. I want to yell a warning but then hesitate, because I remember they are already acting cautiously on their own. Eve takes off her boots and steps into water reaching to her ankles.

"Ice cold," she says, but does not move away. "My feet tingle."

"That is the effect of the cold," I say to her. Just to be on the safe side, I check whether an extraterrestrial worm is nibbling on her skin, but there is nothing.

A plant is growing in the sea a few meters from us. It reminds me of the grass in the steppe. No animals can be seen, and I proceed to analyze the water, which is slightly salty, but not as much as the oceans on Earth. The drop I look at contains 50 different kinds of microorganisms that are genetically related to the mushrooms. On Proxima b the biological diversity seems to be considerably lower than on Earth. Might our home planet be especially favored? Or do the frequent flares here limit the options for life?

Adam already seems to be fed up with it. I notice his disappointed expression. He walks back toward the forest and starts clearing a small patch of mushrooms. I follow him, since we need a place to rest. Ten minutes later Eve joins us, but no one is saying anything. We have now reached a point where some decisions must be made.

I look at them both and ask, "Are you disappointed?"

Adam nods.

"It's obvious, isn't it?" Eve says.

"I am also disappointed," I admit, "though I don't really know what I expected."

"What about the signal?" Adam asks.

"It led us here, in this direction," I say.

"Yes, but there is nothing here."

"We have to first search the area carefully, Adam."

"You know what I mean."

Yes, I know. There is no one waiting for us here. Even if we did find something, it would be a relic from the past.

"I have a suggestion," I offer. "You two set up a camp for us here. I am going to look around with all of my instruments. There must be something I can find."

Eve nods, and Adam at least does not argue. I unpack the tent and the generator, but the rest will have to wait until later. Then I move toward the shore on my four legs.

"Marchenko, it would be nice if you could walk around on two legs again," Eve calls after me.

I COVER ABOUT HALF A KILOMETER. I AM NOT PLANNING AN extended trip. I want to scan the surroundings with everything available to me. There must be traces of the aliens here.

The ocean has typically offered various resources to most civilizations, at least easy transport.

Initially, as nothing can be seen on the surface, I have to look underground. Close to the sea the soil is very wet, and neither radar nor X-ray offers clear images. I only see a black mass with swirls in it. Sound should be able to help me, because it propagates underground at different speeds depending on the material, and boundaries between materials reflect it differently. Like a doctor examining a pregnant woman, I use ultrasound on Proxima b. I place my pressure sensors on the ground—sound is basically nothing but pressure differences—and then firmly stomp with two legs. The sound waves enter the ground and are reflected back at some point. By repeating this method at various locations I get a three-dimensional image of the ground beneath me, which radar cannot penetrate.

Each measurement requires less than two minutes, with the orientation of the pressure sensors taking up most of it. Then I move ahead a few meters and repeat the process. If Adam or Eve is watching they might be puzzled by my activity. I am walking in a circle, repeatedly stomping the ground with two legs. One might mistake this pattern for a magic ritual. My processors add data step by step, completing the puzzle. After taking ten measurements it is already clear to me I am on the trail of something important.

I radio Adam and Eve, telling them it will take me a bit longer.

"How much longer will it take you?" Eve asks.

"Half a day," I reply.

"That means you found something, right?"

"It could be, yes," I reply.

"But you are not sure?"

"Yes."

That answer is actually not altogether true. I am completely sure there *is* something down there, but I just do not know enough about its dimensions. I want to be absolutely sure about what is waiting below our feet before causing Adam and Eve to develop unfounded hopes.

One kilometer further south, I walk in another circle. Here there are fewer mushrooms and the ground is harder, but the result is similar to that of the first series of measurements. Then I walk another thousand meters southward and repeat the diagnosing process. *This thing is large, really large,* I observe. I have already spent three hours, but I have to know what it is.

I walk another kilometer along the seashore and repeat my measurements. Now the picture is becoming complete, and I am quite satisfied. I walk back to Adam and Eve as fast as I can. I use the time to have the fabricators produce two-dimensional projections of my measurement images. I want to have something to show to both of them.

"It's about time," Adam says to me in welcome. The words sound surprisingly friendly. He must realize I did not stay away so long without having a good reason.

"And what do you have?" Eve asks.

"This." I put the pictures on the improvised table. There are six sheets, and Adam and Eve look at them one at a time.

"What do you think?" I finally ask, ending a quarter hour of silence.

"They look like aerial photographs of an airport," Adam replies.

"No," Eve retorts, "take a closer look. What you consider runways are really rail tracks. The rails connect several octagonal platforms... there!" She points at one of the octagons.

"It's a spaceport!" Adam exclaims.

This is also my assumption, but it is good to have someone else affirm it. I nod in confirmation.

"Something else might land on these platforms. Think of helicopters," I say.

"Then they wouldn't be connected by rail," Eve objects. "They must have transported something especially heavy. What could be heavier than a fueled rocket that is supposed to leave a planet that has one and a half times terrestrial gravity?"

"Perhaps they had long ago advanced to antigravity and other exotic things?"

"Then they wouldn't need tracks, Marchenko."

"But wouldn't it be odd if their technology resembled ours so much?" I ask. *It is fun arguing with Eve.*

"Under identical conditions, similar problems often lead to similar solutions," she replies. "You taught us what this is called in nature: convergent evolution."

Nice. Eve really paid attention during my lessons. Transport on smooth rails is associated with less rolling friction, so any civilization might discover this method at some time, unless it does not need to move heavy loads at all. The same applies to having a roof over your head. It protects against the weather, so any sentient creature living on the ground will eventually create house-like structures.

"And what does this tell us?" Adam inquires, asking an important question.

"This is no single picture," I reply. "I surveyed the coast for five kilometers southward. These platforms, connected by tracks, are everywhere. Of course we might have found a large spaceport by chance, but we have to start considering the idea this civilization left the planet a while ago, because it knew the megaflare was coming."

"Then where did the signal come from... the message?" Adam asks.

"I don't know."

"That's why we absolutely have to find its source."

"Yes, Adam, we must."

February 7, 19

We started moving again yesterday, wandering southward along the coastline. Our main goal is to discover the true scope of the spacefaring activities. If there really was a mass exodus of the civilization, then the entire coast should be a single launch site. But the question is, how was all this coordinated? I did not tell Adam and Eve that it is my secret hope to discover something like a control center, where we might find out exactly what happened here, and most of all, where those beings went who long ago called Earth with their message.

Solving these mysteries will not be easy. The wave of emigrations happened a very long time ago. The inhabitants of this planet might not have known precisely when the deadly eruption of their sun was going to occur, so therefore they packed their bags as quickly as possible.

By now, nature has completely reclaimed this area, and we will only find relics of the past below ground. I run ultrasound scans at regular intervals, and at this point I am carrying a considerable number of printouts with me. I will leave it to Adam and Eve to evaluate them, since they like to unravel the mystery about the purpose of these structures. So far, they have only found storage buildings, transport routes, and a launch platform. Twice we even dug at exact spots, but the storage buildings we found turned out to be thoroughly empty. The continuing activity keeps the two of them in a reasonably good mood. I worry, though, about the moment we reach the vicinity of the South Pole and have nothing left to do but plan for the next 80 years on Proxima b.

"Marchenko, wait a moment. Can you make sense of this?" Eve holds up one of the printouts for me.

I identify the sector and call up the original file from my memory module. "What, specifically, do you mean?" I ask.

"Here. The shadow near the edge," Eve says, pointing.

"That could be a wall... or an echo of tree roots. It looks pretty close to some of the wall readings."

Normally we scan the area between the shore and the forest, but the precision of the measurements decreases toward the margins.

"We've never seen a wall like this one. The intensity curve —" Eve says.

"Yes, that's true," I say, interrupting her. "The wall must be at least three meters high. You are very attentive."

Eve is obviously happy about being praised. I am skeptical whether this observation will help us, but at least it offers a welcome change.

"Adam, we are turning around. Eve has discovered something," I say.

He grumbles, but then follows us. It is only a few hundred meters to the spot in question. I compare the picture with my recordings. We are no more than five meters from the forest, so it is amazing the scan even recorded anything here. If this is a wall, it must be huge. Perhaps there is only a large boulder buried here.

I start to dig a hole at a place where I should find the wall at a depth of one meter. This way we will quickly discover whether it is worthwhile to excavate the entire structure. Ten minutes later one thing is clear. We had better set up our camp here for today. The wall is made of a special alloy containing titanium, among other things, and it is coated with platinum. Platinum is rare on Proxima b, just like on Earth.

What we first identified as a wall probably has a different function, either as something of great significance or as a work of art.

The wall is about 20 centimeters thick. As far as I can see, it is not anchored anywhere, but its own mass might give it stability. I am sending a drilling probe downward, and two additional ones to the right and left. According to the data, the wall has a height of 5.20 meters and is 37 meters long. It is an artifact of enormous size and was definitely created by someone.

What might its purpose be? I get a clue after I uncover half a meter along the top edge and spray it clean with water. The material is a shiny jet black, covered with numerous silver-colored symbols. The texts are clearly visible, as if they had been embossed on this surface just yesterday. This wall was made for eternity—perhaps even for us.

February 8, 19

I work through the night to get results more quickly. Eve has been keeping me company since 3 a.m. Earth time. She takes care of the intricate work and wipes the surface clean, so that the symbols are recognizable. Based on the few signs that we have already translated, Eve tries to run a pattern recognition for them, even though she really does not have a chance of success. We have already completely exposed over six meters of the wall. Fortunately the soil here is very firm, so I do not have to bother with shoring up the sides of the dig.

I simultaneously start to analyze the symbols. Groups of eight of them always seem to form a semantic unit, probably a sentence. Only a few symbols are repeated often, and those might have grammatical functions. I believe the others are a kind of picture writing. This complicates deciphering them, because the images might have meant something to the society that once existed here, but be alien to us. Yet I am still optimistic, if only because of the sheer number of symbols. The more material I have available, the better my algorithms will work to detect patterns in the extensive data, then maybe make connections, and finally produce meaning.

However, this requires considerable patience from Adam

and Eve, as a quick answer is unlikely. Eve seems to be able to handle this much better than Adam.

February 9, 19

It's done. The complete text of the wall, which we refer to as the 'blackboard,' is now visible. Once we see it in all its size and beauty, we recognize what an impressive monument has been left to us. The jet-black surface is iridescent and seems to glow from inside. This makes it possible to read the blackboard, even though its front side, the one facing the sea, lies in eternal shadow. I have discovered that the material converts reflected UV radiation into visible light, an ability that the inhabitants must have copied from the local mushrooms.

The text represents a kind of history book, combined with a message expressing gratitude. It thanks the past, the planet, and the builders—of the spaceport, I assume—that provided the entire population a future in space. I do not understand every detail in the history of this civilization, though. Some things are described in a flowery, vague language, while others assume a knowledge of places whose geographical locations are unknown to me. Unfortunately this also applies to the destination the millions of rockets aimed for. Yes, it must have been a huge fleet. The number is unmistakable.

Toward the end the text mentions those who had to stay behind, in the east and the west. It also thanks them, yet it is not fully clear what function they fulfilled. The meaning of their name lies somewhere between 'guardian' and 'keeper.'

Adam and Eve listen very attentively while I present the contents of my neither perfect nor complete translation. They are particularly excited about the last paragraph, as it indicates our journey is not over yet.

"Then we have to go to the east, obviously," Adam says.

This is true, because we have already been in the west. But there is one problem I mention. "We don't know whether the guardians survived."

"That's why we have to go and see," he replies.

"In the east there is the ocean, and then the dark side begins," Eve says. "I can't imagine someone voluntary waiting for something in eternal darkness and icy cold."

"That means we have to look in the sea," Adam says, and Eve nods. I shudder when I recall my odyssey in the dark ocean of Enceladus. At the end of that voyage I lost my body... I suppress the claustrophobic memory. I need to focus all my energy on caring for Adam and Eve.

"A substantial layer of water would definitely present a shield against the radiation of the flare. We should even be able to survive the megaflare at a depth of 3,000 meters," I say.

"When are we starting?" Adam asks.

"I can send out a couple of ISUs today. The ocean is large. The sensor units are better at searching it than we are."

"And we are supposed to just sit around in the meantime?"

"No, Adam. I am going to have the fabricators start building *Valkyrie* today."

"What is that, a submarine?"

"Yes, with a water jet drive. If we hit ice, we can drill through it."

"Are you expecting ice?"

"No, but it is the only model whose blueprints I remember precisely. It might take the fabricators three or four days, but I have a lot of practical experience with this vessel."

February 12, 19

I DID NOT EXPECT SEEING *VALKYRIE* AGAIN WOULD BE SO painful for me. Despite the vessel being a technically modified replica, it is a direct connection to my earlier life as a human. In particular, my mind harkens to Francesca, the woman I love, the woman who is now so far away from me, separated by time and space.

I open the hatch to let Adam and Eve climb inside. The moment I can only see the top of Eve's head, her hair, as she is disappearing into the darkness of the vessel, my mind instantly flashes back to Francesca, and I also visualize Francesca when Eve sits down in the pilot seat. I have to be careful not to let these memories impede my ability to function, and if necessary I can delete them from my memory module. But I would rather die.

Adam and Eve must have noticed that something is wrong with me. They are actually being courteous to each other. Perhaps this has to do with the voyage lying ahead of them? It certainly will be less arduous than my adventure on Enceladus. *If I'd only had fabricators back then!* With their help, I have now solved the energy problem that I constantly had to deal with on Enceladus. We will gain energy for the electric drive by exploiting temperature differentials within the ocean. For this purpose we will drag a specialized centerboard along, reaching down more than 500 meters. It is already swimming in the ocean, and we will only have to grab it.

I am ready to give the order to start. Then I receive a message from one of the ISUs and switch its signal to the pilot screen. It is hard to believe, but the drone has already found something. There is a strong energy source on the sea bottom approximately 50 kilometers northeast of our location. It is not a volcanic vent or anything of that sort, because the object is clearly alien-made.

"This could be it," Eve says. You can tell that she is trying to suppress her hopeful excitement a bit.

"No matter what it is, we have to get there as soon as possible!" Adam insists. He stands next to her and knocks against the monitor.

"It could..." I briefly wonder if any natural source could possibly be responsible for the signal but cannot think of one. So I end my statement with "... be dangerous."

"Well, the idea of sitting around uselessly for the next 80 years is definitely dangerous," Adam replies.

I cannot argue with his sentiment, so I start the engines. I swerve to the south to pick up the generator and then follow a northeasterly course. We should cover the 50 kilometers in one day.

TWO HOURS LATER WE ARE GLIDING CLOSE TO THE BOTTOM OF the sea. We run almost soundlessly, moving at a depth of 2,000 meters. It is pitch dark. The searchlights illuminate the area directly in front of *Valkyrie*, but that only serves to alleviate our boredom. Otherwise, not much is happening. The hair plants, we learn, also cover the bottom of the ocean. Could life down here have been more varied before the great eruption? Perhaps the few resistant species used this chance to occupy all ecological niches.

I wonder how we should approach the source of the signal. How do I know if its inhabitants will have peaceful intentions toward our sudden presence? Perhaps they consider anything different from them to be enemies? Have they been waiting for us—maybe for a thousand years—or do they want to be left alone? We will not know any of these answers unless we try. *If we die doing so…* I catch myself wishing for it. In some respects, wouldn't that be better than finding more ancient relics and having to spend the coming decades alone on this inhospitable planet?

Eve is constantly watching the monitor that depicts the sea floor gliding past. Nothing happens, but she is taking notes.

"What are you recording?" I ask.

"The vegetation density," she answers. "This gives us indications about how supportive of life the sea floor is, and also about the variability of this species."

Eve will find something to keep her busy in the future. Adam glances over her shoulder, tapping a foot and twiddling his thumbs.

THE ENERGY SOURCE IS TWO KILOMETERS DISTANT. ALL scanners are working at maximum level, but we do not get a clear image of the target. However, they detect something else.

"Fast object moving toward Valkyrie. Impact in 40 seconds," the computer says, and then a shrill alarm is heard.

Through the hands of J the robot, I immediately take over the controls, and the engines slowly turn the vessel. I hope that the object racing toward us cannot modify its course.

"Impact in 30 seconds."

The thing takes aim at us again. We have gained ten seconds.

I give the command, "Eject ISUs 5 and 6."

Those are the last two sensor units. I had reserved them in order to examine our target more closely, but now I am sending them on a collision course with the object threatening us.

"Is that a torpedo coming for us?" Adam's voice sounds completely calm.

"I have to assume so," I reply. "If it keeps up its speed and hits us, it will puncture the hull."

"Then we should put on our suits," Eve suggests, "or are we going to swim?" She looks down at her lower belly, where the gills are hidden. Her voice proves how excited she is.

"You'd better not try it at a water temperature of six degrees," I warn them.

"Impact in 20 seconds."

What are the ISUs doing? Can they stop this thing? The mysterious object zig-zags when it notices the two small sensor units, but the ISUs are very agile and manage to keep pace with it. The countdown continues. *19, 18, 17,* ... At 15 seconds ISU 5 magnetically attaches itself to the torpedo, and at 12 seconds ISU 6 has also reached its target. Once the countdown arrives at 10, both generate a strong electrical field that should incapacitate any unshielded electronic systems. I hope the extraterrestrial technology is not based on completely different principles.

"Impact unlikely," the computer says. The electrical shock has worked!

"Oh man, oh man," Adam says, and sinks back into his seat. Eve wipes the sweat off her forehead.

"I have to pee," she says.

"The toilet is in the stern," I say, pointing her in that direction.

I look around, but there is no second projectile. Our opponent might now assume we can deactivate any of these projectiles. I alone know that we have no additional ISUs.

I decide we should establish a dialogue. I send a standard

message that was developed on Earth to use in first-contact situations, broadcasting it on all possible channels.

The answer arrives very quickly.

"This is Marchenko," our adversary greets us. "I am glad you are here. Sorry about what just happened, but you obviously triggered my automatic defense system. I had completely forgotten I installed it shortly after our arrival. I absolutely did *not* want to attack you!"

"Marchenko?" Adam says, flabbergasted. "What? There are two of you?"

"I don't know anything about this," I reply. "However, anyone with a sufficiently criminal mindset could easily have copied my consciousness, even though that would violate the AI laws of Earth. But my very existence is already incompatible with those laws. Officially, I don't even exist."

"But how did the other one get here?"

"Probably the same way we did, Adam, with his own *Messenger*. But right now the more important question is, how do we react to his radio message?"

"Can we believe in and trust the other Marchenko?" Adam asks.

"I cannot say. I would give my life for you. But then we three have a common history, and I raised you with the help of *Messenger*. I don't know anything about the other AI calling himself Marchenko. Perhaps the AI was manipulated in some way, but we won't be able to find out about that."

"I am more optimistic," Eve says. "We can hear and see him and then judge him by his actions."

"So we should risk contact?" I ask.

"It's not what I expected from this journey, but at least it's something new. So, yes," Adam says, and Eve nods in agreement.

After I reply to the greeting sent by my alter ego, the other Marchenko invites us to his station, as I expected.

"A *Valkyrie*. How original," he says. "I have an extension attached to the west wing, and it has an airlock. Unfortunately, you will have to swim through the cold water, briefly, because your vessel does not have a coupling port."

We slowly approach the station, and no one is shooting at us. I switch the camera image to the main monitor screen.

"Do you recognize this?" I ask.

"Looks like *Messenger*, but with various additional arms," Eve suggests.

I point at the monitor and say, "The long one here has an airlock at the end, which the voice mentioned. We are going to enter the station that way."

"So we have to swim after all?" Adam says excitedly, rubbing his hands at the added adventure factor.

"Only out of sheer necessity..." I remind him, "... and in your space suits."

Once again it is a difficult moment for me having to flood *Valkyrie*. The vessel only has a simple hatch at the top, so it gets flooded whenever people enter or leave. This is cumbersome and represents a design flaw, but fortunately it does not damage the equipment. The last time I opened this hatch was shortly before my 'death' on Enceladus.

Eve launches herself out first, followed by Adam, and I—in J's body—am the rearguard.

"Why don't you come over via radio data transmission?" the other Marchenko asks me. "You don't have to get poor J wet."

"I prefer mobility," I reply, "and I am a bit overprotective where the kids are concerned. You know how it is. I can't leave them alone."

The other Marchenko laughs and opens the airlock chamber. It is not large enough for the three of us, so I let Adam and Eve go in first, since I do not mind the icy-cold water as much. I cannot suppress a feeling of unease, however, as the door closes behind them. What if the other Marchenko simply locks me out of the station? But then again, what reason would he have to do that? We should be glad we found each other. Six have a better chance of survival than three. Where there is a second Marchenko—'Marchenko 2' I decide to call him, as my sanity demands I be number 1—surely Adam 2 and Eve 2 cannot be far away.

The airlock stays closed, longer than technically necessary. I am getting more nervous, but then the door opens.

"Sorry for making you wait, but the system is used so rarely that it sometimes doesn't work properly," Marchenko 2 says apologetically.

I pull my heavy body into the airlock and then push the close button on the inside. The water is pumped out and replaced by air. I automatically measure the oxygen content: 17 percent, more than Adam and Eve need.

The two of them are waiting for me directly outside the chamber.

"They absolutely insisted on waiting for you," Marchenko 2 says with a slightly mocking tone. "They seem to be a bit timid. Would you now please come to the control room?"

We walk side by side through the corridor that is eight-meters wide and obviously built by fabricators. Only fabricators can create such seamless structures from any available materials. Everything still smells brand new, as if it had just now been made for us. The only thing the builder skimped on is lighting, which consists of just two fluorescent strips. I believe I can detect the fluorescence molecules of the mushrooms.

A door opens as soon as we approach the end of the corridor, and we arrive in a large, brightly lit circular room.

"Welcome to our home," says *my* voice, which in this case does not belong to me. "Make yourselves comfortable here."

There are two pilot seats. Even as he speaks, they are automatically turning into couches.

"Aren't those Adam and Eve's seats?" Eve asks. She must also be assuming that Marchenko 2 hardly arrived here alone.

Surprised, Marchenko 2 asks, "How do you know their names?"

I am startled every time I hear my own voice speaking sentences I did not form in my own mind.

"I think the Creator has predetermined all of our names. You also call yourself Marchenko."

"Because I *am* Marchenko," the other one says.

"Are you sure?" Eve asks. "The Creator might have manipulated your memory. It would only take a few storage locations."

The other one laughs and says, "Marchenko, your little girl is really cute. But to answer her question: Adam and Eve are usually sleeping upstairs. They just aren't here today."

As if on cue, a round hatch opens in the ceiling and a ladder descends.

"You two youngsters can see this for yourselves," Marchenko 2 offers. "And of course *you* are invited into the main computer, Marchenko. I don't even want to imagine how long you've had to manage without a quantum computer. *Messenger* certainly has enough resources."

The idea of using a quantum computer is practically electrifying for me. I have almost forgotten what a great feeling it is to produce new knowledge in next to no time, to draw conclusions more quickly than all of mankind, all those ten billion humans combined, could do it. Well, unfortunately, I had not completely forgotten that feeling. I would very much like to accept the invitation, but something keeps me from it. 'A robot with a gut feeling,' Adam would say, laughing about me.

Both Adam and Eve already feel right at home here. It's no wonder, since the similarities to our *Messenger* are uncanny. They are lounging on their couches, zapping through the entertainment program they've had to do without for almost two months. In a way, this is the 'quantum computer experience' for humans.

"I AM GOING TO STAY MOBILE FOR A WHILE LONGER," I SAY. "Later I will have to tuck the kids in bed. What about your own Adam and Eve?"

"They are currently on an excursion, as they call it," Marchenko 2 replies. "We believe we might have discovered the source of the radio message."

"Where is it?" I ask.

"Here in the ocean, not far away. Less than half a day from here."

"And you let them go all by themselves?"

"Well, you have to trust in them at some point," Marchenko 2 says. "They are over 18 years old now."

My Adam and Eve are two years younger. Accordingly, this Marchenko must have started his voyage two years earlier, or he was awakened sooner.

"The signal," I say. "I definitely have to take a look at it."

"I'll send you the coordinates," Marchenko 2 says, seeming sincere.

I compare the data with the bearing I detected during my trip to the leaf canopy. They match, within the limits of my measurement precision.

"You could check on it tomorrow and see for yourself," Marchenko 2 suggests. "That would be alright with me, as you could then accompany my Eve and my Adam back here. Are you still living according to Earth time? We are used to it here, even though no sunlight reaches us through the water. Accordingly, it is 11 p.m. now. My bedtime. An old man needs his routine." He laughs in a booming voice, which really is mine, and then he disconnects.

"Are you okay?" I ask Adam.

Adam raises his thumb. Somewhere he found something that resembles potato chips. Eve laughs at some scene on her private monitor. I need neither food nor comfort. I roll J's body to a spot near the door and consider some interesting questions: What does this new situation mean for all of us? Marchenko 2 somehow managed to bring his entire spaceship down here. Could this help us in the future? Would it be worthwhile to fly after the former inhabitants of this planet?

February 13, 19

"MARCHENKO, PLEASE COME IN." IT IS ADAM'S VOICE THAT sounds in the central module, even though Adam was lying quietly asleep on his couch just a moment ago.

"This is Marchenko. What's up?"

My voice answers, even though I did not utter anything. In the long run, these duplications will confuse me to no end. We will have to do something about it if we are to stay together for a longer time. It should not be a problem to change my voice to no longer match the voice of Marchenko 2.

"We found something," the other Adam says. "But we can't get it open. I'm sorry, but you will have to get yourself here."

"There is some news you two are not aware of," my alter ego says.

He hasn't told them about *us* yet?

"I wanted it to be a surprise," Marchenko 2 explains. "Yesterday, a second *Messenger* team arrived. A different Marchenko is already planning to visit you out there. He is more mobile than I am, and is currently located within J, the robot. I am sending him over there right now!"

"That's fine, Marchenko," the other Adam says. "We are looking forward to meeting your twin. Adam, out."

"You heard it," Marchenko 2 says to me. "So it would be nice if you could head out soon."

"By the way, how are the two able to stay so long in the cold ocean?" I ask.

"They took along an inflatable dome and lots of oxygen," he replies. "I think they just wanted to get out of here and be independent for once. You know how it is."

My robot head nods.

"And as I mentioned, the quantum computer invite still stands."

"Once I get back," I say.

I SAY GOODBYE TO ADAM AND EVE. I DON'T THINK THE TWO of them will miss me very much. Then I head toward the airlock. It will not be necessary for me to have a lengthy preparation period, because my steel body has no problem with the high pressure on the bottom of the ocean. My destination is about three hours away by speedy walking, and Marchenko 2 has sent me a detailed map of the ocean-floor environment.

I leave the airlock chamber and slowly sink to the bottom. If I were completely dependent on eyes, the impenetrable darkness might frighten me, but there is plenty of light in other areas of the spectrum. The landed *Messenger* practically glows because it gives off so much energy. It looks a little like a fairytale castle that has been transported to an enchanted land. It is readily apparent it does not belong here.

My software projects the planned course over an image of my environment. The overlay feels real, just as if somebody put up signposts at the edge of my field of vision. The ground has slight waves, but my path slowly leads me deeper. I am making good progress. Even though the pressure down here is high, I am moving in long leaps, as if in zero gravity. Now and then I step on the hair plants common here, which gain energy from currents. There are only a few very small varieties of mushrooms, probably due to the water above us shielding so much of the light.

I remember an old folksong about a miller who liked to wander around, and the tune reverberates through my consciousness. It feels good knowing Adam and Eve are safe. Today, I am only responsible for myself. I look around. The landscape is surprisingly boring. Due to the strong magnetic field that requires a partially liquid mantle, I would have expected more geological activity, but I only see a wavy semi-desert stretching across many kilometers. Without the water above me, it might as well be the Sahara on Earth.

The fact that this sea is not teeming with life like the oceans on Earth is certainly related to its location at the edge of the inhabitable hemisphere. Life always depends on its sun, and existence in a realm of eternal twilight leaves less room for evolution. Perhaps it was high time the inhabitants of this planet had started looking for a new home. Will Earth reach this point at some time? A long time ago, when I was still human, it seemed questionable whether the planet's environmental degradation could be curbed.

Now the automatic system alerts me that an energy source has been detected on the horizon. This must be my destination. What might Adam and Eve 2 have found there? Is this really the transmitter that led us to this planet? During the last meters, the gravitational force rises immeasurably.

"Adam, please come in," I radio to the other Adam and Eve. I really do not want to frighten them. For them, the darkness of their surroundings must be impenetrable. If suddenly a robot emerged from the shadows...

I do not get a reply.

"Adam, Eve, I will be there in a moment," I say.

The radio channel stays silent.

I radio back to my alter-ego, "Marchenko, did you receive any message from Adam and Eve?"

My question to Marchenko 2 also goes unanswered. This can only mean my radio module must be faulty. I try again to reach the landed *Messenger*, but no one replies.

Shit! Now of all times. But it is not a disaster. I will reach the signal source in ten minutes, and there I should be somehow able to communicate with Adam and Eve 2. They know I am on the way and will be able to handle a bit of a shock when I suddenly stand in front of them.

Didn't Marchenko 2 say they had an inflatable dome? I am scanning the area for a slight rise but am unable to locate one. The signal source is emitting too much energy for me to detect its precise shape. Perhaps its emissions mask the habitat dome, or Adam and Eve 2 have already dismantled it to start on the return trip with me.

Another 100 meters. Now I recognize what Adam and Eve 2 found. It is beautiful, a work of art. A slender and elegant pylon rises above a seemingly-fragile transparent dish with a diameter of at least 15 meters. At the same time, spheres float around the mast at distances representing a geometric progression.

I take a closer look. The spheres measure almost a meter and they really float, as there is nothing visibly holding them. I also do not detect a forcefield surrounding any of the individual spheres. Therefore, their density is adjusted precisely to that of the surrounding water, so that their buoyancy is equal to their mass. Considering that water density changes with the temperature, there must be an active process inside the spheres to balance that. An exciting technology! We could use it to construct airships that automatically stay at a certain altitude.

I cannot determine if the spheres fulfill a specific function. The dish and the pylon clearly form a transmitter, as I can measure energy emissions at many wavelengths. The transmitter basically seems to be active, but it is not sending a signal. It cannot have been built by humans, because the technology is completely alien. Was it constructed by the beings that took off from the spaceport millennia ago? And why did they call us now, and not back then?

I look around. There is something wrong here. *Where are Adam and Eve 2? What am I supposed to open for Adam?* I cannot find anything that needs to be opened. Did they endanger themselves by trying to manipulate alien technology?

"Adam, please come in, where are you?" I radio again.

A dark lump separates itself from the ground below me. It is an ISU, and the automatic system classifies it as non-threatening. Yet, it is also not one of the sensor units that I had sent out.

Then a sudden impulse hits me. It is an electrical field, the same weapon I used to deactivate the torpedo, the sensor informs me before it fails. Things go dark around me. I can neither see anything nor move anymore. I am locked inside my hardened memory modules.

February 14, 19

"ADAM, WAKE UP!" EVE STANDS NEXT TO HIS COUCH AND shakes his shoulder.

Jolted out of his sleep, he asks groggily, "What's going on?" He looks at his watch. "It's four o'clock! What do you want?" He sees Eve frowning and realizes she is very worried.

"Marchenko is still not back!" she exclaims.

"He is probably glad to be rid of us for a while and is exploring the signal source to his heart's delight."

"I am sure he would have contacted us."

"We will just ask Marchenko 2 and then we'll know."

"No, Adam. I don't trust him. I don't know why, but I don't."

Adam sits up and thinks, *Eve and her strange intuitions.*

"This can't go on," he says, "we need some facts. Let's look over their room once more." He points upward, and Eve's gaze follows his index finger. There is the hatch that Marchenko 2 mentioned yesterday.

"Computer," Eve says.

"No, don't. Otherwise Marchenko 2 will notice what we are up to," Adam says. "I am sure we can open the hatch manually."

He looks around. There is a handle next to the hatch, and it might be enough if he pulls on it. However, the handle is at a height of three meters. If they push the table from the wall to the middle of the room and he stands on it and lifts Eve upward, it should work. He describes his plan to Eve. One minute later the hatch opens and the ladder slides down. Both of them jump from the table and slide it to the side to make room for the ladder.

"Let's go," Adam says.

"Are we allowed to do this?" Eve asks.

"Marchenko 2 invited us, don't you remember?"

Adam climbs up first. They enter a chamber with a dome-shaped roof that is considerably lower than the ceiling of the command module below them. Couches are to the right and left, neatly covered with bed linens. There are two monitors, both turned off, and also two chests that probably store the other Adam and Eve's personal belongings. Adam tries to open one of them, but it has a code lock.

"Come on, help me," he says. Eve bends down and looks at the lock. It has a keypad for entering numbers. She pushes the 1, then 2, 3, and 4. Nothing happens. Then Eve tries the combination 0-0-0-0, and the lock opens.

"Wow, cool!" Adam says. He lifts the lid of the chest. It even has a built-in light. He sees a single screw at the bottom. Otherwise, the chest is empty. He goes to the other chest, which is also locked.

"I don't think we have to open it," Eve says, and he agrees with her. They have seen enough.

"Marchenko to base." Marchenko's voice sounds from the loudspeaker in the command module. The two of them hurry down. Marchenko 2 is already answering.

"This is the base," he says, "what took you so long?"

Marchenko is coming back, Adam thinks. He is relieved and at the same time surprised about this feeling. Adam smiles at Eve, but she does not smile back.

"Something is wrong here," she whispers to him. "We only can talk about it with our Marchenko when he is actually standing in front of us."

Adam feels unsure. At first he assumes Marchenko will solve the problem, but then he starts feeling doubts.

"There were a few problems here," they hear the voice from the loudspeaker, "but I managed to solve them."

"What about Adam and Eve?" the Marchenko 2 asks.

"They wanted to stay out here a little longer."

"Didn't you tell them we have guests?"

"You know what they are like, always following their own ideas," says Marchenko, then utters a booming laugh over the radio. To Adam's ears, it sounds labored and fake.

But half an hour later Marchenko actually comes out of the airlock, while Adam watches him closely. There is no doubt it is J's body from which the last drops of seawater are dripping, forming a small puddle underneath.

"And what did you find?" Adam asks.

"There is a transmitter, just as I thought," Marchenko replies. "But it is no longer active."

"What was the other Adam trying to open?"

"He wanted to repair the power supply and suspected it was located in the pedestal. But that is made of solid metal and can't be opened."

"Next time you should take us with you," Eve interjects. "I definitely want to practice using my gills."

"Did you say gills?" Marchenko says, hesitating for a moment. "Yes, sure. You can practice with your gills."

"Do you actually have them with you?" Adam asks, realizing this is a test. "I thought you left them behind in our last camp."

Eve looks surprised.

She is really good at this, Adam thinks.

"I specifically asked you to pack them and bring them along," Eve says with feigned disappointment. "Marchenko, don't tell me you forgot, too." She sits down in her seat and pouts.

The robot body shrugs. "I'll check on it later," he says. "If I left them behind, I'll make you some new ones."

February 14, 19

I exist in complete darkness, and I am slowly going insane. Nothing from the outside can reach me. The only things I have left are the images I remember. But can I exist with them for many thousands of years until my body is so corroded that even the protected memory modules decay, which is all that remains of my consciousness? *Won't I inevitably go mad?* Like phantom pain, I can already feel fake impressions spreading through my mind. I will not be able to delay this process for much longer.

I check my hardware for the millionth time. Hope really offers a strong impetus. I once again determine that the electric shock completely destroyed my electronics. This robot body will never walk again, and its sensors will not be able to provide me with information. Only the specially-hardened memory section has survived, together with the interface to transmit my consciousness via radio to different hardware. But there isn't any.

For quite a while I thought I might be able to use the alien transmitter, because it must be connected to a kind of computer. Unfortunately, its protocols are so foreign to me I cannot find a way inside. The base is much too far away, and I cannot actively search for some alternative option. I will have to wait until some suitable device comes within the range for a transfer. But in the middle of the ocean, where is something like that supposed to come from? I am waiting for a miracle, but there are no miracles.

The waiting time grows worse because I worry about the children. What is Marchenko 2 planning to do with *my* Adam and Eve, and what happened to the other two passengers? There is no trace of them. Did he murder them, and is he now searching for new victims? Or did they die accidentally, and in some perverse way he wants substitutes? Being condemned to inactivity is the worst part of all. I cannot protect Adam and Eve, even though this is my only purpose in life.

Something just moved into my field of vision. While I seem blind and deaf, I felt a sunbeam tickling my metal surface. *What could this be?* I try to decipher the code and learn the 'sunbeam' is pulsing in a familiar rhythm. *ISU 4.* It is the signal buoy I sent out at the beginning of our undersea expedition.

This might be my salvation! A sensor unit is perfect. I remember the feeling of unlimited freedom when I switched from *Messenger* to such a mini-spaceship to explore the cosmos, or should one say, *I absorbed the cosmos into myself?* The ISUs follow a random course that will eventually allow them to map the entire ocean floor, and this means I have to hurry. I cannot remotely control the ISU until I have transferred my consciousness to it. And I have to finish the transmission before the ISU once again moves out of reach of my radio interface.

Thus I begin the transfer process immediately, even though this could be dangerous for me. The robot J contains standard protocols in order to fulfill Earth laws, and according to these laws, cloning an artificial intelligence is prohibited. I am not allowed to duplicate myself— any information transmitted to the ISU is immediately deleted from J's memory. If the process is not finished because my target leaves the transmission range too soon, my consciousness will be split in two. I have no idea what this would mean, since it probably depends on which parts of my mind stay behind. *I cannot control it. Or can I?* My mind is racing.

Yes, I think I can do it. I will transfer the most active parts of my consciousness first. From now on I have to avoid thinking of the past. Reminiscences are taboo, and only my plan is important. My intention is to reach the base via the ISU in order to thwart whatever plans Marchenko 2 has. I concentrate on this goal to consider how to get on board and how we can neutralize this enemy together. Francesca, Enceladus, my life as a human being—none of these play a role anymore. I leave that all behind. *Base, I am coming, and I know what to do now.*

The connection between ISU 4 and the memory module in the hardened head of the robot J is interrupted.

February 14, 19

Adam once again sits on his couch, which he has turned into an easy chair. An observer might think he is entertaining himself by watching videos, as he repeatedly calls up new episodes, stares at the screen, and occasionally laughs. In reality, though, he and Eve are thinking about how to get rid of the fake Marchenko. They have created a protected text channel between their terminals that cannot be cracked, even by a quantum computer. Of course there is the risk of Marchenko 2 noticing that they are planning something, but it would be even more dangerous if they talked about it openly.

"We have to deactivate him," Adam writes.

":-O," Eve writes in response.

"Do you think the station has a main switch?" he writes.

"That only happens in bad novels."

"I don't have any other ideas :-(:-(Damn!"

"We have to lure him outside somehow," Eve types.

"And then? Do we hit him over the head? The robot is ten times stronger than we are."

"Wait, I have to check something," Eve writes.

Adam starts twiddling his thumbs. He tries to think, but not too intensively. Otherwise, he might have to realize that they have probably lost their own Marchenko. What does this mean for their future? Could they even survive on their own? Wouldn't it be better to offer to cooperate with the fake AI?

"I know," Eve writes. "The AI laws. They have also been implemented here. AIs are not allowed to duplicate themselves. It is a kind of copy protection."

"This means while he and J are outside, the computer in here would be free for our Marchenko," Adam replies.

"This is true. But also, there always has to be an emergency switch for AIs. That was introduced after the 'Watson Incident.' Supposedly, that AI took over an entire spaceship because it feared for its life."

"But we don't know where it is, and we'd better not ask him," Adam types.

"Well, then we need to go on a little excursion," Eve writes. "I just have to whine about something, don't know yet about what."

"Or even better, offer to show him your gills," Adam types. "Say you brought them along after all. If he is anything like our Marchenko, he will be curious enough to follow you outside. In the meantime I will look for the emergency switch."

"Sounds like a plan. :-)"

"Eve, what do you think he did to our Marchenko? :-/"

"I don't know."

From the corner of his eyes, Adam watches Eve casually rising and stretching her body after typing the last message.

"Marchenko," she says, "I am bored. I can't stand sitting around any longer. Are you coming outside with me?"

"The water is pretty cold, Eve," the familiar voice says.

"I don't mind. Now and then I have to practice using my gills."

"I thought you didn't have them with you?"

"Adam was just teasing me. He did pack them."

"Yes, I know. Well... okay. But we will stay close to the station." The fake Marchenko does not show any sign of a guilty conscience, but this is to be expected.

"Let's meet at the airlock," Eve says.

Eve undresses down to T-shirt and panties and then walks toward the exit on bare feet. Isn't she exposing herself to a lot of danger by going without a pressure suit? Yes, she can breathe under water like a fish, and fish can survive even at a water depth of 2,000 meters, but she also has lungs. *Is this really such a clever idea? The gills will work, but can lungs survive here?* Question after question flits across her mind as she continues toward the airlock. She hopes the people who put the gills into her DNA also thought of this.

Clenching his fists, Adam watches on the monitor screen as Eve and the robot enter the airlock chamber. In a moment the exterior door will open, and then water will come flooding into the chamber. Eve may only have a few seconds left.

Adam sees her glide out of the hatch with strong swimming strokes. She has managed the first step. Now he has to find the AI deactivation switch. He jumps up and crosses the command module. Up there, in the room allegedly belonging to the second Adam and Eve, there was no control console. Here in the central module there is a console for the environmental system.

Adam tries to understand all the button labels. He could really use Eve's help now. *How long will she be able to distract the fake Marchenko?* He has to hurry, but none of the buttons appear to have anything to do with artificial intelligence.

Adam examines the entire room. Directly below the ceiling hatch he sees a circle on the floor. *Is this also an opening?* Adam feels around the area. There might be a round door below the rubbery floor covering, but he needs a knife. *Where does Marchenko keep his tools?* Adam runs frantically through the central module, looking inside boxes. *There! A pair of scissors. That should work.* He removes the rubber floor covering as quickly as possible, and below it is a hatch with a handle in its center. He pulls, but this is not enough to get the opening mechanism functioning. He twists the handle in all directions. *What is the trick here?* Then he realizes he is standing on the hatch. *What an idiot I am!* Adam steps to the side. The hatch opens and a narrow ladder extends downward. It is dark there, but as soon as he places a foot on the ladder, the light is switched on.

"What are you doing, Adam?" the voice says from the loudspeaker. "The service module is none of your business and could be dangerous."

Adam disregards the voice and keeps climbing downward.

"I am sorry, Eve, but Adam is doing something stupid right now. I have to go and check on him. You can just keep on swimming."

The service module is small and smells of grease and old machine oil. It is apparent this Marchenko must have used it as a workshop. In the flickering light, Adam spots the sole control console here, and he reaches it in three steps. It seems to be a kind of fuse box, and it is here where one can temporarily deactivate individual systems in order to do repair work. The AI emergency switch stands out, though, because of the bright red lettering and the larger size. Just to be sure, Adam reads the explanation printed below it. Yes, if he pushes this button, all AI within a radius of 200 meters will be permanently disabled. He raises his arm and aims for the button.

February 14, 19

INSIDE THE ISU, I FEEL STRANGELY LIGHT, AS IF NEWBORN. There is no more past, not even regret about it, as only my task and I are real. *What is my name?* I forgot. But I am here. I live on board ISU 4. Perhaps I am its control core, but all that is irrelevant, as I only have one objective: I have to reach the base and save Adam and Eve by eliminating Marchenko 2.

The sensor unit is moving at top speed, but unfortunately this will also use up all of its energy. It won't be able to fulfill the function it was designed for anymore, but this does not matter now. I have to get to the base as quickly as possible. The ocean floor seems to race past me. I have the impression that I've seen this before, but I cannot recall exactly.

But this is unimportant, I tell myself. The station comes closer. *Another two minutes.* I must not warn Marchenko 2, so I maintain radio silence. My sensors detect two figures. They are moving around directly in front of the airlock I will have to use to enter the station, and I identify one of them as the robot J. My hope increases. It probably contains the consciousness of Marchenko 2.

I only have one chance. I can completely disable the robot by using an electric shock against it. I vaguely remember something like that happening to me a short while ago. But then there better be no human beings nearby, because water —especially the salty water of an ocean—conducts electricity all too well. I approach from a direction where the airlock entrance visually shields me from Marchenko 2. He must not know that I am coming. This is the only way to use this opportunity and surprise him. I am only an ISU, and as soon as the robot notices me, I do not stand a chance.

The human, as I see now, is Eve. Strangely enough, I am not surprised at seeing her swimming around without a pressure suit, but she will die if I activate the shock too early. I am ten meters away when Marchenko 2 begins talking to Adam via radio, and I listen to him. Adam seems to have opened up the service module. I know the plan of the station down to the last detail. Down where Adam is going now, there is an emergency switch that deactivates and kills all artificial intelligences in the near vicinity.

'Adam, No! I am almost ready!' I want to yell out, but that would alert Marchenko 2. I rapidly calculate: If I draw attention to myself, there is a 50 percent probability of Adam's plan failing. If I remain calm, there is a 90 percent probability that Marchenko and I will die, but Adam and Eve will survive. The results are clear: I will not say anything.

Now Marchenko 2 is moving toward the airlock. He must have realized what Adam is up to. More than likely, he must hope that he can cover the 15 meters to Adam's position faster than he would be able to leave the 200-meter radius of the emergency shutoff function. I approach very closely, but he does not notice and seems to panic because he might be deactivated.

I have to act swiftly now. Eve indicates she wants to go inside the airlock with him, but he ignores her. *That asshole!* If she has to stay much longer in the 6-degree water she is going to die. Marchenko 2 is starting to close the exterior airlock door behind himself. *This is my chance.* I accelerate, and in the nick of time slip into the chamber alongside him. The door closes. Eve, who remains outside, will be safe now if I can accomplish my task quickly.

If Marchenko 2 had taken her inside with him, I would have had to hold back. He notices me and immediately realizes this ISU did not get into the airlock by accident. He tries to hit me with his arms and legs, but it is too late. I trigger the charge and burn his brain. It is over.

February 14, 19

THERE IS A LOUD HISSING SOUND, AND ADAM JERKS BACK. *What happened?*

"Marchenko?" Adam calls out.

No answer. He carefully pulls back the finger still aiming at the AI emergency switch. Or, should he use it, just to be safe? No, he first has to check what is going on. *Why is Marchenko suddenly silent?* Adam frantically climbs into the central modules and checks the camera feeds, one after the other. The view through the exterior camera shows Eve hammering against the airlock door. *She must be chilled to the bone.* He quickly orders the door to open. She crawls inside and closes the door behind her. He hears her voice, and then sees her on the monitor screen.

"Adam, the robot with the fake Marchenko has been deactivated. It was done by the ISU, which slipped in here," Eve says. She holds up the sensor unit to the camera.

"Okay, I'll let you come in," Adam says.

"No, wait. I am sure that the consciousness is housed in a protected area. While J's electronic systems have been destroyed, Marchenko 2 could flee into the onboard computer if you open the door. Right now, he is prevented from doing so, because the airlock chamber is a Faraday cage."

"But you can't just stay in there forever."

"I can get out as soon as you deactivate the computer. Then the fake Marchenko has no alternative."

"I understand. I already know where I can switch off the IT system."

Adam turns around and climbs back down into the service module. He deactivates the main computer and returns.

"You have to open the airlock manually now, because the automatic system isn't working anymore," he instructs.

"I can do that," Eve says.

Ten minutes later Eve is back with him. They hug for a long time.

"You did well," he says.

"You, too."

They do not need any more words. But then there is an important issue to clarify.

"What about Marchenko. Our Marchenko?" Adam asks.

"There are two possibilities," Eve explains. "If he was on board the ISU, he is dead. The electric shock that neutralized the robot must have killed our Marchenko. The memory modules of the sensor units are not shielded like the robot head is. Marchenko sacrificed himself for us."

Adam looks pale. "But he still could be out there," he says in a near-whisper.

"That's right. I suspect the fake Marchenko also deactivated him with an electric shock. That's why he lured our Marchenko to the signal source. And then he used his own robot to pretend he was our Marchenko, the original one."

"You think the ISU was remotely controlled by the real Marchenko?" Adam wonders.

"I am not sure how, but that must be it," Eve replies.

"But that would mean his consciousness is still out there somewhere. Then we have to go and get him as quickly as possible."

"We should try it. During that time the computer will be turned off, so the fake Marchenko cannot flee. And we just get inside *Valkyrie* and start looking."

This time they leave the base in their pressure suits. Afterward, the airlock chamber remains locked on both sides. This way, the robot head will be a prison from which the AI inside cannot escape. Adam and Eve activate *Valkyrie*, pump out the water, and set course in the direction where the instruments detect a strong energy source.

Shortly before reaching it, they encounter a lonely figure that appears frozen to the sea floor. Adam activates a data connection, and the computer reports finding a huge amount of data. Adam starts the download, which takes half an hour. Then he gives the start command, and...

My consciousness awakens. "What are you doing here?" I ask. "And where is J?"

"It's nice to have you here again!" Adam says, happily.

"Oh, Marchenko. It is wonderful that you're back with us!" Eve cries.

It turns out I have forgotten all the events of the last three days. I cannot even explain how that happened. They tell me about the struggles that occurred, and I am really amazed.

"Then I really have to thank you," I say. "You have been great!" My voice cannot hide my overwhelming emotion.

Once inside the base I am allowed to occupy the onboard computer. We once again deactivate *Valkyrie*, and after doing all this we open a secure channel to the impostor.

Marchenko 2 does not try to justify his actions, nor does he want to explain his motives. He does admit, however, that his two passengers were killed by the flare wave when they were four years old, and it was impossible to restart the gestational system then. Therefore he landed all alone on Proxima b, and this period of solitude seems to have cost him his mental health. Why hadn't he simply been happy about having new companions? No answer.

We discuss what to do with the impostor and murderer. Adam votes for destroying him completely, while Eve wants to give him a second chance. I myself do not want to become a murderer, but a life in which we constantly have to be afraid of the other AI is out of the question.

Therefore, we agree to send him into exile, but before doing so, we repair the defective robot body and I insert program restrictions so that, from now on, Marchenko 2 is forbidden to leave the dark hemisphere of Proxima b. We do not expect we will ever have to visit that half of the planet.

Author's Note

Welcome back! Covering nearly 5 light years, this was by far the longest trip you have made with me yet, so I hope you made it safely home. If you liked the trip, just head over to Amazon and leave a review at

hard-sf.com/links/610639

Proxima b seems like a very distant target that we may never reach. But still, the basic idea of *Proxima Rising* is rooted in actual plans that the privately financed Starshot program is trying to make a reality in a few years. Technology nowadays allows engineers to keep spaceships so small that we could propel them by shining strong lasers on them. The logical next step would be to allow these ships to grow like *Messenger* does in *Proxima Rising.*

However, there are two major roadblocks, both based on our human nature.

First, we need nanomachines to build such spaceships, able to grow by themselves. This could be a very harmful technology if used in the wrong ways by the wrong sort of people.

Second, we would need huge lasers in space—outside Earth's atmosphere—to propel these ships. But these beasts could also be used in bad ways. Think *Star Wars*. Building the lasers on the surface of Earth works too, but it is much more expensive and notably less efficient because the beams would have to travel through our atmosphere.

You see, we could get to the edge of space much more easily if all of humanity could just agree on not harming each other. I often wonder why that's so hard. But maybe I'm just naive. I sincerely hope that science fiction tales of our seemingly-endless possibilities may help at least a little to overcome this contrary behavior by showing what could await us. Like Proxima b.

If you read about writing stories, you will often find the recommendation to 'kill your darlings.' But fear not, I do not follow those guidelines—usually. People rarely die in my novels. I cannot promise it will never happen as this would reduce tension. This is especially true in my next book as you can figure out from its name, *Proxima Dying,* and from the color of its cover you can see at the order link

hard-sf.com/links/652197

Proxima Dying is my darkest book yet, and not only because it is set on the dark side of Proxima b. Marchenko, Adam, and Eve will each meet their fate here. The book's name tells you that it might not be the lightest kind of reading material. And, maybe, someone or something will be dying too. *Proxima Dying*, the second part of the Proxima trilogy, is like the second part of any *Star Wars* trilogy—very dark. Still, the seeds of something new are there.

Is there anything you would like me to know? I would love to hear from you. Just write to me at brandon@hard-sf.com. Thank you so much!

Due to the fact that exoplanets like Proxima b play an important role here, you will find a section entitled *Exoplanets – A Guided Tour*. If you register at hard-sf.com/subscribe/ you will be notified of any new Hard Science Fiction titles. In addition, you will receive the color PDF version of *Exoplanets – A Guided Tour.*

facebook.com/BrandonQMorris

amazon.com/author/brandonqmorris

bookbub.com/authors/brandon-q-morris

goodreads.com/brandonqmorris

Also by Brandon Q. Morris

Proxima Dying

An intelligent robot and two young people explore Proxima Centauri b, the planet orbiting our nearest star, Proxima Centauri. Their ideas about the mission quickly prove grossly naive as they venture about on this planet of extremes.

Where are the senders of the call for help that lured them here? They find no one and no traces on the daylight side, so they place their hopes upon an expedition into the eternal ice on Proxima b's dark side. They not only face everlasting night, the team encounters grave dangers. A fateful decision will change the planet forever.

3.99 $ – hard-sf.com/links/652197

Proxima Dreaming

Alone and desperate, Eve sits in the control center of an alien structure. She has lost the other members of the team sent to explore exoplanet Proxima Centauri b. By mistake she has triggered a disastrous process that threatens to obliterate the planet. Just as Eve fears her best option may be a quick death, a nearby alien life form awakens from a very long sleep. It has only one task: to find and neutralize the destructive intruder from a faraway place.

3.99 $ – hard-sf.com/links/705470

The Death of the Universe

For many billions of years, humans—having conquered the curse of aging—spread throughout the entire Milky Way. They are able to live all their dreams, but to their great disappointment, no other intelligent species has ever been encountered. Now, humanity itself is on the brink of extinction because the universe is dying a protracted yet inevitable death.

They have only one hope: The 'Rescue Project' was designed to feed the black hole in the center of the galaxy until it becomes a quasar, delivering much-needed energy to humankind during its last breaths. But then something happens that no one ever expected—and humanity is forced to look at itself and its existence in an entirely new way.

3.99 $ – hard-sf.com/links/835415

The Death of the Universe: Ghost Kingdom

For many billions of years, humans—having conquered the curse of aging—spread throughout the entire Milky Way. They are able to live all their dreams, but to their great disappointment, no other intelligent species has ever been encountered. Now, humanity itself is on the brink of extinction because the universe is dying a protracted yet inevitable death.

They have only one hope: The 'Rescue Project' was designed to feed the black hole in the center of the galaxy until it becomes a quasar, delivering much-needed energy to humankind during its last breaths. But then something happens that no one ever expected—and humanity is forced to look at itself and its existence in an entirely new way.

3.99 $ – hard-sf.com/links/991276

The Enceladus Mission (Ice Moon 1)

In the year 2031, a robot probe detects traces of biological activity on Enceladus, one of Saturn's moons. This sensational discovery shows that there is indeed evidence of extraterrestrial life. Fifteen years later, a hurriedly built spacecraft sets out on the long journey to the ringed planet and its moon.

The international crew is not just facing a difficult twenty-seven months: if the spacecraft manages to make it to Enceladus without incident it must use a drillship to penetrate the kilometer-thick sheet of ice that entombs the moon. If life does indeed exist on Enceladus, it could only be at the bottom of the salty, ice covered ocean, which formed billions of years ago.

However, shortly after takeoff disaster strikes the mission, and the chances of the crew making it to Enceladus, let alone back home, look grim.

2.99 $ – hard-sf.com/links/526999

The Titan Probe (Ice Moon 2)

In 2005, the robotic probe "Huygens" lands on Saturn's moon Titan. 40 years later, a radio telescope receives signals from the far away moon that can only come from the long forgotten lander.

At the same time, an expedition returns from neighbouring moon Enceladus. The crew lands on Titan and finds a dangerous secret that risks their return to Earth. Meanwhile, on Enceladus a deathly race has started that nobody thought was possible. And its outcome can only be decided by the

astronauts that are stuck on Titan.

3.99 $ – hard-sf.com/links/527000

The Io Encounter (Ice Moon 3)

Jupiter's moon Io has an extremely hostile environment. There are hot lava streams, seas of boiling sulfur, and frequent volcanic eruptions straight from Dante's Inferno, in addition to constant radiation bombardment and a surface temperature hovering at minus 180 degrees Celsius.

Is it really home to a great danger that threatens all of humanity? That's what a surprise message from the life form discovered on Enceladus seems to indicate.

The crew of ILSE, the International Life Search Expedition, finally on their longed-for return to Earth, reluctantly chooses to accept a diversion to Io, only to discover that an enemy from within is about to destroy all their hopes of ever going home.

3.99 $ – hard-sf.com/links/527008

Return to Enceladus (Ice Moon 4)

Russian billionaire Nikolai Shostakovitch makes an offer to the former crew of the spaceship ILSE. He will finance a return voyage to the icy moon Enceladus. The offer is too good to refuse—the expedition would give them the unique opportunity to recover the body of their doctor, Dimitri Marchenko.

Everyone on board knows that their benefactor acts out of purely personal motivations… but the true interests of the tycoon and the dangers that he conjures up are beyond anyone's imagination.

3.99 € – hard-sf.com/links/527011

Ice Moon - The Boxset

All four bestselling books of the Ice Moon series are now offered as a set, available only in e-book format.

The Enceladus Mission: Is there really life on Saturn's moon Enceladus? *ILSE,* the International Life Search Expedition, makes its way to the icy world where an underground ocean is suspected to be home to primitive life forms.

The Titan Probe: An old robotic NASA probe mysteriously awakens on the methane moon of Titan. The *ILSE* crew tries to solve the riddle—and discovers a dangerous secret.

The Io Encounter: Finally bound for Earth, *ILSE* makes it as far as Jupiter when the crew receives a startling message. The volcanic moon Io may harbor a looming threat that could wipe out Earth as we know it.

Return to Enceladus: The crew gets an offer to go back to Enceladus. Their mission—to recover the body of Dr. Marchenko, left for dead on the original expedition. Not everyone is working toward the same goal. Could it be their unwanted crew member?

9.99 $ – hard-sf.com/links/780838

Proxima Rising

Late in the 21st century, Earth receives what looks like an urgent plea for help from planet Proxima Centauri b in the closest star system to the Sun. Astrophysicists suspect a massive solar flare is about to destroy this heretofore-unknown civilization. Earth's space programs are unequipped to help, but an unscrupulous Russian billionaire launches a secret and highly-specialized spaceship to Proxima b, over four light-years away. The unusual crew faces a

Herculean task—should they survive the journey. No one knows what to expect from this alien planet.

3.99 $ – hard-sf.com/links/610690

The Hole

A mysterious object threatens to destroy our solar system. The survival of humankind is at risk, but nobody takes the warning of young astrophysicist Maribel Pedreira seriously. At the same time, an exiled crew of outcasts mines for rare minerals on a lone asteroid.

When other scientists finally acknowledge Pedreira's alarming discovery, it becomes clear that these outcasts are the only ones who may be able to save our world, knowing that *The Hole* hurtles inexorably toward the sun.

3.99 $ – hard-sf.com/links/527017

Silent Sun

Is our sun behaving differently from other stars? When an amateur astronomer discovers something strange on telescopic solar pictures, an explanation must be found. Is it merely artefact? Or has he found something totally unexpected?

An expert international crew is hastily assembled, a spaceship is speedily repurposed, and the foursome is sent on the ride of their lives. What challenges will they face on this spur-of-the-moment mission to our central star?

What awaits all of them is critical, not only for understanding the past, but even more so for the future of life on Earth.

3.99 $ – hard-sf.com/links/527020

The Rift

There is a huge, bold black streak in the sky. Branches appear out of nowhere over North America, Southern Europe, and Central Africa. People who live beneath The Rift can see it. But scientists worldwide are distressed—their equipment cannot pick up any type of signal from it.

The rift appears to consist of nothing. Literally. Nothing. Nada. Niente. Most people are curious but not overly concerned. The phenomenon seems to pose no danger. It is just there.

Then something jolts the most hardened naysayers, and surpasses the worst nightmares of the world's greatest scientists—and rocks their understanding of the universe.

3.99 $ – hard-sf.com/links/534368

Mars Nation 1

NASA finally made it. The very first human has just set foot on the surface of our neighbor planet. This is the start of a long research expedition that sent four scientists into space.

But the four astronauts of the NASA crew are not the only ones with this destination. The privately financed 'Mars for Everyone' initiative has also targeted the Red Planet. Twenty men and women have been selected to live there and establish the first extraterrestrial settlement.

Challenges arise even before they reach Mars orbit. The MfE spaceship Santa Maria is damaged along the way. Only the four NASA astronauts can intervene and try to save their lives.

No one anticipates the impending catastrophe that threatens their very existence—not to speak of the daily hurdles that an extended stay on an alien planet sets before them. On Mars, a struggle begins for limited resources, human cooperation, and just plain survival.

3.99 $ – hard-sf.com/links/762824

Mars Nation 2

A woman presumed dead fights her way through the hostile deserts of Mars. With her help, the NASA astronauts orphaned on the Red Planet hope to be able to solve their very worst problem. But their hopes are shattered when an unexpected menace arises and threatens to destroy everything the remnant of humanity has built on the planet. They need a miracle—or a ghost from the past whose true intentions are unknown.

Mars Nation 2 continues the story of the last representatives of Earth, who have found asylum on our neighboring planet, hoping to build a future in this alien world.

3.99 $ – hard-sf.com/links/790047

Mars Nation 3

Does the secret of Mars lurk beneath the surface of its south pole? A lone astronaut searches for clues about the earlier inhabitants of the Red Planet. Meanwhile, Rick Summers, having assumed the office of Mars City's Administrator by deceit and manipulation, tries to unify the people on Mars with the weapons under his control. Then Summers stumbles upon so powerful an evil that even he has no means to overcome it.

3.99 $ – hard-sf.com/links/818245

Exoplanets – A Guided Tour

Introduction

MESSENGER IS ON ITS WAY TO PROXIMA B, THE FIRST—AND SO far only—known planet of Proxima Centauri, the star closest to our sun. Is it coincidence that we found an earthlike planet in our immediate cosmic neighborhood? No, not at all. It would be strange if we had looked for one in vain. Today astronomers know that most stars develop a planetary system during their lifetime. It is estimated that the number of planets exceeds that of stars. On average, each star possesses between one and two planets. The Milky Way, with its 200 billion stars, might accordingly contain about 300 billion planets.

However, great variability exists. There are gas giants that closely orbit their mother star and are almost as hot. Far on the outskirts there are ice planets, like Neptune in our solar system. Then there are planets comparable to Earth, and there are also a large number of cosmic loners racing through the solitude of space without a star. What these systems specifically look like—and if life could develop there—depends on the local circumstances.

We are now going to examine possible characteristics and variations. I am going to use the terms 'planet' and 'exo-planet' as synonyms—actually any planet not orbiting our sun is an exoplanet. This, however, is a very 'human-centric' perspective, since any extraterrestrial would clearly classify Mars, Venus, and Earth as exoplanets.

Naming of Exoplanets

ONCE PLANETS ARE DISCOVERED, THEY USUALLY RECEIVE THE name of the star they orbit, but with an additional letter. The naming system starts with b, as a is reserved for the star itself. If several planets are discovered in a system, the innermost one receives the b, and then the other ones become c, d, etc. going outward. Planets orbiting a binary star system receive a letter after the two letters designating the two stars. For instance, HD202206 AB b follows its course around the binary system consisting of HD202206 A (sun-like) and HD202206 B (brown dwarf).

In 2014, the International Astronomical Union gave 'real' names to a number of exoplanets: Ægir, Amateru, Arion, Arkas, Brahe, Dagon, Dimidium, Draugr, Dulcinea, Fortitudo, Galileo, Harriot, Hypatia, Janssen, Lipperhey, Majriti, Meztli, Orbitar, Phobetor, Poltergeist, Quijote, Rocinante, Saffar, Samh, Smertrios, Sancho, Spe, Tadmor, Taphao Kaew, Taphao Thong, and Thestias.

Types of Planets

Before a planet comes into being, a young star—or two or three, which is the norm—grows within a cosmic disk of gas and dust. The cloud condenses more and more strongly at its center, until it becomes so hot and dense that the fusion of hydrogen nuclei—i.e. protons—begins. Yet, this does not use up the entire material of the cloud. Normally, considerably less than ten percent of the total mass remains, which is still located within the rotating disk of gas and dust. The heat of the young star allows only elements with a high atomic number to condense in the inner area—iron, nickel, silicon, and so on. These then form the rocky planets. Further out, where it is colder, the lighter hydrogen and helium atoms can condense. Accordingly, the planets developing in this region contain more of the plentiful gases.

This explains the basic division of planets into rocky planets and gas planets. Later, there still might be some changes. Gas planets can wander inward and push smaller rocky planets into the sun, or even completely out of the system. Sometimes the mass available in a certain orbit is insufficient for a complete planet. Then an asteroid belt forms, like the one between Mars and Jupiter. At the outer fringes of the system, the cloud is too thin for larger objects to develop. Here dwarf planets or comets come into being. In our solar system, the Kuiper belt and the Oort cloud represent these celestial garbage dumps.

However, the planets also change during their lifetime. A gas planet, for instance, might lose its gas under the influence of its star—then only its core remains as a rocky planet.

It might be a bit Earth-centric again, but exoplanets are often classified after their counterparts in our solar system.

Gas Giants (Jupiters)

Gas giants consist mostly of light gases like hydrogen and helium, and they do not have solid surfaces. Instead, the gas becomes more dense with increasing depth, and at some point it reaches a solid state. Hydrogen can even become metallic. These factors make it difficult to precisely measure the size of gas giants. Therefore, the point where the atmospheric pressure equals that on the surface of Earth is defined as a gas planet's surface, while everything above it is considered atmosphere.

Gas giants cannot exceed 13 times the mass of Jupiter, which is about 1.2 percent of the mass of the sun. If a planet gets heavier, the pressure in its interior becomes so high that deuterium fusion processes set in... and it becomes a brown dwarf. Brown dwarfs assume a position between planets and stars because no hydrogen-helium fusion happens inside them. This type of fusion is a defining feature of true stars, but it only occurs at about 70 times the mass of Jupiter.

Hot Gas Giants (Hot Jupiters)

Hot gas giants are gas giants with one special characteristic: They move around their mother star in a very tight orbit, with an orbital period shorter than ten days. They can form in either of two ways: when a gas giant wanders too far inside the system; or when a rocky planet sucks up so much gas it becomes a gas giant. Due to their proximity to a star they are extraordinarily hot, some exhibiting temperatures of several thousand degrees. The chance of life existing on them is minimal. Due to their large mass and their short orbital periods they were among the first exoplanets to be discovered. Some of them have been expanded by the heat of their star, reaching gigantic proportions. Then they are called 'Hot Saturns'—Saturn also has a relatively low density.

Ice Planets (Neptunes)

Ice planets have a structure similar to gas giants, but instead of primarily consisting of light hydrogen and helium atoms, they are composed of compounds with nitrogen, oxygen, carbon, or sulfur. The 'ice' in their names does not refer to water ice, although water is usually present in liquid form in the interior of these planets. However, other compounds such as methane, ammonia, or sulfur dioxide can exist here in frozen form. Sometimes, though, the ice planets have a hydrogen layer that can amount to almost a fifth of their mass.

Hot Ice Planets (Hot Neptunes)

If an ice planet ventures too close to its star, it is no longer an ice planet, since the heat of the star also warms up its interior. Then it is designated a 'Hot Neptune.'

Earth-like Planets

Compared to gas giants, rocky planets like Earth are much harder to discover due to their small size. On the other hand, they are very common. According to some estimates, one in five sun-like stars might have an Earth-like companion in its habitable zone. That means there could be 11 billion potentially-habitable planets in the Milky Way alone. In addition, there are planets orbiting smaller stars such as red dwarfs, for which no good statistics yet exist.

Earth-like planets might not look like exact replicas of

Earth. The only common defining feature is that they have a solid surface with rock underneath it. The interior is often structured in layers, with a hot, sometimes liquid core of iron and other heavy elements. Above that might be a mantle of silicates and a crust, which is also made of silicates and other light components. This is sometimes followed by a layer of air, i.e. atmosphere. Some planets have water on the surface—a hydrosphere.

Hot Earth-like Planets (Venus-like)

These rocky planets have a very high temperature—several hundred degrees, like Venus in our solar system—either because of proximity to their sun, or because they have dense enough atmosphere to create a greenhouse effect.

Super-Earths

So far, most of the rocky planets discovered belong to the group of Super-Earths, meaning their masses are greater than that of Earth. There are various definitions, ranging from between 1 and 14 times to between 5 and 10 times Earth's mass. However, the measurements are often subject to errors. Determining the diameter is insufficient to distinguish between a planet with a small rocky core plus a large gas cover, and a genuine rocky planet.

If the original dust disk is large enough, huge rocky planets can form, so-called Mega-Earths. This would, in particular, be the case for planets in orbit around giant stars of the spectral classes B and O, that have up to 150 times the mass of the sun. Such giant Earths could weigh up to 4,000 times as much as our Earth.

However, this is certainly not the only classification system, and scientists consider it rather impractical. A different method does not look at the outside of a planet, but instead focuses solely on its composition. This distinguishes between:

- Metallo-silicate planets, similar to Mercury and Earth
- Silicate planets like Europa and Io; and Earth's moon
- Hydro-silicate planets, comparable to Ganymede, Callisto, Titan, and Pluto
- Ice planets like Enceladus, with very low silicate content
- Gas giants with methane clouds below 80 degrees Kelvin
- Gas giants with ammonia clouds below 150 Kelvin
- Gas giants with water vapor clouds, 150 to 350 Kelvin
- Gas giants with an albedo around 12%, 350-900 Kelvin, 'Hot Jupiters'
- Gas giants with alkali absorption, 900-1500 Kelvin
- Gas giants with silicon dioxide clouds above 1500 Kelvin

Planets in Systems with Multiple Stars

Planets can also develop in systems with multiple stars. In these systems, however, it is more difficult for them to reach permanently-stable orbits. Conditions are most favorable if both stars are very far away from each other—or very close. In the former case we basically have separate planetary systems. For instance, Proxima b orbits its mother star Proxima Centauri, while that star moves around a common center of gravity with the binary pair, Alpha Centauri A and Alpha Centauri B. In the case of stars being close together, planets usually move around both and are called circumbinary planets. Such combinations seem to be relatively common. The Kepler telescope investigated 1,000 binary star systems and has found seven with planets.

Planets without Stars

There is another class of planets which is so exotic that scientists have not even agreed on a name for it. These are objects that travel all alone through interstellar space, far away from the light and warmth of a star. Up to now, we only know of a handful of these lonely wanderers, but there are probably many more of them. Astronomers' estimates diverge considerably: For *each* of the approximately 200 billion stars in the Milky Way, there might be a handful or up to 100,000 loner planets.

The term most often used for them is Planetary Mass Object, sometimes shortened to Planemo, or simply PMO. Before we can determine their origins—and therefore their number—more precisely, we first have to find and examine one, and this is an enormous challenge. All the search methods for exoplanets, to be discussed in the next section, fail here. An Earth-like PMO far out in space is a frozen stone ball almost impossible to detect unless it happens to move in front of a star that, from our perspective, lies behind it. This bends the star's light, which astronomers can record as a gravitation lens effect.

There are a few of these planets, though, that radiate in certain wavelengths, one reason being that they stored enough of the heat generated during their development process. An exciting example, cataloged as PSO J318.5-22, was discovered by a team in 2013.

Where do these lonely wanderers come from? Some, especially the smaller, Earth-like ones, are probably cosmic runaways that originally formed like normal planets in a protoplanetary disk. But then some accident hurled them out of their system—for example, the influence of a heavy neighbor or another star that approached the system. Many others have been solitary all their lives. They developed from interstellar nebulas in the same manner as stars or brown dwarfs. Astronomers believe there is a lower mass limit for objects to form this way. They estimate it to be between two and three Jupiter masses.

Habitability and Life

It is very difficult to determine from afar whether a planet could, in principle, harbor life. The problems lie in the fact that we only know one system of life so far: life on Earth. It is generally based on surface water in its liquid state. There might be many other types of life that would be based on completely different preconditions.

But the researchers had to agree on something. Therefore, they define the habitable zone around a star as that area in which water could exist on the surface of a planet orbiting it. This does not mean that water actually exists. And what if some lifeforms do not acquire their energy from sunlight but instead from heat? Then they could also use water below the surface, which is closer to the core of the planet.

How far the habitable zone reaches depends on how much energy a star emits. And this can change due to the aging process. If the sun keeps increasing its output, which is a typical phenomenon of aging, Earth will at some point no longer be in the habitable zone, as it will get too hot. And if the sun becomes a red giant at the end of its lifecycle, then conditions near Jupiter and Saturn will turn more advantageous. Then Saturn's moon Titan might become the most fertile place in the solar system.

But apart from the size and the distance of the habitable

zone, the nature of the main star has a great influence on the possibility of life. Very bright giant stars often do not last long enough for life to develop on their planets. Red dwarfs, on the other hand, emit strong X-ray and UV radiation. This could be an obstacle for the development of life, because in these cases the habitable zone would be very close to the star. It is very important for the development of life that the star should provide a constant energy output over a long period of time. Sudden eruptions or fluctuations can have disastrous consequences. The 11-year solar cycle has a significant effect on the climate of Earth, even though the energy output only changes by 0.1 percent. Therefore stars with stronger cycles are presumed problematic for the development of life.

Several other characteristics of the planet also must be considered. A dense atmosphere can retain solar energy better than a thin one, due to the greenhouse effect. Mars, for instance, would be noticeably colder than Earth, even if it had the same orbit around the sun. A strong magnetic field prevents the solar wind from ripping away the atmosphere over time. It also protects against radiation eruptions of the star, which is particularly helpful in the case of red dwarfs like Proxima Centauri. The issue of whether a planet always faces its star with the same side or whether it has a strongly elliptical orbit can also influence the chances for life on its surface.

Life as we know it is very particular, and the planet must not be too small. Smaller planets do not have enough gravity to retain a dense atmosphere. Their interior also cools off soon after they develop, leaving neither plate tectonics nor a magnetic field, both of which presuppose a liquid core. Therefore it is probably no accident that Earth is the densest of all rocky bodies in the solar system. Studies estimate that the lower limit for habitability is 0.9 Earth masses—looks like we humans were lucky—as the Earth is only slightly above that. However, with a growing planetary size, the risk of the atmosphere becoming too dense also increases. Then the greenhouse effect would make the surface too hot, so that a

Super-Earth would have to orbit its star at a greater distance than Earth does around the sun.

And the planet had better move around its star in an almost circular orbit, because otherwise it would sometimes get too hot, and then too cold. The Earth is exemplary in this aspect, as the eccentricity of its orbit—a measure of being close to a circle—lies below 0.02. The exoplanets discovered so far, and whose eccentricities are known, have values above 0.25. Their oceans would alternately freeze and boil with the changing seasons.

Two final aspects: If a planet does not meet the criteria, either because it is too large or made of gas, it is possible that its moons, which usually are made of ice or rock, could still carry life.

And finally, life itself plays a role in its spread. The fact that there is so much oxygen in Earth's atmosphere—which animals can breathe—is based on the good preparation by plant-based life that produces oxygen as a side product. So if we find a planet that seems to be suitable but does not have enough oxygen, we would just have to sow plants—and then wait a few million years. Patience is always helpful in space.

Methods for Discovering Exoplanets

Compared to stars, exoplanets are small, light, and extremely dim. It is therefore not surprising that the first ones detected were not near normal stars, but around a rotating neutron star, the Pulsar PSR 1257+12—also called Lich—2,300 light years from Earth. Pulsars send radio signals with extreme regularity due to their rotation, but in the case of Lich, astronomers noticed tiny delays. These could only be caused by several companions. At first they suspected the existence of two planets, but now we know there are three planets, Draugr, Poltergeist, and Phobetor, as well as the 'exocomet' PSR 1257+12 e. Pulsars are the remnants of a supernova explosion. These three companions must either have survived the supernova, or they developed later and were captured by the pulsar. Up to now, only one other planet has been found this way.

What other methods are there which astronomers successfully used to discover planets?

Transit Method

The transit method presupposes that the course of the planet moves directly across the axis between the Earth and a star. This reduces the brightness of the star in specific intervals, which can be measured by telescopes. Space telescopes like Kepler are especially suited for this.

Using the transit method allowed scientists to detect about 80 percent of the currently 4,062 exoplanets in 3,038 systems as of May 2019.

The procedure is successful, but it suffers from a major disadvantage: The mass—and therefore the type—of the planet cannot be determined, only its size and orbit. Furthermore, only about one percent of all existing planets can be detected this way, as the others may be moving in different courses around their stars.

Radial Velocity Method

When considering the rotation of the Earth around the sun, one often imagines the sun as if it were stationary, twirling the Earth around it on a string, so to speak. This image is incorrect. In reality, both the Earth and sun—planet and star—move around a common center of gravity. So the star also turns in circles, though small ones, when it is influenced by the planet. We cannot see this circular motion from the Earth, but we can see this star move back and forth, away from us and toward us. The speed with which this happens is called the 'radial velocity,' and via the Doppler Effect, this slightly shifts the star's spectral lines. We can measure this shift with special instruments and then calculate how heavy the planet—or planets—pulling on this star must be.

If just this technique is used, though, it yields only a lower limit for the planetary mass. In order to calculate the exact mass, and thus the density, the planet would also have to be detected by the transit method. About one in five of all planets has been found using this method.

Gravitation Lens Method

If the light of a background star passes by another star on its way to Earth, it can be bent and magnified, just like going through a lens. However, if the star in the foreground has planets, this effect will change periodically. With the help of this method, 19 planets have already been identified, often at large distances of several thousand light years. Unfortunately, such gravitation lenses are hard to find. In addition, these observations cannot be repeated, as the stars move on in the meantime. One advantage of this method, though, is that it also works for planets with a wide orbit or low mass. Scientists hope to get an overview this way, to determine how common Earth-like planets really are.

Direct Observation

Ten years ago, nobody would have considered observing an exoplanet through a telescope. Now significantly improved technology has increased the number of planets discovered this way to more than 20. Once the E-ELT at the ESO or NASA's James Webb Telescope become operational in a few years, we should gain exciting new data about many planets in our neighborhood. A direct view of your target offers many more details than an indirect proof.

Today this method works well for young planets. They retain enough heat from the period when they came into being that they still radiate energy. The coldest exoplanet detected this way is 59 Virginis b, which is no more than 500 million years old and has an average temperature of 240 degrees. The smallest planet that has been directly observed is Fomalhaut b, with approximately two Jupiter masses.

Exoplanet Records

Which planets exhibit the most extreme features?

- Farthest away: SWEEPS J175853.92-291120.6 b —27,700 lightyears
- Closest: Proxima b—4.22 lightyears
- Heaviest: DENIS-P J082303.1-491201 b—28.5 Jupiter masses
- Lightest: Draugr—0.02 Earth masses
- Biggest: HD 100546b—6.9 Jupiter radii
- Smallest: Kepler-37 b—0.3 Earth radii
- Densest: PSR J1719-1438 b—at least 23 g/cm3
- Hottest: Kepler-70 b—several thousand degrees
- Coldest: OGLE-2005-BLG-390L b—50 Kelvin or -223 degrees Celsius
- Youngest: V830 Tau b—2 million years
- Oldest: PSR B1620-26 b—13 billion years
- Longest year: 2MASS J2126-8140—about 1 million Earth years
- Shortest year: PSR J1719-1438 b—2.2 hours
- Farthest away from its sun: HD 106906 b—about 650 astronomical units
- Closest to its sun: PSR J1719-1438 b—0.004 astronomical units

- Closest to other planets: Kepler-70 b approaches Kepler-70 c to within 0.0016 AU
- Heaviest mother star: HD 13189 b—mother star with 4.5 sun masses
- Lightest mother star: TRAPPIST-1b, c, and d—mother star with 0.08 sun masses
- Most extensive planetary system: HD 10180—9 planets, 7 of them confirmed
- Most mother stars: Kepler-64—orbits in a system with 4 stars

Eleven Exemplary Exoplanets

EXOPLANETS APPEAR IN THE MOST DIVERSE FORMS—ALMOST as if they sprang from the imagination of a science fiction writer.

Proxima b

Proxima b is the exoplanet closest to our sun and therefore the obvious destination for the expedition depicted in this novel. If you ever go there, you will find most things just as described. I imagined the life forms on my own, based on scientific knowledge, of course. The planet is 30 to 50 percent heavier than Earth. Due to the planet's tight orbit, its star surely must have forced it to always direct the same side toward the sun, as the moon does to Earth. One orbit around its mother star takes 11.2 days. However, one would not notice this on the planet, as there are no seasons, and it is always day if you're on the 'front' side. Proxima b is located within the habitable zone, so water could exist on its surface in liquid form. Compared to Earth, 30 times more UV radiation and 250 times more X-rays reach the surface. Whoever wants to live there has to adapt to high radiation levels. A magnetic field, which has not yet been proven to exist, could mitigate their effects considerably. This also applies to the radiation eruptions of the mother star.

WASP-17b

Almost all known planets rotate the right way—meaning that their orbits follow the rotation of their central star. This is only logical, because planets form from the swirling disk of matter around a rotating protostar. It is different in the case of WASP-17b. This world has an orbital inclination of 149 degrees, which means it completes a retrograde orbit around its star every 3.74 Earth days. In addition it is very bloated and therefore has an extremely low density.

The reason for this strange orbit is unknown: Some researchers suspect that a near-collision, or the gradual gravitational effect of another planet might be responsible for it. WASP-17b was the first of the retrograde-orbiting planets to have been discovered. The mass of the planet is 0.5 of Jupiter's and its radius 1.5 to 2 times the radius of Jupiter.

Kepler-70b

Kepler-70b is really fast—the planet moves around its central star, a red giant, in only 5.76 Earth hours or 0.24 Earth days. This is the shortest orbital period of all planets known today, and the velocity lies slightly below five percent of the speed of light. It is believed that this planet used to be a Hot Jupiter, but that now only a remnant of the former gas giant is left, with less than half the mass of Earth. Due to the tight orbit of Kepler-70b, 65 times closer to its sun than Mercury is to ours, it has such extreme temperatures that it is one of the hottest exoplanets.

Its central star probably expanded into a red giant approximately 18 million years ago and in doing so swept away the planet's atmosphere. This is what might happen to Earth a few billion years from now. The planet might have been engulfed by the atmosphere of its star at one time, but its rocky core survived, nevertheless.

WASP-12b

When WASP-12b was discovered in 2008, it ran counter to all expectations. Since then, it has been considered one of the hottest planets. It is more than 50 percent larger than Jupiter. But this Hot Jupiter is particularly interesting because it is being eaten alive. It orbits its sun so closely—one revolution takes 1.1 Earth days—that it probably loses 6 trillion kilos of mass every second, while its atmosphere is being blown away. It is assumed that the planet will die within 10 million years.

In addition, the planet might exhibit a high concentration of carbon in the form of carbon monoxide and methane. This means it could have a solid core containing a lot of diamond. Perhaps millions of years from now only a gigantic diamond will be left of WASP-12b. In addition, this planet was long considered the fastest-moving known planet. It moves at an impressive speed of 830,000 km/h.

Gliese 436 b

Gliese 436 b acts like a comet, because it drags a long tail behind itself. In its orbit, it seems to lose between 100 and 1,000 tons of hydrogen per second. It is assumed that during its existence Gliese 436 b has lost up to ten percent of its atmosphere. But its huge tail, which is approximately 50 times larger than the central star, obscures the sun during its orbit of less than three days.

There had been suggestions that planets with comet-like tails might exist, but Gliese 436 b was the first one actually discovered. Due to its size and proximity to its central star, it is called a Hot Neptune. Its gaseous tail might continue to exist for a longer period, because the sun that the planet orbits is a relatively cool red dwarf.

Janssen

On this world, one of the few with a real name, diamonds aren't just a 'girl's best friend.' Janssen, alias 55 Cancri e, is a Super-Earth and one of the five planets orbiting its star, the A component of the binary system Copernicus. We used to believe that a lot of water exists on 55 Cancri e. However, today researchers assume that the planet consists mainly of carbon in the form of graphite, diamond, and other minerals. An entire third of the planetary mass, about three times the mass of Earth, could be a single huge diamond.

Due to these findings, it is assumed that far-away rocky planets don't have to be similar to Earth. They could be completely different, and Janssen was the first rocky planet to be detected that had a totally different composition than ours. On the day side, the planet reaches temperatures up to 2,400 degrees, while the night side is refreshingly cool with a maximum of 1,100 degrees.

HAT-P-1b

When astronomers discovered HAT-P-1b in 2006, they were amazed to find that it is almost twice the size of Jupiter, while weighing only half as much. Accordingly, its density is only a quarter of the density of water and it is lighter than cork. In a giant bathtub, it would float three times higher than Saturn. So far, nobody knows why this is the case. Perhaps additional heat reaches the interior of the planet, but there is also no explanation for that. One possibility is that the planet might be 'lying on its side' and rotating vertically to its orbit, like Uranus in our system. However, as this position is very rare, and other 'bloated' planets have already been discovered, this theory definitely does not apply to all of them. The planet's star, by the way, is part of a binary system.

Gliese 1214 b

Gliese 1214 b is a Super-Earth. Its mass reaches almost 7 times that of Earth, and its radius is estimated to be more than two and a half Earth radii. It orbits its star at a distance of only 2 million kilometers. The most interesting aspect is that observations indicate its atmosphere consists mostly of water vapor.

The density of the planet might be around 2 grams per cubic centimeter. For comparison, that of Earth is 5.5 grams, and water weighs 1 gram per cubic centimeter. Scientists concluded that there must be lots of water there from the time the planet was farther away from its sun, in the habitable zone. The current close orbit and the high temperatures evaporate the water into a hot haze enveloping the planet. The planet is still considered one of the exoplanets most likely to have an ocean, but with a surface temperature of 120 to 280 degrees it would be so hot you'd better not jump into the water.

HD189733 b

The next time you stand in the rain, you might want to think of the inhabitants of HD 189733 b, even though it is rather unlikely they exist. On this planet there is not only a scorching temperature of 850 degrees, but perhaps also a rain of glass falling sideways, driven through the atmosphere by winds reaching up to 8,700 km/h. The cobalt blue color of the planet is not caused by oceans but by silicate particles in the clouds of its atmosphere. When these silicates condense in the extreme heat, they are turned into small drops of glass, which not only create the blue light, but are also carried around the planet by hurricanes. The planet is 30 times closer to its sun than Earth is to ours, and it has a captured rotation, meaning it always faces its star with the same side. The enormous temperature difference further reinforces the storms.

HD80606 b

All the planets in our solar system have relatively circular orbits, so that their closest and most distant points from the sun are not so different. The orbit of HD 80606 b, on the other hand, is strongly elliptical. During an orbit lasting 111 Earth days, the distance of HD 80606 b from its sun varies between 0.03 AU and 0.88 AU, where one astronomical unit equals the distance from the Earth to the sun. When it approaches the point closest to the sun, the temperature rises from 500 to 1,200 degrees within just six hours. Accordingly, the seasons on HD 80606 b are not determined by the angle of inclination but by its orbit. If you stayed high up in the atmosphere of the planet for one orbit, you would observe its star getting 30 times as large as the apparent size of our sun in our sky, while increasing its brightness by a factor of 1,000. The extreme temperature changes must create storms just as extreme, with winds blowing at 18,000 km/h.

TrES-2 b

Could there be a world that is darker than the color black? Of course! The best example is TrES-2 b, one of the darkest exoplanets discovered so far. It only reflects one percent of the incoming sunlight, but it glows in a dull red like a heating coil, because an extreme heat of more than 1,000 degrees exists there. TrES-2 is about 750 light years away from us, in the direction of the constellation Draco, and it orbits its star at a distance of only 5 million kilometers. Unlike Jupiter, this planet apparently has no reflective clouds that can repel sunlight—in Jupiter's case, more than a third of it. Instead, it contains many light-absorbing chemicals that capture 99 percent of the radiation.

Here is a tip: If you register at hard-sf.com/subscribe/ you will be notified of any new Hard Science Fiction titles. In addition, you will receive the color PDF version of *Exoplanets – A Guided Tour.*

Glossary of Acronyms

AGCT – ADENINE, GUANINE, CYTOSINE, THYMINE (THE BASE amino acids of DNA)

AI – Artificial Intelligence

ALMA – Atacama Large Millimeter Array

AU – Astronomical Unit (the distance from the Earth to the sun)

DNA – DeoxyriboNucleic Acid

E-ELT – European Extremely Large Telescope

ESO – European Southern Observatory

ISU – Independent Sensor Unit

IT – Information Technology

NASA – National Aeronautics and Space Administration

PMO – Planetary Mass Object, or Planemo

RNA – RiboNucleic Acid

UV – UltraViolet

VR – Virtual Reality

Metric to English Conversions

IT IS ASSUMED THAT BY THE TIME THE EVENTS OF THIS NOVEL take place, the United States will have joined the rest of the world and will be using the International System of Units, the modern form of the metric system.

Length:
centimeter = 0.39 inches
meter = 1.09 yards, or 3.28 feet
kilometer = 1093.61 yards, or 0.62 miles

Area:
square centimeter = 0.16 square inches
square meter = 1.20 square yards
square kilometer = 0.39 square miles

Weight:
gram = 0.04 ounces
kilogram = 35.27 ounces, or 2.20 pounds

Volume:
liter = 1.06 quarts, or 0.26 gallons
cubic meter = 35.31 cubic feet, or 1.31 cubic yards

Temperature:
To convert Celsius to Fahrenheit, multiply by 1.8 and then add 32
To convert Kelvin to Celsius, subtract 273.15

Brandon Q. Morris
--
www.hard-sf.com
brandon@hard-sf.com
Translator: Frank Dietz, Ph.D. Editor: Pamela Bruce, B.S.
Final editing: Marcia Kwiecinski, A.A.S., and Stephen Kwiecinski, B.S.
-- --
Technical Advisors: Michael Paluszek (President, Princeton Satellite Systems), Dr. Ludwig Hellmann
Cover design: BJ Coverbookdesigns.com

Made in United States
Troutdale, OR
04/07/2025